"What exactly does this mean?" Katherine appeared infuriatingly unruffled by the news, entitled almost.

"It means the house is yours, along with all of Luella's belongings."

"So we sell it?" Katherine arched one perfectly groomed eyebrow.

"If you want." He looked somewhat deflated. "Oh, I almost forgot. There's a bit more to this." He shuffled through another pile of papers. "Here it is. Yes, that's right. Per Luella's last wishes, the two of you will need to clean out the house, split up, sell, or donate her possessions as you see fit, and make sure the house is in tip-top shape, should you want to put it on the market. Then and only then you can divide the money between you." He studied both of them carefully.

"That's preposterous. I can't stay in Vermont to clean out and fix up a house." Katherine shook her head. "I'd be happy to pay someone to do it."

"Fine by me." Laney's jaw clenched. How *dare* she throw her money around, even if it did make things easier on both of them?

"Oh no. That won't be possible, I'm afraid." Richard Newman wagged his index finger back and forth. "Luella was quite clear in writing and when I spoke to her, on more than one occasion. She specifically wanted you ladies to do this together."

"Not possible." Katherine huffed.

"At least we agree on something," Laney confirmed.

"Maybe this will change your mind." He scribbled something on a notepad, mumbling numbers to himself at the same time. One final flick of his pen and he looked up again, smiling triumphantly. "The house is worth one-point-four million dollars. Along with Luella's belongings, that means each of you stands to walk away with well over a half million after taxes. Now, how does that sound?"

Neither Laney nor Katherine said a word. They both just stared straight ahead.

"This is good news, ladies. Great news, really." He narrowed his eyes and tapped his pen on his desk. "Luella said you were the best of friends."

"We used to be." Laney sniffed.

"Actually"—Katherine's voice softened just a little—"we used to be sisters."

you knew me when

EMILY LIEBERT

NEW AMERICAN LIBRARY

New American Library
Published by the Penguin Group
Penguin Group (USA), 375 Hudson Street,
New York, New York 10014, USA

USA | Canada | UK | Ireland | Australia
New Zealand | India | South Africa | China

Penguin Books Ltd., Registered Offices: 80 Strand,
London WC2R 0RL, England
For more information about the Penguin Group visit penguin.com.

First published by New American Library,
a division of Penguin Group (USA)

First Printing, September 2013

 REGISTERED TRADEMARK—MARCA REGISTRADA

LIBRARY OF CONGRESS CATALOGING-IN-PUBLICATION DATA:
Liebert, Emily.
You Knew Me When/Emily Liebert.
p. cm
ISBN 978-0-451-41944-6
1. Homecoming—Fiction.   2. Female friendship—Fiction.   I. Title.
PS3612.I33525Y68 2013
813'.6—dc23   2012051780

Printed in the United States of America
1 3 5 7 9 10 8 6 4 2

Set in Palatino
Designed by Spring Hoteling

For my boys, Jaxsyn Alvin and Hugo Grey.
I love you to the moon and back.

Acknowledgments

Before I became an author, I was an avid acknowledgments page reader, consuming the lists of names as if they held the secret to my literary success. Now that *You Knew Me When*, my second book, has published and I'm working on my third, I understand that—in some ways—publishing a book is like being a parent. You simply can't do it alone.

Alyssa Reuben, my beloved agent and dear friend, you deserve as much credit for the evolution of this novel as I do! Throughout the process, I was blown away by your fierce dedication, keen editing skills, and ability to read draft after draft (after draft) with a renewed sense of purpose. You told me over and over (which clearly I needed to hear) that we would sell this book! And we did. Well, let's be honest: YOU did. Not only did you sell *You Knew Me When*, but you landed me a two-book deal, for which I will forever be indebted to you. I look forward to being your favorite author (fine, my words not yours) for many, many years to come.

Huge thanks also go to Jason Yarn and Laura Nolan at Paradigm.

This novel would not have been a reality without my editor extraordinaire, Kerry Donovan, at New American Library/ Penguin. I have never, in my many years as a writer, worked with an editor as smart, perceptive, and supportive as you are. You have a unique and outstanding ability to take a "complete" book and see exactly how, with very specific nips, tucks, and additions, it could be a million times better. Thank God for that! I can't wait to work on my next novel together and many more after that.

Thank you to everyone at New American Library and Penguin who contributed to the birth of this book: copy editors, publicists, graphic designers. . . . The list goes on.

Not to be forgotten, my fabulous publicists Sarah Hall and Julie Chudow along with the remarkable team at Sarah Hall Productions. You are all dynamos and, without you, who would know about this book? You've worked and continue to work tirelessly on my behalf. Thank you, thank you, thank you!

Many, many thanks to my outstanding partners in this effort. After all, these days it's not just about the writing! A heartfelt thank-you to Erin Giddings and Leo Reyzis at Zoya for all of your hard work in developing the *You Knew Me When* collection of nail polishes named after the leading ladies in this book. I can't wait until everyone is wearing them this fall! The sincerest thank-you to Alessandra Meskita, the most talented fashion designer I know, who poured her heart and soul into creating five dresses—three also named for the characters in this book and two named after me—to wear to my launch parties. You are a genius. Thank you also to Marc Bagutta—your eye for fashion design is truly remarkable.

And now a special thank-you to the people in my life—friends and colleagues alike—who've supported me throughout my career: Kerry Kennedy; Mariah, Cara, and Michaela Kennedy Cuomo; Andrew Cuomo; Tom Yellin; David Goffin; Dean Waters; David Eilenberg; Ken Gillett; Jason Corliss; Sara Haines; Jodie Boies; Zoe Schaeffer; Jayne Chase; Vanessa Wakeman; Jene Luciani; Monica Lynn; Lisa Lineback; Mindy Smith; Holly Alexander; Jill Kargman; Jennifer Heitler; Blake

Harris; and Lauren Becker—best intern ever! To my friend, fellow author, and one-woman-literary-support-system Shari Arnold—you read multiple drafts and gave honest feedback— THANK YOU!

Jessica Regel, you will always receive a heartfelt thank-you in my acknowledgments. You took a chance on me, which is everything.

This book is about best friends, which I know a thing or two about, because I have the best of the best: Melody Drake. How many years has it been? I won't date us. You're the only one who really gives it to me straight. And I love you for that and so many other reasons.

Thank you to my in-laws, Mary Ann Liebert, Peter B. Liebert, Peter S. Liebert, and Karren Liebert, and to my sister-in-law and brother-in-law, Sara and Alex Liebert.

Without my family, I would be nowhere. My parents, Tom and Kyle Einhorn, tell me how proud they are of me practically every day. I love you both more than words can express. Zack Einhorn—you're an amazing brother and friend, and I'm so proud of your growing success. My grandmother Ailene Rickel is one of my best friends and my biggest fan. I love you a million times over. Thank you also to my grandmother Pat Einhorn— I love you!

And, finally, to my three boys . . . Lewis, you are my love and you are the most wonderful husband and father to our "little men." I couldn't do what I do without your endless support. Jaxsyn and Hugo, my sweet pumpkins . . . I love you to the moon and back.

you knew
me when

For what it's worth, I'm sorry for everything.
It doesn't have to be this way.
I miss my best friend. I miss my sister.

Katherine

C lick, click, click. Her sandals rattled against the pavement, ten toes pinched and bonded by silvery strips of crisscrossed leather, iridescent in the oppressive sunshine. She squinted at her mother ten paces ahead, finally slowing down as they approached the corner. Click, click, click. The bulky red truck careened around the bend, pointing its bulbous nose at the diminutive green sedan hurtling through the intersection. Click, click, click.

The shrill cry of a passerby. Her mother's body soaring through the air, limbs flailing like a marionette.

Katherine jolted upright, her creamy white sheets slick with sweat. She inhaled the bittersweet smell of lavender and perspiration; slid her smooth, tanned legs over the edge of the bed; and walked toward the bathroom determinedly. Surveying her reflection in the mirror, she grimaced at each new wrinkle and splashed cold water on her face. Her workout gear, which she'd arranged neatly on her makeup chair the night before, confronted her. Predictably, she met the challenge.

It was only six a.m., but light was already peeking through the sheer, billowing curtains garnishing the floor-to-ceiling windows in her personal gym, affording the treadmill a godly presence. "A spacious guest bedroom," the Realtor had dubbed the clean space with pristine white walls and dark hardwood floors. *A gym,* Katherine had thought, nodding politely. She skimmed the channels on her flat screen, scanning e-mails on her iPhone with the other hand. Half the world had been doing business for hours, and she couldn't help but feel breathlessly behind every morning as soon as she woke up. There was always a launch in London or Paris or China, and people depended on Katherine's directives. Sometimes when she couldn't sleep in the early-morning hours, she'd ease her insomnia with an hour on her laptop. Just a little leverage over her fellow cosmetics executives who dared to get a full night's sleep.

"Shit," she sighed dramatically after reading a new e-mail. One of the VPs in her department had failed to sign off on ad copy, and now the head of advertising, waiting for his six thirty a.m. flight out of JFK, was pissed. Why was it always so fucking difficult to get people to do things the right way at the right time? Katherine increased her speed to a sprint. Two-minute intervals for every five minutes of jogging. Every morning, in sickness and in health. Her relationship with the treadmill may have been her most successful to date.

She set her phone down and raised the volume on the TV. Matt Lauer was interviewing a morose-looking Karrie Kashman, who—despite the headline "Another Failed

Marriage"—had managed to pour herself into a searing-red Herve Leger bandage dress.

"Fifty-eight days. A full two weeks less than last time." Matt shook his head and leaned toward her sympathetically. From anyone else it would have come off as a reprimand.

"Yeah." Her glassy eyes were comforted by the longest pair of fake lashes Katherine had ever seen. She'd have to ask her assistant to find out the brand.

"Where is Kurtis now?" Matt prodded, as a photo of Karrie's estranged media mogul husband flashed on the screen.

"I'm not sure." Karrie sniffled.

"I know this is hard for you." *But I'm just getting started.* Karrie nodded. "Is there a chance of reconciliation in the future?"

"No." Karrie was unwavering. "But my sisters and I have a lot going on, like the launch of our sixth perfume, and our new line of kids' clothing for Target." Katherine upped the incline on the treadmill, pumping her arms to the beat of Karrie's PR pitch. *That a girl.*

"And this isn't your first divorce—not even your second," he reminded, in case it had slipped her mind.

"No." She gazed longingly at nothing. Poor Karrie wasn't exactly on her A game.

"Something to think about." Matt turned to the camera. "We'll be back with more on Karrie's devastating *third* divorce in a few minutes."

The rest of the interview was a bloodbath. After the commercial break, Karrie had promptly disintegrated into a heap of heavy makeup and designer duds, no doubt leaving her entourage withering in the wings. Most people couldn't put their finger on the public's fascination with the Kashman clan, but Katherine knew. It was obvious, really. Not only did you want to *be* them, but also you *were* them. There was Karrie's sister Kleo at a movie premiere, looking flawless in some dress you'd never own. And there she was the next day, fleeing the room as her drunken baby daddy smashed his fist into a mirror. And that you could relate to.

Sure, Katherine was an executive at one of the top cosmetics companies in the world, a thought leader in the way of brand marketing, but still she had to admit that the Kashmans had mastered the art of spinning grass into gold. Pretty grass, sure. Plump-assed grass, absolutely. Still grass, though.

Karrie had worn Blend Cosmetics on more than one occasion. She'd even tweeted about their pomegranate cheek stain, which had promptly sold out in every store across the globe. And now Katherine was in talks with Karrie and her sisters to become faces for the brand. Some of the male execs had scoffed at the idea, feeling particularly smug when the whole divorce debacle had reared its ugly head *again*, but Katherine hadn't flinched. The divorce would be old news within two weeks' time and, if anything, it had only amplified her popularity. Nothing like a practiced pout to sell lip gloss.

Katherine sprinted for the last five minutes of her workout, running through the day's schedule at the same time. She'd be at her desk by eight fifteen, which would give her forty-five minutes to go through the rest of her unanswered e-mails and tie up any loose ends. She had back-to-back meetings until two, when she'd return to her office to play catch-up until at least five. She'd need to sit down with her assistant at the end of the day to regroup, and then it was back to unreturned e-mails and departmental issues that only she could address. There was probably an event or two tonight where she could swoop in, swap air kisses, schmooze, and treat herself to a glass of champagne before heading home by eleven to once again conquer the breeding e-mails that lived in her in-box around the clock. And maybe catch a late rerun of *The Real Housewives of Somewhere or Other.*

She spent the next hour playing out the same meticulous routine as every other morning. It no longer took careful attention, much less effort. She could shower, straighten her glossy, shoulder-length black hair, and line her piercing green eyes while composing a speech for next week's board meeting and keeping up on her e-mails, her phone affixed to one hand, a hot iron in the other, with nary a singed strand.

Coiffed to perfection, she strode through the lobby, oblivious to the lavish holiday decorations already up the week before Thanksgiving. Click, click, click. Her heels punished the marble floor. There was a plump Christmas tree adorned with silver and white ornaments—no tinsel on the Upper East Side, thank you. A small menorah sat on the windowsill, a nod to the many Jewish residents of 1152 Park Avenue, who still preferred the tree. Wreaths dressed the tops of the elevators—front, back, and service. But Katherine bypassed it all, staring down at her iPhone, her fingers dancing the quickstep on the keyboard. Click, click, click.

"Good morning, Ms. Hill." Her doorman, Roberto, rushed around from behind his desk. She nodded and smiled, but not in his direction. "Taxi?" She nodded again, striding through the open door, which miraculously gave way as she approached. Click, click, click.

And then she stopped, awareness returning in that moment only. But always in that moment. She stood back from the curb until the cab had come to a full stop.

After all, accidents did happen. Even twenty-three years later.

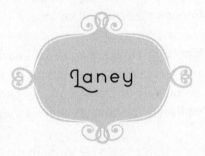

Laney

"Coffee." Laney padded into the kitchen in her tattered bathrobe and fluffy pink slippers, her wild blond curls raging.

"The Twisted Sister look really works for you." Rick smiled and grabbed his wife around the waist, burying his nose in the side of her neck.

"Funny. Coffee." She pulled a bowl from the cabinet, filled it with Cheerios, and poured milk over the precarious heap. Stray Cheerios trickled onto the floor, and Laney scooped them up with her spoon and into her mouth.

"Classy," he laughed.

"We'll be friends when you share some of that black stuff. You know, with the *caffeine*." Rick reached across the table and emptied the pot into her mug. Laney had never been a morning person. Even as a baby, she'd slept in until nine most mornings. It was one of her mother's all-time favorite stories. That and a million others. She clasped her hands around the warmth, inhaled the delicious aroma, and sipped. Three more gulps and she'd be legitimately awake.

"What's on the agenda today?" Rick cut into his waffle, wielding a large bite on his fork. Maple syrup oozed down his chin.

"Classy." She laughed. "Oh, you know. Same old fun." Laney had been working at Oasis, a day spa in Manchester, since a year after graduating from the University of Vermont. She'd started as a receptionist, and eleven years later she was running the joint. She loved the work, just not the domineering boss. "Massages, facials, verbal abuse."

Tina, the owner, was a gangly, gaunt woman with a pinched nose, angular jaw, buglike eyes, and a permanent scowl on her pallid face. Her husband had purchased the spa four years ago as a gift to her—perhaps intended as more of a diversion—and overnight Laney's job had plummeted from heaven to hell. Gone were the days of Bob and Francine, the sweet elderly couple who'd opened its doors three decades ago and treated her like their daughter, extolling every decision she made. In many ways it had been like Oasis was hers.

"Just tell the bitch to screw herself."

"Nice, Dad." Their twelve-year-old daughter, Gemma, swaggered into the room dressed in dark-washed skinny jeans, a fitted purple V-neck sweater, and tall motorcycle boots. Apparently, they were in at the moment. Until they were not.

"Oh. My. God." Laney looked up, alert for this first time. "Is it Tammy Faye Day at school?"

"Who's Tammy Faye?" Gemma opened the refrigerator, as if breakfast was a meal she'd deign to eat.

"She's the only person in the world who's had more makeup on her face than you. Wash it off." Laney pointed her thumb over her shoulder, motioning in the direction of the bathroom.

"But, *Mo-om!*" Hands on hips.

"But, *Gem-ma!*" Laney mimicked.

"You're being *beyond* ridiculous. I wear makeup every day."

"Okay, well, today you're looking a bit more tranny than preteen, and it's not flying. Rick?" Laney broadened her hazy blue eyes at her husband, who was never much help in the discipline department. Fortunately, Gemma had been an easy child. She still was, really. It was hard to believe Laney and Rick had been only ten years older than Gemma was now when they'd become parents.

"What your mother says. Sausage?" He pointed a link at his wife and daughter, who both scrunched their perfect noses.

"Dad," she sighed in protest.

"Go on." He shrugged his shoulders and pulled a face in Laney's direction while her head was down, prompting Gemma to giggle like the twelve-year-old girl she was.

"We're leaving here in fifteen minutes. I can't be late today." Laney shoveled the last bite of cereal into her mouth and stood to clear their plates.

"I got it, sweetie." Rick jumped up. "You go tame that mop."

"You live for this mop." She slapped his arm.

"Yes. Yes, I do."

Laney was wrong. There were, in fact, girls with more makeup on their faces than both Gemma and Tammy Faye. Put together. There were also girls dressed in shirts cut so low you could practically see their shoes. Even worse, there were boys who were interested; their shredded jeans cinched mid-ass in order to properly showcase their plaid boxer shorts. Was that attractive to her daughter? Her beautiful, smart, good-head-on-her-shoulders daughter?

"It looks like his pants are falling off." Laney tested the waters. She didn't want to be *that* mom, but really? It seemed so impractical. Not to mention chilly.

"Tacky." Gemma glanced out the window. She'd been preoccupied with her Droid—no doubt updating her Facebook status: "Gemma Marten is in the car with her very uncool mom"—for the length of the five-minute ride. The Droid had been a Valentine's Day present from Rick, who'd had a particularly good year in the construction business. People weren't necessarily buying houses during the recession, but they were adding on to their existing ones. Laney had received a pair of diamond studs. Small, but still diamond. Rick had received a blow job.

"Totally," Laney agreed straight-faced, but bursting with pride on the inside. Gemma reached for the door handle. "Eh-hem."

"Embarrassing." Yet she leaned over and kissed her mother on the cheek. Laney noticed Gemma's makeup bag shoved into her purse. She'd probably head directly to the girls' bathroom and reapply everything Laney had made her wash off.

"Do you need a ride home?" Laney had convinced Tina to let her take her lunch break at three thirty on the days when Gemma couldn't carpool with a friend. It hadn't been an easy negotiation. It never was.

"Nope. I'll hitch with Hillary." She was already out the door, calling over her shoulder, same blond curls as Laney's own whipping violently in the wind. Laney was still young enough to remember the profound humiliation of slipping out of her mother's beat-up Oldsmobile before anyone she knew could spot her.

"Okay. Love you!" Laney called out as the car door slammed. "Love you too, Mom. Have I told you lately how completely awesome you are?" she sing-songed, as if someone were listening.

Laney pulled out of the school parking lot, her cell phone trilling from inside her purse. "Where *are* you!?" Tina's voice screeched as soon as Laney answered.

"I'll be there in five minutes, Tina. It's only twenty after." Laney heard her huff.

"This place is a *mess*." Tina could barely complete a sentence without stressing something. You are *so* late. That woman is a *complete* witch. I am just *sick* to my stomach. When Laney and Rick were in particularly silly moods, they took great pleasure in reenacting their version of Tina's sex talk. You are so *big*, Laney would start. I just *have* to lick your nipples, Rick would counter. Not before I *mount* you like a horse. And on and on until they'd thoroughly grossed themselves out. Mr. Tina was a rich man, but not a terribly attractive one, and his ever-expanding paunch was *so* not hot.

"What's a mess?" Laney had been the last one to leave the previous evening, as she always was. And the place had been spotless, as per Tina's obsessive-compulsive guidelines.

"Well, there are loose papers all over the desk, for one." Laney could make out the muffled sounds of shuffling and crinkling. She cringed.

"Tina, those are bills. I left them stacked on the desk because you need to pay them." *And I left them stacked in a perfect fucking pile.*

"All right, all right." One thing Tina didn't like to talk

about was money. Who knew why, since it just materialized whenever she needed it. "Just *get* here so we can have this place in order before our first appointment."

"On my way." Laney clicked off and threw the phone into her cup holder. "AAAAGGGHH!" She wasn't sure how much longer she could take it.

Maybe there was only so much happiness to go around for each person and she'd filled her quota with Rick and Gemma. Long-term professional contentedness was apparently more than her fair share.

Katherine

"Jesus fucking Christ." Katherine shook her head. "Brooke!" she called out from behind her barren glass desk.

"I'm here." Katherine's assistant materialized in the doorway, taking short tentative steps forward.

A crisp cream backdrop with pops of color—jewel tones. No clutter and nothing gaudy was how Katherine had described her vision for her office to the company's interior decorator. And, in typical fashion, her wish had been granted. The carpet was an unspoiled cream, as were the walls, which were adorned with two large Miró originals—Katherine's personal donation to the space. Three purple leather club chairs faced her desk, and a round glass table surrounded by six more leather chairs in a rich asparagus green sat in the corner, reserved for private meetings. There wasn't a family photo or trinket in sight, much less a stray piece of paper.

The only accoutrement was a tall black hand-blown glass vase bursting with white calla lilies, placed in the center of the table. Katherine had been upgraded to a larger office five years ago, with the expectation of even longer hours. She'd figured as long as she was going to live at work, she might as well feel at home.

"I'm sorry, but how hard is it to get an egg-*white* omelet with tomato and onion and *without* cheese?" She strummed her glossy red nails on the desktop. Despite Blend's closet full of vibrant colors, free to employees, she wore Zoya's "Katherine" polish exclusively, because it never chipped and because she couldn't help but feel like it'd been created expressly for her. Katherine had neither the time nor the patience for constant touch-ups. And nothing was tackier, in her opinion, than a messy manicure.

"I'm so sorry. That's what I ordered." Brooke scuttled over to Katherine's desk to remove the takeout container.

"Of course you did." Katherine nodded. "It's not *your* fault they're idiots."

"I'll get them to bring another one immediately. The right way." Brooke was a plain-looking girl—tall, a little scrawny, and certainly no older than twenty-four, with long, straggly blond hair and forgettable brown eyes. When she'd first started working at Blend, Katherine had treated her to a haircut and highlights at New York's swanky Frédéric Fekkai Salon, at least a week's salary for Brooke. She'd also sent her home with bags of cosmetics, explaining—in the least offensive way—that Blend employees were expected to maintain a certain appearance. Brooke had taken the hint in stride and her presentation had improved over time, but there was only so much Katherine could do. In the end, what mattered most was that she was consistently prompt, organized, and ambitious enough to follow Katherine's neurotic way of doing things. To the letter. And so far she'd proven herself in spades.

"Don't worry about ordering another one. I have a meeting with sales in fifteen minutes." She knew what Brooke was thinking, even though she'd never say it. Why couldn't Katherine just eat a regular omelet with a little cheese? Would it kill her to consume a few extra calories? Probably not. But that wasn't really the point. Was it? She wanted things the way she wanted them. And it was impossible for her to wrap her mind around the fact that people were incapable of filling very simple orders and following even simpler directions. Surely the line cook who'd made her omelet didn't appreciate the hours she spent on the treadmill. Or understand that in order to maintain her lean figure, given her crawling metabolism, stringent dietary restrictions were her only option. Katherine had never been the pretty girl growing up, and for that very reason, she'd spent years manipulating the best out of her looks. She was always tweezed, waxed, highlighted, tanned, and smoothed every which way possible. Botox injections came every six months, though it was looking like four-month intervals were in her near future.

"Do you want me to take that?" Katherine closed the lid to the omelet and handed it to Brooke.

"Tell them if they fuck up once more, no one from Blend is ordering from there again." She refocused on her laptop. "That reminds me. I need to see Tom Birnbaum."

"Absolutely. I'll go call him." Brooke turned on her two-inch heel—a marked improvement, Katherine observed, from the shabby ballet flats she used to wear.

"Thanks. Tell him to hurry. He's already fucked up royally." Katherine typed as she spoke. Multitasking was like breathing.

"Will do." Brooke swiveled back to face Katherine. Sometimes it was hard to tell when the conversation was over.

"Obviously, omit that last part."

"Right."

"Sorry. I know you're not stupid." Katherine smiled sheepishly at Brooke. "I'm just irritated about the omelet."

"Of course." Brooke nodded. "You know Tom's wife is eight months pregnant." This got Katherine's attention. Was Brooke implying that she should overlook Tom's apparent gaffe because he was about to become a daddy? If so, she had a lot to learn. Pregnancy and children were considered unacceptable, even humiliating excuses when offered by female executives. But, then, if you were a woman without kids in your mid-thirties, like Katherine, you were considered frigid and unforgiving, unable to relate to the bottomless pit of warmth, devotion, and empathy reserved only for mothers.

"Well, I don't think his impending child has anything to do with his egregious error. Plus, I know his wife, Judy. She'd sooner give birth on the conference-room table at Goldman Sachs than miss a meeting." Katherine regarded Brooke's confused expression.

"Oh no, I wasn't suggesting her pregnancy had anything to do with his mistake. I only mentioned it because I thought you'd like to send them a gift."

"Yes, of course. A gift. You're always one step ahead." Katherine quelled her embarrassment. "See if you can find out the sex. And get Tom in here, okay?" She smiled again. "Thanks."

Katherine scribbled manically with her red pen, wondering how many people's eyes had perused and approved the new marketing campaign in her hands. How many presumably competent people had overlooked the nine misspelled words she'd already flagged and the fact that the "d" in Blend was obstructed by the tip of their latest red lipstick?

Today had been one of those days wrought with complications at every turn. Back-to-back meetings in which the buck had been passed like a hot potato around the room. Irate messages from heads of three different departments. And those little annoying glitches that seemed to procreate as the hours flew by—spilling water on her brand-new Chloé silk blouse, the notable absence of red peppers at the salad bar, her iPhone freezing at the worst possible moments, and so on. Finally, back in her office at six o'clock, Katherine had been welcomed by a pile of marketing materials that needed her sign-off and a list of urgent calls that had to be returned immediately, and she still hadn't seen Tom Birnbaum, who was—according to Brooke—on his way upstairs. She rested her elbows on her desk and bent her head forward, massaging her eyelids with the tips of her fingers. Managing people was not a part of her job she relished. The creativity, yes. The negotiating, absolutely. The power, undoubtedly. But definitely not the boss-employee discourse. It always became personal. And Katherine didn't do personal, at least not well.

"Katherine?" Brooke knocked cautiously and cracked the door to her office. "Tom is here to see you."

"Thanks. Send him in." She straightened up instinctively and tucked her hair behind her ears, smoothing it down with the palms of her hands. One of the first things Jane Sachs, the founder of Blend, had taught her was that perfect posture was everything. *No one likes a slouch.* Those words had stuck with Katherine through the years, along with Jane's overall philosophy that the way you looked and carried yourself was the way people perceived you. *I always wear my most flattering outfit on my shittiest day*, Jane had once told her, swearing up and down that this tactic was the key to her success.

"Hi, Katherine." Tom walked toward her desk, looking more disheveled than she'd ever seen him. Typically, his metrosexual tendencies resulted in fashion-forward Prada suits and accessories one could only assume had been selected and laid out by a woman, but not in Tom's case. If anything, Judy could stand to benefit from her husband's style sensibilities.

"Tom, what—" she started.

"Listen. Before you say anything, I know. I totally fucked up with Stan's ad stuff, and then I was late this morning." He sat down in one of Katherine's purple leather chairs and hunched his body forward. *Posture*. She resisted saying it, though Jane would have. "There's no excuse. It will never happen again."

"This is so unlike you." Katherine was relieved not to have to run through his shortcomings. It was one thing she particularly liked about Tom. He rarely screwed up, and when he did, he owned it. No hot-potato buck tossing by Tom.

"I know." He sighed, raking his fingers through his thick brown hair. "Honestly, this pregnancy is killing me."

Katherine laughed. "Well, you look great. It shouldn't be too difficult to lose the baby weight."

He managed a smile, pained as it was. "It's ridiculous, right? I'm not even carrying the damn child." *Damn child*. Didn't seem like an auspicious start, but who was Katherine, frigid woman in her mid-thirties, to judge?

"What's going on?" She felt like she had to ask, even though the two hundred e-mails in her in-box were beckoning her.

"Yesterday the doctor told Judy that she has to be on bed rest for the remainder of the pregnancy."

Katherine snorted.

"Right. You know Judy. That didn't exactly fly."

"Well, isn't that the sort of thing you have to listen to?" Katherine didn't know much about bed rest or babies, but she'd heard enough from colleagues.

"In theory, yes. In Judy Land, no." He sighed again. "So, I know this is no excuse, but I was a little distracted yesterday, what with Judy completely ignoring the doctor's orders, and then this morning I actually had to wait at home until her mom got there so she didn't try to sneak out."

"That's tough." She nodded, though it was hard for her not to empathize with Judy. Katherine would jump off the roof of her building if faced with lying in bed all day long. "Look, Tom. I'm not going to waste my time telling you personal issues can't impact your work."

"I know."

"I know you know. Stan's pissed, but I'll handle him."

"Thank you, Katherine. You have no idea . . ."

"This time, Tom. I'll handle him this time."

Katherine glanced at the clock. Nine. Jesus. There was barely time to catch the tail end of one of the four cocktail parties on her social calendar. She leaned against the back of her chair, resigning herself to an air kiss–less evening. Her stomach growled. She hadn't eaten anything all day but a small salad, minus the red peppers. She'd pick up sashimi on the way home, but not before making a dent in the pile of mail Brooke had placed on her desk. Reluctantly, she sifted through the stack, tossing the junk and setting aside anything of remote importance. A thin FedEx envelope, addressed to Ms. Kitty Hill, caught her eye immediately. She stared at the label, her heart suddenly throbbing against her chest.

Kitty Hill lived in Vermont and wore no makeup. She dressed in bulky corduroys and shiny snow boots. Kitty Hill was insecure and reserved. Thicker and hairier. Kitty Hill was another person, a nobody. Katherine tore at the cardboard to find a smaller white envelope with a single sheet of paper tucked inside.

Richard P. Newman, J.D.
16 Hitchcock Road
Manchester, Vermont 05255

November 9, 2011

Dear Ms. Hill,

This letter is to inform you that you've been named in the last will and testament of Mrs. Luella Hancock.

The reading will take place at the following address on November 17, 2011, at two p.m. If you are receiving this letter, you're required to appear in person on the aforementioned date.

If you have any questions, please feel free to call my office: 802-362-4315.

Regards,
Richard P. Newman

Katherine read the letter again. Not Luella. Not the woman who had loved her so purely and with every morsel of her being. It must be a mistake. It had to be a mistake. Unexpectedly, tears began tumbling down Katherine's cheeks, falling hard and fast and catching her off guard. And then she knew. She'd have to go home. After twelve years, she'd finally have to go home and face her past.

Only a four-hour drive, but still a lifetime away.

Laney

"Yes, Tina. I do understand the way you want the appointment book organized, and so does Annie." Laney rolled her eyes and smiled at Annie, their new receptionist, who did not respond well to criticism. In the three weeks she'd been working there, Annie had already cried seven times. Laney felt sorry for her, but she didn't mind the crying because it really unnerved Tina. Like most bullies, Tina didn't actually view herself as a bully. *What in the world is she so upset about?* Tina had asked all seven times, flapping her emaciated arms in the air. *You'd think I was abusing her.* She'd pursed her thin lips. *Well, yes,* Laney had thought. But she'd kept her mouth shut, as always.

Laney was not someone who typically did well with keeping her mouth shut. *Spirited* was how she'd been described as a young girl, which had given way to *spunky,* and later *fiery* during her teen years, much the same way she'd characterize Gemma. When it came to Tina, though, she didn't have much of a choice. She doubted Tina would ever fire her, and if she did, she'd have a hell of a time running Oasis. Still, a boss was a boss. A job was a job. Sure, they could make ends meet on Rick's salary alone, especially when he was having a good year. That was just it, though: Rick's annual income was always something of a question mark. And, God knows, someone had to keep Gemma in clothing and makeup.

"Well, then, why is this waxing appointment in *red* when it's supposed to be in blue?" Tina questioned, exposing a triumphant expression. There was nothing Tina savored more than catching a mistake. The only thing Laney could guess was that it made her feel involved. Like the ship would sink without her clever color coordination.

"Because she's getting two treatments," Annie chimed in, wearing an equally triumphant expression. She'd yet to learn that Tina was right, even when she was wrong.

"Was I *talking* to you?" Tina snapped, and Annie looked as though she were about to cry. Again.

"Because Mrs. Kane is getting two treatments," Laney echoed. "Even though she's coming in for a bikini wax, she's having a facial after. We do multicategory treatments in red."

"Well, that seems stupid." *You were the one who came up with it.* "But who am I to argue?" She tittered. "Just the boss."

"We can change it if you'd like." Laney's shoulders stiffened. It seemed like she and Tina had these conversations every few weeks. Micromanagement at its finest. *Why do we fold the towels in three? Why is the wax so hot? Why don't we have green nail polish? Why don't we offer Japanese hair straightening? Why is the sky blue?* BECAUSE YOU WANTED IT THAT WAY!

"No, no, no. You do it *your* way." Tina slithered into her

expensive-looking leather jacket and reached directly across Annie for her Louis Vuitton purse, completely oblivious to her physical presence. Annie dodged the swinging bag. "I'm off to yoga. Don't burn the place down," she crowed on her way out the door. It was her signature departing line.

Laney turned to Annie. "Please kill me before I kill her."

Much to everyone's delight, Tina never returned after yoga, which had led to a string of jokes about her being stuck in Downward Dog or Bent-over Bitch. The latter had been their hair colorist, Pierre's, contribution. His heavy French accent had made it all the more amusing. "Bent-over *Beetch*." Laney knew it was unprofessional to poke fun at Tina with her staff, but she couldn't help herself, and it seemed to improve morale. There'd been a startling amount of employee turnover since Bob and Francine had sold the spa. At first it had been like a mass exodus, including multiple middle fingers wagging at Tina.

Laney kept praying she'd take the hint and start treating people more respectfully, but no such luck. In the past three years they'd flipped the entire Oasis staff seven times. *Seven times.* But Laney had held on, impervious to Tina's tyrannical behavior, at least initially. Lately, it was getting to her more and more. She was going home irritable at the end of the day, which wasn't fair to Rick or Gemma. Sometimes she'd snap at them for nothing in particular, desperate to relinquish the ugliness, for fear it would consume her.

Laney had never expected to still be living in Manchester into her mid-thirties. On the contrary, she'd always sworn she'd get out of the small town where she grew up, convinced that she was destined for greatness or at least glamour. Not that there was anything wrong with Manchester; she just wanted more. Something better, bigger, glossier.

Deep down, she probably felt entitled to it. As a teenager, Laney had delighted in scouring the village for hours, especially during ski season, when the wealthy Manhattanites descended on the outlet stores, waving their mint green American Express cards this way and that. Oh, what she would have given for a mint green American Express card. Laney hadn't been content to simply rub elbows with the beautiful people, as she'd called them. She yearned to *be* one of the beautiful people. *I'm going to live the glamorous life in New York City*, she'd told anyone who would listen. Given her fiery personality, no one had doubted it for a second.

Except life didn't always work out exactly how you planned. Did it? And here she was, twelve years later, one of Tina's minions. At least she could still dream about an alternate existence while lying in bed at night.

Laney stumbled through the door at seven thirty, balancing four bags of groceries on either side, the plastic handles digging into the crooks of her arms. The sweet aroma of Rick's homemade tomato sauce permeated her senses and drew her toward the kitchen like a malnourished zombie.

"Taste this." Rick held out a wooden spoon smothered in sauce, cradling the underside with his free hand.

"That's heaven." Laney licked the spoon clean. "When I die, bury me in a vat of that." She kissed Rick on the lips and heaved the groceries onto the counter.

"I feel like I'll be too sad to cook that much, what with you dead and all." He turned back to the pot, stirring the sauce as gently as he'd handle a newborn baby. "Though if we have a little advance warning, I could stockpile it in the freezer."

"Absolutely. I'll do what I can to die a slow death." Laney smirked. "All in the name of the sauce, of course."

"Of course." Rick hovered over a large boiling pot of penne and cracked open the oven to check on a thick, bubbling loaf of garlic bread.

"That's all for me, right?" Laney eyed the bread like it was the last morsel of food on Earth. Thank God for good genes.

"Every crumb." Rick switched the burner to simmer, added a sprinkle of sea salt to the pasta, and started unpacking groceries alongside his wife.

"Where's Gem?" The house was way too quiet. Despite the fact that Gemma could mainly be found in her room, plugged into her iPod and mesmerized by her Droid, somehow her presence, or lack thereof, was palpable.

"She's eating at Casey's house tonight." Rick put up a hand. "I know what you're going to say." He drained the pasta in a colander and dumped it back into the pot, giving his sauce another tender stir.

"I'm sorry, but I don't like that girl." Laney hoisted herself onto the counter, her legs dangling over the edge.

"You're kidding." Rick poured the sauce over the pasta and folded it in.

"She's got an attitude problem. And she's spoiled." Laney pulled two bowls from the cabinet and handed them to Rick. "Don't be shy. I didn't eat lunch."

"I'm pretty sure Gem can handle herself."

"I'm not worried about Gemma. I mean, I am. I don't know. I just don't like her. Okay?" Casey was, simply put, a mean girl, unless you were her friend, in which case she seemed like the greatest thing since Uggs. Gorgeous, clever, popular, and occasionally devious. She lived in a ridiculously large house on the other side of Manchester Village that had a pond for skating in the winter, a tennis court, an Olympic-sized outdoor swimming pool, and an indoor lap pool. For obvious reasons, Gemma preferred chilling there rather than at her own house, which was, by traditional standards, perfectly suitable. There was no pond or tennis court or swimming pool—indoors or out—but there was a finished basement with Ping-Pong and pool tables, not to mention a spectacular eat-in kitchen with a huge marble island as the centerpiece. Rick had built it himself with great care and attention to detail, considering what Laney and Gemma would love above all else.

"Fine by me." He lifted her down from the counter and hugged her to his chest. "I forgot to mention a FedEx came for you today."

"Ooh!" Laney's mood elevated instantly. Mail meant someone was thinking of her, even if it was the electric company. And packages? Well, even better. "I hope it's something good," she commented as she sashayed into the foyer.

"I doubt it. It's just a flat envelope."

"Never know. It could be a check from Ed McMahon," she called from the other room.

"Not likely," he called back.

"You're such a pessimist." She returned to the kitchen, shaking her head of tangled blond curls, and yanked on the cardboard strip to open the envelope.

"Sorry to disappoint you, but Ed McMahon's been dead for a few years."

"No way!"

"Yes way."

"Well, maybe it's from whoever took his place." Laney retrieved a smaller white envelope from inside the FedEx envelope. "Here's my big fat check. Better be nice, or I won't buy you anything." She opened it and found, much to her chagrin, only a single sheet of paper. Minus any dollar signs.

Richard P. Newman, J.D.
16 Hitchcock Road
Manchester, Vermont 05255

November 9, 2011

Dear Mrs. Marten,

This letter is to inform you that you've been named in the last will and testament of Mrs. Luella Hancock.

The reading will take place at the following address on November 17, 2011, at two p.m. If you are receiving this letter, you're required to appear in person on the aforementioned date.

If you have any questions, please feel free to call my office: 802-362-4315.

Regards,
Richard P. Newman

"No check?" Rick looked over at Laney, who was sitting at the kitchen table, staring at the piece of paper. "Everything okay?"

"Luella Hancock died."

"Oh, wow. That's really sad." He came over and put his hands on her shoulders, leaning down to kiss her cheek.

"I can't believe my mom didn't tell me."

"They didn't keep in touch much, did they?"

"No. I mean, not for years. And I haven't seen Luella in ages, not even at the supermarket."

"Maybe your mom doesn't know."

"I guess not. I'll have to call her." Laney's eyes were still transfixed on the letter. "She always loved Luella. We all did."

"I'm sorry, sweetie. I know she was important to you."

"It appears I was important to her too." Laney handed Rick the sheet of paper. "Luella named *me* in her will."

August 1988

Kitty

t's totally weird how everything can change all at once. One day you're a normal family, living in a normal house, with a normal life. Okay, maybe things weren't *completely* normal, but at least no one ever talked about me or pointed at me from across the cafeteria. I wasn't worthy of gossip. Lana Park was worthy of gossip. Justin Grills was worthy of gossip. And, unfortunately for Tanya Barker, she was worthy of gossip too, only not in a good way.

After the accident, I got lots of attention. There Goes That Poor Little Girl Whose Mother Got Killed kind of attention. And, of course, the She Watched Her Get Hit by the Car kind of attention. It definitely made me more popular at school. The cool girls were suddenly interested in me, inviting me to sit at their lunch table so they could ask me all sorts of questions about the accident, like I was some kind of circus freak. Sabrina Montag even lent me her pink fluorescent scrunchie in gym class. Unfortunately, having your mom pass away isn't exactly the reason you want to be popular, and mostly it made me want to run and hide. Some days I skipped school altogether; it's not hard to get out of class when your mom just died. The thing is, being home wasn't any better. It only made me sadder. That's when my dad decided it was time to move. He told me the bottling plant he worked at in Bennington really needed a new director of operations at their Manchester office, but I overheard him talking to his boss on the phone, begging to be transferred because we needed a change "in light of everything that's happened." In other words, my dead mom.

Sometimes I think it was better when I was invisible at school. My mother was never invisible. She stood out like a supermodel in our small town, always wearing beautiful dresses, with bright red lipstick and long red nails even if she was just running her regular errands, never track suits, like the other moms. She liked to be noticed, looked at, listened to, complimented, and waited on. No one else could get into Giorgio's, the fanciest Italian restaurant in Bennington, without a reservation *and* have Giorgio himself bring a free bottle of wine to the table. No one else had their groceries carried to their car by the manager of the supermarket like she did. She expected it. I don't expect it, because I'm not beautiful or special the way she was. It's okay. I know it.

My mom wanted to be an actress. She was living in New York City and going to auditions for commercials and soap operas every day before she met my dad. It sounded really exciting. She said once she left Iowa, where she grew up, she never wanted to go back. One night she was out with her friend, another actress, who introduced her to my dad, who was visiting one of his friends in New York City. My mom didn't really like my dad that much at first. He wasn't as handsome as the men she usually went out on dates with and he was a little annoying, but he was so in love with her, she finally decided to go out with him. She said being an actress was no way to make money, and that my dad liked taking care of her, treated her really well, and had a good job. I guess he had enough money for both of them, so she went with him to Vermont. My dad tells a whole other story. He says they fell in love the first time they saw each other. I think she always missed her life in New York City. My mom would have been a great actress.

I'm not really sad to be leaving Bennington. It's been totally strange living in the house with all of her things for the past four months. My dad tried to pack up as much as possible. He said he'd save her clothing and jewelry in case I wanted them one day. But even with her stuff gone, everything still looks and smells like her. It's like she's gone, but she's not. It's hard to explain, but in a way, it's sort of like my dad and I never lived here to begin with. It was her house. It still is. Dad's never said anything about it, at least not to me, but I think he feels it too. It doesn't mean I don't miss her. I do. I guess it comes in and out. Some days I feel relieved. I know that sounds mean, but it's nice not to worry you're always disappointing someone. Other days, I'm sad a lot, sometimes from the time I wake up to the time I go to sleep. It's weird to think I'll never see her again. I hope I don't forget her.

Moving day came faster than I thought. Once you know you're leaving, it's hard not to feel nervous about it. I didn't sleep at all last night. I couldn't stop thinking and mostly worrying about what my new life is going to be like. I haven't even seen our new house yet. My dad said he knows I'll love it. So I'm sure I will. He knows what I like. And my room is going to be much bigger, which can't be a bad thing. My dad says we're a team now.

I walked out onto the porch and sat on our stoop for the last time, watching him load the rest of our stuff into the trunk of our gray Chevy. I can't help but feel like we're leaving my mom behind. The house and her things are really my last connection to her. On the other hand, I want to run away from this town as fast as possible—the people who know, who point their fingers and stare at me with sad faces, and mostly all the little things that remind me of her every day. Like the way our dish towels still smell like her perfume.

"Ready, Kitty Kat?" My dad called from the car and slammed the trunk closed. He squinted at me and smiled. The sun was brighter than ever—a good omen, I hope.

"Yup!" I picked up my pink suitcase and ran toward the car, nervous and excited for our future together. I tried not to look back, but I did anyway. I needed one last look.

Laney

"When do you think they'll get here?" I followed my mom around the kitchen, feeling antsy, kind of like my skin was tingling all over. She'd made the four of us a huge pancake breakfast, and there was still yellow batter splattered everywhere. Mom loves to cook, but she's a bit messy at it.

"I don't know, love. Soon, I guess." She swiped a wet dish towel down the length of the counter and patted it dry with a paper towel.

"Did you see her?" I twirled in circles on the shiny brown tile.

"Laney, I told you I didn't see her, only her father." She washed a bunch of red grapes in the sink and added it to a bowl of big pink peaches.

"Well, what was he like?" I sat down at the kitchen table, hugging my knees to my chest. I was *desperate* for every last detail.

"He seemed lovely, sweetheart. I'm sure they'll be here soon enough."

"I'm sure they won't. Soon enough would be *now*." I stood up again. "What color is his hair?"

"Brown."

"Like, a lightish brown? Or is it real dark, like, almost black?"

"I don't know. Sort of medium. Why do you care what color his hair is?"

"I'm trying to imagine what his daughter's going to look like." So far she looked like a man with medium brown hair. "And his eyes?"

"What about them?"

"What color are they?"

"Laney, I have no idea. I didn't study him. We talked for maybe five minutes. Just long enough for him to say they were moving in next Saturday."

"*Next* Saturday!?"

"*This* Saturday, love. *Today*. I'm just telling you what he said then."

"Tell me *exactly* what he said."

"For the millionth time, he said he and his daughter are moving into the house next to Luella's, and that she's eleven, just like you." Didn't sound like a five-minute conversation to me.

"I wish they'd just get here already."

"Patience, Laney. Patience." It's a word I hear a lot, mainly from my parents. I guess because I don't have any. I once tried to explain to them that clearly I wasn't born with patience, and eleven years later it has yet to arrive. They told me that it's not something you're born with or something that arrives out of the blue, but it's something you have to develop. Seems like a waste of time.

"Can I take the pie and wait on their porch?" Yesterday Mom and I baked them a gorgeous raspberry pie with golden crust and oozy red goodness all stuffed inside. It took lots of willpower for my brother, Grant, and me not to eat it for dessert last night.

"I don't think so, Lane. We should let them get settled in before we jump down their throats." She took off her flowery apron, folded it neatly into the drawer next to the stove, and kneeled down in front of me. "I know you're excited, but this is a big change for her. And for her dad."

"What happened to her mom again?" I knew the answer, at least part of it, but I wanted to hear it one more time. If I was about to meet my new best friend, I had to know everything there was to know about her.

"Laney, I told you her mom passed away." She shook her head. I heard her tell my dad it was a "real travesty." I'm not quite sure what that means, but it can't be good.

"From what?"

"Lane. Come on. It's not important." She peeled one side of a peach and cut me a slice. "All I'm saying is that I think we should give them a little space and, once they're settled in, you can go over with the pie. Okay?"

"Fine." I sighed, though I still thought it would be nice to welcome them as soon as they got here. Who wouldn't want a sweet girl like me with a delicious pie waiting at their door? I'd be happy to help them unpack boxes too! "Do you think she knows about me?"

"I'm not sure, love, but I have no doubt she will soon enough."

The house two doors down from ours has been empty for three years now. Mom told me a really rich family from New York City used to use it as their ski home when I was little, but I don't remember them much and it seems like forever ago. It's similar to our house. Medium-sized, white on the outside, with black shutters and window boxes, where I hope they'll plant some pink tulips. Pink tulips are my favorite. My dad buys them for me every Valentine's Day. I've only been inside the house once. It's nice. But nothing like Luella Hancock's. Her house is enormous, and since it's right between my house and the new girl's house, it makes ours look kind of little, even though they're not. I was beyond excited when Mom told me a girl exactly my age was about to move in. Jackpot, right? I'm sort of over most of the kids at school. They're so boring. Now I'll have a brand-new friend to do *everything* with. Plus, it's a huge deal to have your best friend live practically next door. Best friends *and* neighbors. I hope her dad told her about me.

"I'm just going to watch out the window, okay?" I hopped onto the window seat by the front door, leaning my back against one side and stretching my tanned legs down the blue-and-white-striped cushion. I look eons better with a tan, especially in the white Cavariccis I got for my birthday. Grant and I have been swimming at Luella's pool almost every day this summer. He's my older brother, but only by a year, and he can do a backward dive. I can't yet, but I'll have mastered it any day, and then I can teach the new girl. Unless she already knows how. Well, I'm sure there will be plenty of other stuff I can teach her. Summer is my absolute favorite time of the year, especially since winters are so cold and dark in Vermont. Mom always says, "Even when it's cold and dark, our home has a sunny disposition," but I still like summer best.

"Suit yourself. I'm going to the supermarket. Are you sure you don't want to come?"

"Yup."

"Might make the time pass more quickly. Maybe they'll be here when we get back."

"No, thanks. I'll stay here." I spotted their gray Chevy
the day my mom met the new girl's dad. Of course, I didn't
know whose it was at the time, otherwise I'd have been out
there immediately to introduce myself. Anyway, they have
to pass our house to get to theirs, so if I just sit here and
watch it'll only be a matter of time. I do *not* want to miss
their arrival, because as soon as they get here I can start
counting down their "time to settle in" before I pop on
over with the pie. Maybe she'll want to go for an afternoon
swim at Luella's; she says we can come over whenever we'd
like. Luella doesn't have any kids. I once asked her why and
she said it wasn't in the cards for her. I told my mom, and she
said not to be such a busybody. Funny word, but I don't
see what the big deal is. It's not like she *killed* her kids; she
just didn't have any of her own, which is fine by me, because
we get her pool all to ourselves.

"Okay, but do not run over the minute they get here." She
gave me a warning look, and I nodded back when she was
facing the other direction. "Did you hear me, Laney?"

"Yes, Mom." She gathered her purse and car keys. "You
said don't go over as soon as she gets here." *But you didn't say
don't get her to come to me.*

Kitty

We got to the house really quickly. I almost wanted a little while longer to imagine it. But here it was—big and white, with black shutters and a cherry-red door. I like a cherry-red door. It reminds me of my mom's nails. On the way over, my dad told me that there's a girl my age who lives on the other side of this mansion that's next to our house. He said that when he met her mom, she said her daughter would be thrilled to have a new friend. I'm not really getting my hopes up. That's what parents always say. And her daughter is probably cooler than I am. She probably wears tight acid-washed jeans and tortoiseshell sunglasses. Plus she probably has all the friends she needs. I thought about telling everyone in Manchester that I was very popular in Bennington, but I'm pretty sure very popular people don't tell people they're very popular. Although I couldn't really say, since I'm not. Anyway, that would be lying, which I try not to do, because then I need to apologize at church.

"Let's go, Kitty Kat. Grab what you can," my dad said cheerily. I took my pink suitcase, which I'd held on my lap on the way over, and two other small bags and followed him into the house. "So?" He looked at me, waiting to see what I thought.

"Wow. It's so . . ." What was the word? "Fancy!" My mom would have loved it. She loved fancy. I felt a little sick knowing she'd never live in this house. There was a huge, shiny kitchen with a refrigerator bigger than I've ever seen. Connected to the kitchen was an even bigger living room. My mom didn't cook, but I could still imagine her in this kitchen, heating up a can of beans in the microwave and looking beautiful. "Can I go see my room?"

"You bet! Up the stairs on the right." My dad seemed happy. I knew this was hard for him too. Even if the place was gross, I would have said I liked it. And then I would have had to apologize at church.

My bedroom was twice the size of the one in Bennington. It could fit at least six friends for a sleepover, if I made any friends. The walls were painted a light pink, my favorite color, and there were two large windows taking up one whole side of the room, with empty window boxes on the outside for flowers or plants or something. I ran back downstairs.

"I love it, Daddy!" I squeezed him tight around the middle and he held me for longer than usual, kissing the top of my head.

"I'm so happy, Kitty Kat. So, so happy."

"Me too!" I might have seen some tears in his eyes.

"Hey, there's a letter here for you. Someone dropped it through the mail slot." My dad handed me the purple envelope which had "NEW GIRL WHO'S 11 WHO JUST MOVED IN" written on it in red marker. I turned it over and the other side said, "VERY IMPORTANT—READ IM-MEDIATELY." So I did.

> Dear New Girl,
>
> Welcome home! My name is Laney, and I live on the other side of the really big house (in the white house that looks like yours). We need to meet immediately!! Don't unpack! It can wait! Come over as soon as you get this!!!!!!!!! It's very, very, very important.
>
> Sincerely,
> Your New Best Friend

I stared wide-eyed at the note. I've never had a best friend. I've never had anyone think it was very, very, very important to meet me. Not even one *very*. Could it be a joke? Could news of the girl with the dead, beautiful mom from Bennington already have gotten to Manchester? I showed the note to my dad.

"Wow! Go on over." I'm pretty sure he was as surprised as I was. All parents like to think their kids have loads of friends, but when no one ever comes to the house and no one ever invites your kid for sleepovers, it's hard to ignore.

"Really?" I looked around the first floor at all of the un-packed boxes, bags, and furniture wrapped in blanket-type thingies. "I'll just help you here and go meet Laney tomor-row." Part of me wanted to rush over. Another part of me wanted to wait. What if she realized I'm not her new best friend? It's one of the problems with being an overthinker,

as my mom used to call me. *You take everything too seriously,*
she'd say. A lot.

"Are you kidding? Get out of here! I've got this under
control."

"Okay. I'll just say hello and be home really soon." He
gave me a thumbs-up, and my mind started sprinting immediately. Should I change my clothing? What would a best
friend of Laney's wear? Probably not knee-length brown
shorts, which made my legs look like pork sausages, or a
dark green collared Izod shirt, which made me look like a
boy. But all of my stuff was packed and, honestly, most of it
wasn't much better. I didn't bother asking my dad. I knew
what he'd say. *If Laney doesn't like you for who you are, she's no
friend of yours.*

On the other hand, my mom would have said, *Beggars
can't be choosers.*

Standing at Laney's front door, I wished I'd changed my
ugly outfit. She'd probably take one look at me and realize
her mistake. My stomach was all flip-floppy and, as I rang
the doorbell, I decided I should have waited until tomorrow.
Maybe she wouldn't be home. Or maybe she wouldn't hear
the bell, and I could just slip back to my house and help my
dad unpack. Not my first choice of things to do, but at the
moment it sounded pretty good. I turned around and started
walking away.

"Hello?" a woman's voice called out just as I'd reached
the bottom of the steps. "Are you the new girl from three-oh-
five?" She stood in the doorway, wearing a light yellow sun-
dress with a blue-and-white checked apron tied around her
very thin waist. Her long, curly blond hair was pulled back
in a loose ponytail. She wasn't beautiful like my mom, but
she was pretty in a natural kind of way.

"Oh, hi. Yes." I made my way back onto the porch. "I didn't mean to bother you. It's just that I, um, I got this. I think it's from your daughter, Laney." I handed her the letter.

"I see." She read it and shook her head, laughing, which made her whole face light up. "That would definitely be my Laney. I told her not to bother you."

"It's no bother, really. I'll just come back at a better time."

"Nonsense!" She smiled brightly. "I'm Carol Drake. Laney's mom. It's such a pleasure to have you as our new neighbor. Laney is simply over the moon to have a friend her age living so close. Please come in. . . ." She paused.

"Kitty. Kitty Hill." I followed her inside. Laney's house looked a lot like ours, only lived-in. Carol walked me into the kitchen, where there were big bowls overflowing with fresh fruit and glass containers filled with cereal and crackers and cookies, even one tall one with uncooked spaghetti. Most of the food in my old house was either canned or from the deli department.

"Can I get you something to drink, Kitty? A snack?" She didn't even wait for me to answer before putting a bowl of the biggest red grapes I'd ever seen in front of me and pouring me a glass of lemonade.

"Thank you." I picked a grape off the stem. My dad and I were so busy getting everything together for the move we'd barely eaten anything all day, unless you count the bag of corn nuts we shared on the car ride over.

"I'll just be a minute. Laney's next door at Luella Hancock's house for a swim."

"Oh, you don't have to get her. I could just come back later when she's done, or tomorrow."

"No, no. Laney has been dying to meet you. I literally had to shove her out the door to keep her from staring out the window all day! Don't go anywhere."

"Okay." I smiled. It was impossible not to. Laney's mom was so *happy*. I don't remember my mom being like that—at least not most of the time. There were some great days. Days where she'd wake me up and say, "No school today!" and we'd go shopping and have strawberry milk shakes at the Bennington Diner. But then the next day, she'd be all snippy again. Still, Carol made me miss my mom a little. There's just something about moms that dads don't have, no matter how hard they try. I can't explain it.

I sat for a little while, eating the grapes as slowly as I could until I heard voices coming from the back of the house. A second later, Laney spun into the kitchen like a tornado, soaking wet in a red-and-white polka-dot bikini. At first glance, I knew she was everything I expected her to be, but had hoped she wasn't: blond, blue-eyed, skinny, and perfectly tanned from head to toe. She even had a sparkle in her eyes—the same one my mom got when she talked about her days as an actress in New York City.

"Kitty!" Laney threw herself at me, wrapping her wet arms around my sweaty back. "I can't believe you're finally here! This is so exciting! It felt like *ages*. I almost jumped out of my skin! What should we do? Do you have a bathing suit? Do you want to go to Luella's pool? Are you hungry? Do you need help unpacking? Did you get my note?"

She spoke without taking a breath, dripping a puddle onto the kitchen floor. I must have sat with my mouth hanging open, because she just kept going. I didn't know what to make of it. What to make of her. It was like she'd known me forever and we hadn't seen each other for the longest time, even though we'd never met before. I watched her carefully, wondering why anyone who looked like her or acted like her—the little bit I'd seen—would be interested in someone like me, sitting like a lump in poop-colored boys' clothing.

"Laney, relax." Her mom handed her a fluffy white towel and wiped up the pool of water that had formed under her feet with a bunch of paper towels. "Kitty just got here. Maybe she's not ready to rush over for a swim."

"I think all my bathing suits are packed." I nodded.

"Oh." Laney twisted up her perfect face. What I wouldn't give to look like her, twisted face and all. "Well, Luella invited us both for tea and biscuits tomorrow. Wanna go?"

"Sure. I just have to ask my dad."

"Okay." Laney looked a little disappointed. "Do you want to stay for dinner?"

"Laney, she just got here. I'm sure her father wants her home tonight."

"Probably." I nodded again. It was a lot to take in all at once.

"Kitty, you and your father are welcome at our house anytime, and I hope you will accept a dinner invitation for next week, once you're settled." Carol put a hand on my back. I was thankful Laney had hugged me all wet, otherwise her mom would have known how grossly sweaty I was from the move.

"Thank you. I'll tell my dad." I smiled. I couldn't do much more than smile and nod. "I think maybe I should be getting home. There are still a lot of boxes." I stood up.

"No! You only just got here," Laney shrieked. I sat back down.

"Laney." Carol gave her a serious look, which wasn't really serious at all.

"Fine." Her shoulders collapsed. "You'll come to Luella's tomorrow?"

"Okay." I was sure my dad would say yes. I stood up again.

"Pinkie swear?" She held out her right hand, waiting for me to do the same. We hooked our smallest fingers together, and her face lit up like a Christmas tree. The brightest Christmas tree I'd ever seen. "To new best friends."

"To new best friends."

The next afternoon, I showed up on Luella's doorstep with a sad batch of cookies, which my dad had baked after I went to sleep. He said it's really important that we make a good impression on the neighbors.

"My, those look delicious. Thank you." Luella took the cookies and led me inside. Her home was just as beautiful as she was. Crystal chandeliers hung from the tall ceilings, colorful carpets covered the polished wood floors, and everywhere you looked there were trinkets that seemed like they were from far-off places—a shiny gold Buddha, a pair of orangish-pink colored porcelain dogs, and lots of statues with women and men kissing and hugging, which I think were made of china. Luella was definitely older than my dad by a lot, but she was still very beautiful, with silvery gray hair slicked back into a tight bun, skin that glowed, and big brown eyes the color of dark chocolate.

"Sorry they're burnt. We just moved in next door, and my dad hasn't learned how to use the oven yet. I'm Kitty."

"No bother. I'd say they're well-done." When she spoke, it almost sounded like singing.

"Thank you, Mrs. Hancock."

"Luella will be just fine." She nudged me into the kitchen. "Iced tea, dear?"

"Yes, please."

"So, tell me: how do you like Manchester so far?" She carried two tall glasses to the table; sat down across from me, tipping the frosted-glass pitcher of tea into each glass; and pushed a plate of biscuits toward me. "Help yourself, dear." I did.

"It's okay, I guess. Our house is nice. And my room is really big and pink." I was wearing a navy blue skirt and a plain white T-shirt, in the hopes that Laney would forget yesterday's ugly outfit. My dad said he'd give me some money to go shopping before school starts. I hope he doesn't want to come with me. I love him, but he's even worse with fashion than I am. If that's possible.

"Well, that sounds delightful. A good start, I'd say." She took a biscuit for herself. "I hear you've met our Laney, then?"

"Yes."

"A real spark plug, that one. Sucks all the energy into her vortex. Don't you think?"

"I guess." I had no idea what a vortex was.

"But a nice girl. Means well, even though she can wear you down."

"Uh-huh." I bit into the biscuit. I get uncomfortable when people ask me lots of questions. So I just eat, which explains my thighs. "Is she . . ." I looked around the room, thinking Laney might leap up from behind the counter.

"She'll be here any minute now." Luella smiled reassuringly. "I hope you two will enjoy the swimming pool while it's still warm."

"Oh, sure. Thank you." I wiped some crumbs off the table and into a napkin.

"A little mess never hurt anyone." Luella took the napkin. "I mean it. About the swimming. You're welcome anytime, Kitty. I need you kids frolicking about to keep me young, and I like the company."

"Oh, okay." I nodded politely, wondering why she lived all alone, especially in such a big house, but I didn't ask.

"HELLO! LUELLA? KITTY?"

"That'll be Laney, letting herself right in the front door

like she owns the place." Luella frowned a little. "Let's you and I get together for tea later this week. Shall we? Just the two of us."

"Sure." I nodded. I've never had so many people interested in me all at once.

"You've started without me!" Laney appeared, putting on an injured face. "I'll have to catch up!" She sat down and helped herself to a biscuit, practically swallowing it whole. "So, what have you been talking about? Sorry to be late. Mom was crazy about losing her keys again. Grant found them in the living-room plant." She giggled. Her hair wasn't wet from the pool like yesterday, and I'd never seen anything like it. Layers upon layers of wild blond curls everywhere.

"Well, I was just getting to know Kitty here."

"Isn't it absolutely fabulous? A new best friend and neighbor all in one! When Mom told me, I nearly freaked out!" Laney ate another biscuit, talking all the while. "Don't you think, Kitty? I mean, moving here and meeting me! Lucky, huh?" I had to agree.

"I'd say you're both very fortunate to have a friend your age so close by." Luella pulled another glass from the cabinet and filled it. "Iced tea, dear?"

"Thanks." Laney gulped it down. "Have you had any?" She eyed my untouched glass. "Luella makes it with fresh mint from her vegetable garden. She's got tomatoes and lettuce and cucumbers and corn too. Oh, and peppers. Lots of peppers. My mom says Luella is the reason we eat beautiful salads every night in the summer. It's my favorite time of year. What about you?"

"I think I like fall best." The more clothing, the better for me.

"Me too." Luella agreed. "Not too hot, not too cold."

"My mom likes fall too. She sweats a lot in the hot weather. And she doesn't know how to swim. Can you believe that? I mean I love my mom, but . . ." Laney looked at me suddenly. "Sorry."

"Sorry about what?" I sipped my tea.

"I keep talking about my mom. And, I mean, I know . . ." Laney shifted in her seat. It was the first time I'd seen her even a little uncomfortable. It was kind of a relief.

"It's no big deal."

"Who wants to go for a swim?" Luella interrupted. I knew she was trying to help by changing the subject.

"It's really okay," I mumbled, but I don't think either of them heard me.

"I DO!" Laney lifted her shirt over her head. She was wearing a pink ruffled bikini top.

"I didn't bring my suit."

"Run back home and get it!" Laney insisted. "Go on. I'll meet you out there." She jumped up, leaving her mess behind.

"I'll just help you clean up here." I stacked my plate on top of Laney's and carried them to the counter.

"Don't be silly. Go on home like Laney said and get your suit. Only a few hours left of sunshine."

"Are you sure? My dad said it's rude to eat and run."

"Well, your dad is right, under normal circumstances." Luella put the dishes in the sink. "But I'm letting you off the hook." She winked.

"Okay." I smiled. "Thank you again, Luella, for the tea and biscuits."

"It's my pleasure, dear. I hope you'll come often." She walked me to the front door. "It'll be open when you come back. Don't be shy; just let yourself in."

"Thank you." I started down the path until she called out to me, and I stopped to turn and face her.

"You know, Kitty, you remind me of another young girl I once knew."

"Oh, really?" It seemed like a strange time to bring it up, but people in this town are strangely friendly and open.

"A girl I knew very well."

"Who was she?"

Luella stared off into the distance, like she'd suddenly forgotten. And then it came back to her. "Me." She looked in my direction again. "You most certainly remind me of me."

Present Day

Katherine

" I'm going home to visit family and friends." That's what she'd told the overtly intrusive man behind the rental-car counter. It seemed to be the most normal answer, sort of like, "I'm going to grab a burger and fries." Neither of which she'd done in over a decade. The man had gone on to ask whom she was visiting, specifically, where she was going, and how long she'd be staying. "Not really sure" had been all she could manage without biting his head off. Katherine was not looking forward to the four-hour ride. For one, driving wasn't really her forte. Nobody drove in New York City. The price of a parking garage was tantamount to a month's rent for a one-bedroom apartment. Well, not any apartment Katherine would live in, but still. There were so many more enticing ways to spend your money. Like on taxicabs and shoes.

More than that, four hours in the car meant four hours of

idleness. Four hours she would not be able to return e-mails or check marketing copy, or even talk on the phone. There was nothing Katherine could do but sit behind the wheel, her mind buzzing feverishly, as she set out on her tedious journey from present to past.

When she'd told Jane Sachs that she needed a few days off, Jane had furrowed her brow. "This is unexpected," she'd said, narrowing her eyes. "What's going on?" Katherine had told her about Luella, who'd been an old friend of Jane's back in the day. "Well, I'm very sorry to hear about Luella, of course. It's just that I was hoping you were actually taking a vacation. I can't even remember the last time you took a sick day." That was because she never had. Katherine didn't get sick. And she definitely didn't "get" sick days. What could be worse than lying around like a sloth, feeling sorry for yourself when there was so much to be done? She'd never said as much, but it always irritated her when one of her staff called in sick. As far as she was concerned, a runny nose and sore throat were not reasons enough to evade responsibility.

Jane had urged her to take a little extra time, since it was the week before Thanksgiving. "You can't go all the way to Vermont and then turn around and come back right before the holiday, Katherine." Sometimes Jane spoke to her more like a mother than a boss. And when she said her name at the end of a sentence like that, she meant business. Katherine had conceded, momentarily considering whether or not she really had to stay in Vermont for the entirety of the time she'd promised Jane. But, ultimately, she knew Jane was right. And anyway, what would she do at home in her apartment with no work? The mere thought of it was preposterous.

Katherine hadn't seen her father in at least three years. Every so often he'd trek into the "BIG city," as he called it, to visit her for a weekend. He'd bring Hazel, his longtime girl-friend, who would ooh and aah over every last thing. She was enchanted by all of it—from the tall buildings to the glitzy shops and the street vendors. Katherine liked Hazel well enough. She was pleasant-looking, with cropped ashy blond hair and egg-shaped brown eyes. All of her features were soft and simple, like her personality. Hazel had met her father outside the Vermont Country Store the same year Katherine had gone off to college, a fortunate coincidence. Hazel had been selling raffle tickets for an American Heart Association auction, her husband having died from a heart attack two years earlier. Katherine's dad had bought a ticket, they'd gotten to talking, and she'd moved in two months later. Was their relationship erupting with passion? Unlikely. But they filled a very important void in each other's lives: com-panionship. And, if Katherine was being honest, Hazel had made it that much easier for her to stay away for so long. She acted as a buffer of sorts, even if unintentionally.

Hazel and her dad had invited her to stay with them, but Katherine had politely declined. She didn't like being any-one's houseguest, even if it was, in theory, her house. Or at least it had been at one time. Still, she couldn't very well stay in her old bedroom. She was a grown-up now, for God's sake.

Katherine arrived at the Equinox, a historic boutique re-sort just outside Manchester central, with two Louis Vuitton bags and one speeding ticket. It wasn't so much the expense of the ticket that agitated her; it was the fact that she'd been unable to negotiate her way out of it. Cops could be so gall-ingly unreasonable.

The rooms at the Equinox were nice enough—country charm married to modern elegance, with two fireplaces, one in the living area and one in the bedroom. Katherine surveyed the contents of her luggage and laughed. What had she been thinking? Actually, she hadn't been. She'd been so preoccupied with the circumstances surrounding the visit home that packing Gucci slacks and Manolo Blahnik four-inch heels had somehow seemed the rational course of action. Her father and Hazel were expecting her sooner rather than later, but there were priorities. Katherine sat down on the sofa and dialed her own number.

"Katherine Hill's office; please hold." The phone clicked before she could say anything. Brooke was probably frantic in her absence. Who could blame her? No doubt she was being harassed by everyone and anyone who'd been unable to reach Katherine for the better part of the day. "Hello. This is Brooke," she came back on the line, panting.

"Hi. It's me." Katherine put her feet up on the coffee table, fleetingly relieved not to be in the office.

"Oh, Katherine, hi," she puffed.

"Everything okay?"

"Um, well, not exactly." Katherine could hear the crackle of rustling papers. "Alan's assistant, Regina, quit this morning, so he's been giving me all his stuff and . . . Wait. Where is that . . ." she trailed off.

"Brooke?"

"Yup, I'm here. Sorry, there's just a lot . . . it's really amazing how . . ."

"Breathe. It's okay." Katherine bit into a crisp red apple she'd lifted from the lobby. It was the first thing she'd eaten all day.

"Right, absolutely. Don't worry. I'm on top of it all. If I could just . . ."

"Listen, Brooke, I've got to run, but here's what I want you to do. Send me one e-mail with any issues I can deal with when I get back to my hotel this evening. And call my cell with anything that needs my immediate attention in the meantime. Okay? Remember, I'm on *location*, not *vacation*." It was Jane's line, but Katherine had used it more than once over the years.

"Okay, will do," Brooke stammered, while three other lines chimed in the background.

"And I'll call Alan and tell him to give his crap to someone else's assistant. If he tries to pawn anything else off on you, let me know."

"Thanks." Brooke sounded at least somewhat comforted.

Katherine finished unpacking, organizing everything just the way she liked it. She took her own advice and inhaled deeply, and dialed the vaguely familiar number for the first time in too long.

"Hi, Hazel. It's Katherine. I'll be over in ten minutes." She exhaled. "Yes, I'm looking forward to seeing you too."

"Kitty Kat!" Katherine's father answered the door with outstretched arms. She couldn't help but cringe at the designation, and then feel immediately remorseful. Why was it that within seconds of being home, all of the guilt she'd so conveniently kept at bay for twelve years came charging back like a stampede of bulls?

"Hi, Dad." She let him fold her into his embrace, inhaling the spicy scent of his cologne. He looked different, older. A constellation of deep lines splayed from the corners of his eyes, and his salt-and-pepper hair had lost its pepper. Was that a slight limp?

Katherine had almost driven by the house. She hadn't remembered it being quite so small. After living in New York for over a decade, even Luella's mansion appeared somewhat quaint—at least that's what Realtors in Westchester would call it. The same way they called graveyards peaceful and teardowns "projects." But yet there it stood. The same white facade, the same black shutters, the same cherry-red door. She was pleased her father hadn't changed that. Walking inside, she couldn't help but fixate on every little thing. The kitchen was still painted the same robin's-egg blue, and the cabinets still boasted the same maple finish. The identical yellow porcelain napkin holder with hand-painted pink flowers still sat on the same round glass table. Same red shag carpet in the living room. And on and on. She half expected to find her old pink raincoat hanging on the same rusted hook in the mudroom.

"Kitty!" Hazel rushed down the stairs, wearing a bright purple apron, the one thing that did appear to be new. "Oh, my. Look how skinny you are! Look how skinny she is, Joe. Not one inch to pinch."

"She looks perfect to me." Katherine's dad patted her back affectionately and began pulling her jacket off. "Let's get you something to eat." She felt a little awkward being fawned over. But there was no getting around it. As far as they were concerned, she was the pope. Or Barbra Streisand. Her dad had always had a thing for *Funny Girl*.

"Oh, I'm not hungry, thanks. I ate something at the hotel." Not a lie altogether, but it was unlikely that they'd view half an apple as a suitable meal.

"Nonsense. I've made mini quiches and pigs in a blanket, and some of my special ginger cookies for dessert." Hazel smiled nervously. Katherine knew Hazel wasn't sure what to make of her. Unlike Hazel's own daughters, Katherine didn't visit. She didn't have a husband or a family. She didn't cook or own an apron. And she most certainly didn't clean or vacuum. But, more than that, Hazel knew that Katherine was important—even without a husband or a family— she just didn't know exactly why. Sure, there was some kind of high-powered job, but to Hazel that meant little more than the paycheck it resulted in.

"I'll just take a glass of water for now." Katherine felt herself acting polite, as if her very presence might somehow insult them. Did most people have to try this hard around family? She wasn't sure. There'd been a time when Katherine and her dad had a natural, easy relationship, but over the years there'd been a shift. It had probably started when she was a teenager. There were so many things she couldn't discuss with her dad or hadn't wanted to, and it had created a division between them so broad that it had never been mended. A division that had once been filled with the unconditional adoration between a daughter and her father. And then there'd been the real distance. College. A new job. Life.

"Here you go, darling. Come sit down." Hazel ushered her to the kitchen table, placing a glass of water and a plate of quiches and pigs in a blanket in front of her. "They're homemade."

"Thank you. That was really very sweet of you to go to all this trouble." Katherine watched Hazel flutter around the kitchen like a newborn butterfly who'd just grown her wings. Hazel, for her part, did not look a day older than the last time Katherine had seen her or the time before that. It was remarkable, really. She'd certainly never had any Botox. And Katherine was fairly certain Hazel wasn't slathering Crème de la Mer on her face—more likely whatever crappy drugstore brand she could get the best bargain on. But yet her skin was luminescent, one might say flawless, especially for a woman in her early seventies. Her cheeks blushed naturally; almost the exact color of Blend's Really Rosy cheek stain, and her ashy blond hair hadn't even gone completely gray. If only Hazel knew what lengths Katherine went to—both the effort and expense—to maintain her "ageless" beauty.

"Well, it's not every day we have such a special guest." Katherine's dad beamed. There was that guilt again. She couldn't imagine what it had been like for him all these years. In the beginning he'd called every other day to check in on her. "How's the BIG city?" He'd always open with that. Then the calls became weekly, then monthly, until they'd stopped altogether, save for holidays and birthdays. She could hardly blame him. Would you continue to call someone who never had more than a harried thirty seconds to run through the latest life was dishing out? It was awful to say, but it had just seemed easier to gloss over most of it than to start from scratch, explaining the ins and outs of a world he'd neither get nor ever be a part of.

Katherine's cell phone hissed. She glanced at the number. Brooke. "I'll just be a minute," she said, and held up her index finger, excusing herself into the living room, which radiated the same subtle musty aroma it always had. "Hi, Brooke. What's going on?" She sunk into the brown velour couch. "Uh-huh. Okay. I see. What an asshole. Don't worry, I'll deal with it."

Six phone calls later, Katherine returned to the table, where her father and Hazel were waiting patiently. "I'm so sorry. Things are a little frantic at work in my absence."

"Of course, Kitty Kat." Her dad nodded knowingly, even though he didn't understand.

"So, you're here for Luella's will reading." Hazel nudged the plate of quiches and franks toward Katherine. "Such a sweet lady."

"Yes, she was." Katherine pinched the inner corners of her eyes with her thumb and forefinger. She really didn't want to cry again. "I just can't believe she named me."

"You were like the daughter she never had." Her father picked a quiche off the plate and ate it in one bite. "I think it makes a lot of sense, actually."

He was right, and Katherine knew it. Luella had been like a surrogate mother to her, even though she'd also been somewhat of an enigma. Growing up, Katherine hadn't thought much about it. After all, there's a certain level of self-absorption inherent in childhood; people are supposed to focus on you, not you on them—especially adults. And Luella had just sort of been there, like this constant fixture—both she and her home were always open for swimming, tea, a game of gin rummy, or whatever. But, beyond that, Luella was an unfalteringly reliable confidante to Katherine, offering advice when needed and lending a sympathetic ear when there was nothing to be said. She had an uncanny knack for knowing exactly when to keep her mouth shut and when not to. Still, it was hard for Katherine to feel like she ever really knew Luella the woman, despite how close they'd been. She was a widow; that everyone was well aware of. She had no kids of her own, though she never spoke of why. She had lavish parties with throngs of guests, but very few close friends, if any. She was gorgeous, kind, and relentlessly generous, but also painstakingly private. That Katherine could relate to, then and now.

Through the years, Jane Sachs had made only a few passing comments about her old friend, all of which Katherine had taken note of. Apparently, Luella's husband had been about a decade older than she and very handsome; the kind of man that other women ogled on the sidewalks of New York City, where—typically—people didn't take time to look more than two feet in front of them. Jane had once remarked that John had been madly in love with Luella—that they'd had a very special and unique connection that was evident to anyone in their general vicinity. She'd said John's eyes followed Luella everywhere she went, like it was the first and last time he would ever see her, even if she was just excusing herself to the ladies' room. Jane had also confided, on the heels of Katherine's prodding, that Luella and John had been desperate to have children—a big family, actually—but they'd tried and tried to no avail. There'd been more than one miscarriage, Jane recalled, and ultimately they'd decided to leave it in God's hands rather than let it rule their lives. The one thing Jane had never touched on was how and when John had died. And what that had been like for Luella. Of course, Katherine had never asked, given her acute sensitivity when it came to people dying prematurely.

"Joe, your cholesterol," Hazel admonished in her gentle way.

"One quiche won't kill me." He shooed at her tenderly. "You were very important to Luella, and she wanted you to know that."

"So, you knew about this?" Her father looked at Hazel, who nodded.

"We did. Luella told us of her plans before she passed. But she asked us not to say anything. She didn't want you to fuss."

"Do you know what she's left me?" Katherine eyed the mini hot dogs. She wanted to eat one for Hazel's sake alone, but she just couldn't bring herself to. There were so many more tempting things to waste one's calories on. Like chocolate soufflé.

"Not really." Her father looked at Hazel again.

"Not *really*? Or not at all?" Katherine winced at her inherently demanding tone. It was the tone she used for employees, not for her father.

"We've already said too much. You'll find out everything tomorrow."

"Would you like to stay for dinner, darling?" Hazel let him off the hook.

"I wish I could." She could. "But I have so much work to catch up on. I'll probably eat room service in front of my laptop." Hazel looked horrified. She'd definitely never ordered room service. Or felt tethered to a laptop.

"You're staying for Thanksgiving, though?" Her dad walked her to the door, helping her into her coat. They'd been so thrilled when she'd told them.

"Yes, Dad. I promise." She kissed his cheek and he pulled her close to him.

"I love you, Kitty Kat."

"Love you too, Dad."

Katherine got back into her rental car, realizing she hadn't even had the decency to ask how Luella had died. She closed her eyes, praying that it had been peaceful and painless. And then she silently scolded herself for being so detached. For being so far removed from all of it—all of them—that she was only entitled to scant details after the fact. How could she have so carelessly abandoned this woman who gave so much to her in so many ways? She was an ingrate, and Luella was repaying her with even more benevolence, because that was Luella's way.

She forced herself to think about the last time she'd spoken to Luella. When had it been? Three, four, five years ago? Luella had come to visit her sporadically during college and after she'd first moved to New York. There had even been a few fancy lunches at Barneys with Jane Sachs, which had made the other entry-levelers both envious and fearful of Katherine early on. But eventually Luella had told Katherine she was too busy to travel—what with her book club, upkeep around the house, and her charitable commitments.

In hindsight, Katherine figured Luella's reluctance to leave Vermont had probably meant she wasn't feeling well enough. Eventually, Luella's phone calls had become fewer and farther between as well. And what had Katherine done? She'd simply allowed her to pull away, too consumed by her own self-absorption to notice.

Now, staring at the shabby facade of the most lavish home on Pine Street, once so manicured and pristine, Katherine felt profoundly ashamed. And, of course, there standing next to it was Laney and Grant's house, a place so wrought with memories she felt like her head was going to explode. Katherine hadn't let herself think about Laney.

And she certainly hadn't let herself think about Grant.

July 1991

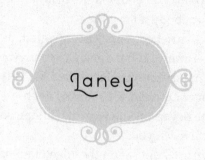

Laney

"He is such a total show-off." I dropped the baby oil on Kitty's lounge chair. She needed major help tanning those pale-as-a-ghost legs of hers. "You are such a total show off, Grant Drake!" I screamed it real loud so he could hear me from all the way up on the diving board, where he's been doing backflips nonstop. It's not that I can't do them. I just don't feel the need to parade around in front of Luella and Kitty, who cannot. Kitty's a bit of a scaredy-cat when it comes to things like that. And Luella, well, she's seventy-three, so she's not flipping anywhere, anytime.

It's been a superhot summer. I'm not sure what we'd do without Luella's pool. Kitty and I meet here every morning at ten, play gin rummy with Luella in the shade, and then we work on our tans. Though Kitty refuses to use the baby oil and insists on, like, 8,000 sunblock. It's no wonder she looks like Casper.

"I told you I'm not using that stuff." Kitty handed the oil back to me. "You might as well hold aluminum foil under your chin." Sometimes she can be a real downer.

"If you want to look all pasty for school, that's fine by me."

"You're gonna fry yourself to death." Grant laughed, shaking his wet body all over us.

"Stop it!" I shrieked, and Kitty giggled, as if anything Grant does is funny. "What do you care anyway?"

"I don't. I'm just saying." He pulled his faded gray Pearl Jam T-shirt over his head. He knows I'm obsessed with that T-shirt and he never lets me wear it. "I hope you're red as a tomato. That'll teach you."

"No, it won't." Grant sat on the edge of my lounger, and I kicked at his thigh. "Get off. I'm lying here. And anyway, Kitty and I are talking about personal things. Aren't we, Kitty?"

"Um, I guess." Kitty squinted and put her hand to her forehead like a soldier saluting her troops. Why she doesn't wear sunglasses is beyond me. She says she couldn't find a pair that looks right on her face.

"I'm sorry. Were you deep in discussion about this week's *90210*? Will Kelly and Brenda fight over a guy *again*? Oh no!" Grant slapped his cheeks with his palms and moved to Kitty's chair. Of course she curled her legs under to make space for him.

"Shut up. Why don't you go find your girlfriend, *Sandy*?" I sneered. "I'm sure she's somewhere pining for you. 'Oh, Grant, I want you sooooooo badly! I want to kiss those soft lips of yours.'"

"At least I have someone who likes me. Someone who's not flat as a pancake, like you!" He got up and walked toward our house. There's a shortcut through Luella's bushes to our back deck, which makes it superconvenient when we're wet from swimming.

"Loser!" I yelled after him, and he gave me the finger. I'll have to remember to tell my mom later.

"Sandy Parker?" Kitty sat up and turned toward me. Everyone knows Sandy Parker. She makes sure of it. There's also the not-so-minor fact that the whole school saw her making out with Greg Baldwin, who was a senior last year *and* the star of the basketball team. Not that I'm jealous.

"The one and only."

"Oh." Kitty scrunched her face up all weird. "What's Grant got to do with her?"

"He ran into her at her dad's hardware store. I guess she was there helping him or something. Then I overheard Grant telling Sam that Sandy told him to call her, so now I use it against him whenever he's annoying me."

"That's mature." Kitty tugged at her T-shirt. She won't take it off, even when it's just the two of us. It's not like she's fat or anything. Fine, maybe she could stand to lose, like, five pounds, but she totally sells herself short. If she'd just let me give her a little makeover, she could look really amazing. "Do you think he will?"

"Will what?"

"Call her."

"I don't know. Who cares?" I rolled over onto my stomach to tan my back. "Can you rub some oil on me?"

"Obviously, I don't *care*. I just don't really see Grant liking Sandy Parker. She's so . . ." Kitty smeared the oil from my shoulders down to the bottom of my legs.

"Lame?" I extended my arms along either side of my body. It's so much more comfortable to fold them under your head, but then they're all white on the underside. Consistent tanning is really an art.

"Well, yeah, she's definitely lame." Kitty was suddenly all fidgety. "I don't know. She just doesn't seem like Grant's type."

"How would you know?"

"I wouldn't." She wiped her hands on her T-shirt. "This stuff is disgusting."

"What has he told you?" Sometimes Kitty and Grant talk when I'm not around. And here I thought it was all boring stuff. "You better tell me, Kitty Hill. He's my brother. I want to know everything he's said to you about girls. Full. Blown. Details. But leave out anything gross."

"He hasn't said anything. I swear." She pulled her heavy black hair off her neck to reveal thick beads of perspiration being absorbed by the collar of her T-shirt.

"You better not be lying to me!"

"I'm not. Can we please drop it?" She let go of her hair. "Do you have an extra ponytail holder? It's a million degrees out here."

I took the elastic band out of my hair and handed it to her. "Fine. Sandy's not worth it anyway." Kitty's so strange when it comes to boys. Not that Grant is a boy. Well, not in *that* way. It's like she's scared of them. She hasn't even had her first kiss yet. "Sandy will probably peak in high school and then end up stuck in Manchester for the rest of her life, working at her dad's hardware store."

"What's wrong with Manchester?" She piled her hair into a high bun. It actually looked good, in a messy-sexy kind of way.

"What's not?" I turned my head to the other side to ensure even side-of-face tanning.

"What do you mean?"

"Duh. It's a total snooze, for starters. It's fine for now, but there's no way I'm living here forever. I'd rather die than end up like my parents."

"Laney! Don't say that. Your parents have a great life. Plus it's bad luck to talk about yourself dying."

"Sorry." I'm always forgetting to be sensitive about the whole death thing around Kitty, what with her mom and all. She never wants to talk about her or the accident.

"I just don't see what you have against Manchester."

"Don't you want to live someplace exciting? Like New York City?"

"Not really."

"What!?" I rolled onto my back and sat up straight, facing Kitty, who was red as a clown's nose from the heat. "You wouldn't want to live in the most exciting place in the world?"

"Maybe I don't think it's the most exciting place in the world." She fanned herself with her hand, which was still glistening from my baby oil.

"Well, you're ruining the master plan." I slipped my tank top over my bikini. My skin was feeling a bit crispy.

"What master plan?"

"The one where we go to UVM together, so we can save our money, and then move to New York after college, get a fabulous apartment, which we'll decorate ourselves any way we like, and host lots of parties. Naturally, we'll get super-glamorous jobs too."

"I don't think you can just *get* a glamorous job." Her face turned serious for a minute. "Plus not everyone makes it in New York. Some of them end up bitter in Vermont and married with a kid."

"Huh?"

"Forget it."

"Kitty, don't be so pessimistic. You don't want to go through life a slave to some shitty job. Do you?"

"I guess not." Clearly, Kitty does not have a master plan, which is just as well, since she's part of mine.

"Come *on*. You're my best friend. I can't do it without you." I pouted for effect.

"Don't you think we should worry about making it through high school first? We're only going to be freshmen."

"Oh, my God, I know! I can't believe we're going to be freshmen. *Finally!* This is going to be our best year ever."

"I hope so."

"Are you kidding? Lisa's brother, Bill, is going to be a senior, and she said he'll get us into all the upperclassmen parties. This is when all the older guys start paying attention to us."

Lisa and Meg are our two other good friends at school. I've known Lisa since we were in music class together at three years old, and we met Meg when she switched to our elementary school in second grade. Lisa's a bit of a drama queen. In addition to Bill, she has four older sisters, so she'll do pretty much anything to draw attention to herself. Meg's more like Kitty, on the quieter side, but she's also superathletic, unlike Kitty. Meg can be kind of boring sometimes, but she's always willing to tag along with whatever we want to do. She and Kitty hit it off immediately. With Lisa it took a little longer— she thought Kitty was a drag at first. But then she came around. Kind of. I think she's jealous that I'm closer with Kitty than I am with her, especially since we've known each other for, like, ever. The thing is, I could *never* spend as much time with Lisa as I do with Kitty. She gets on my nerves. A lot. Usually, we all do sleepovers on the weekends, but this year is going to be different. This is the year it all starts happening.

"You mean this is when all the older guys start paying attention to *you*."

"You too, Kitty. You're always so negative about yourself." I shook my head.

"Well . . ." She ran her hands, palms facing outward, from her head down her body. "Wouldn't you be?"

"No, I wouldn't be. You have to act confident, and people will think you are. You're really pretty, Kitty."

"You have to say that." She frowned.

"I do *not* have to say that! Have you ever known me to lie?" She raised an eyebrow. "Fine. Have you ever known me to lie to *you* about something like this?"

"I guess not." She shrugged.

"Let me give you a makeover!" I must say, I have a special talent with hair and makeup. I could do wonders with Kitty.

"I don't know."

"Come on!" I tilted my head to the side and gave her my most persuasive grin. "We'll make you a supermodel!"

"I doubt that." She rolled her eyes in her judgmental Kitty way.

"Trust me. *Please.* I want you to feel good about yourself for once."

"I'll think about it."

"That means yes! This is so awesome! I'll do your hair, your makeup, and we'll go through all your clothing and put together supercute outfits. Manchester High won't know what hit them!"

"Fine." She smiled, even if just barely.

"Woohoo!!" I leaped onto her chair and hugged her. She rolled her eyes again and laughed. "What would you do without me?"

"You know, I ask myself that question at least once a day."

"Oh, shut up. You know you love me."

"A little."

"Enough to move to New York City?"

"Fine, but I want the bigger bedroom."

"Fat chance, though I like the way you're thinking."

"How about some iced tea and sandwiches before you skip town?" Kitty and I nearly jumped out of our skin. Luella was hovering in the doorway, her tight silver ballerina bun shimmering in the sunlight. She does that a lot. Sneaks up on us. Sometimes I wonder how long she's been standing there.

"Can we have them out here?"

"Of course, dear."

"I'll help you, Luella." Kitty sprang to her feet. Why does she always have to be so damn polite? It makes the rest of us look bad. I guess it's no mystery why Luella favors her.

"Thank you, dear." Luella nodded and swiveled toward the kitchen, her sparkly orange caftan swishing gracefully.

Once they'd disappeared into the house, I lay back down on my lounge chair, closed my eyes, and smiled. Eight more years of boring Vermont, and then New York City, here we come! Master plan, phase one. Completed.

Kitty

Some people think being an only child is special because you get all the attention. But, on the flip side, *you get all the attention*. The spotlight has nowhere else to shine. And I'm not really a center-stage kind of girl.

Laney is the closest thing I have to a sister. The only problem with that is she's already got a brother and parents of her own. Her family is the definition of the word *normal*. The Drakes eat dinner together every night at six o'clock. On Sunday mornings, Laney's mom makes a big breakfast of waffles or pancakes or eggs and bacon with fresh-squeezed orange juice, while Laney and Grant watch *Saved by the Bell*. Their dad helps them with their homework, and their mom goes clothing and school-supply shopping with them. They even take family vacations to Nantucket every summer. Freakishly normal, right?

Mrs. Drake is like one of those TV moms, a real Maggie

Seaver type, with the permanent smile and the after-school-special personality to go with it. She always goes out of her way to make me feel like a member of their family, but as much time as I spend there, and as much as they treat me like one of them, I still can't help but feel like an outsider. It's probably just me and my overthinking. I hate to be an imposition on anyone, and since my dad works late nights and some weekends at the bottling plant, I really am at Laney's house a lot. He's trying so hard to do it all, and I can tell it's wearing him down.

I can't lie. Growing up with just a father has its challenges. Any discussion of boys, my changing body, my period, or, worst of all, sex is beyond awkward for him and completely humiliating for me. Most girls would probably rather lose a father, if they had to choose. But I'm not sure. My dad and I have a special bond. And as much as Mrs. Drake makes me miss having a mom, I'm pretty sure my own mom would never have been like her.

On her good days, my mom could make you feel like the center of the universe—kind of like Laney does. I guess that's what my dad loved about her. There are moments that I wonder if our relationship would be better today, if we'd be really close, but I think I know the answer to that. I would probably still be a disappointment to her—a mutt who got the short end of the stick in the looks and dazzling-personality department. I know I'm not altogether ugly. Let's just say I'm not getting into Giorgio's without a reservation.

Tonight I'm sleeping over at Laney's. Mrs. Drake made an amazing dinner for all of us. Lamb chops so tender they were falling off the bone, creamed spinach, roasted potatoes, and warm apple pie with vanilla ice cream for dessert. So much for my diet. The other really awesome thing about

Laney's parents is that they don't expect any help cleaning up. I always offer, but Mr. and Mrs. Drake just shoo us out of the kitchen as soon as we're done eating. They say we'll have plenty of time to clean up when we're adults. My father does not share their feelings on this, nor does Luella. She thinks Laney's parents are too lenient, which might explain Laney's laid-back attitude toward, well, everything.

"Come on. Let's go to my room." Laney was halfway up the stairs five seconds after we'd finished our pie. "Grant's hogging the TV in the den."

"I don't mind watching together." It's strange that Laney never wants to hang out with her brother. I feel like if I had a brother, especially one as cool as Grant, I'd want to do stuff with him all the time.

"Well, I do. He always wants to watch those stupid cop shows. And, remember, there's that thing we wanted to do." She widened her smoky blue eyes. I wish I had smoky blue eyes.

"Yeah, I guess." I followed her reluctantly. Ever since I got my period six months ago, Laney has been obsessed with teaching me how to use a tampon. I don't understand what she has against pads.

"Trust me. This will change your life." She nodded like she'd never been so sure of anything. Although, come to think of it, Laney is always sure about everything. Like the time she said she was certain that Sun-In would transform me into a blond bombshell. Instead, my hair came out an unfortunate shade of orange, not that there is a good shade of orange in the way of one's hair.

"Whatever." I rolled my eyes. I do that a lot when it comes to Laney. Sometimes I feel guilty, but I can't help myself.

"Take this." She handed me a box of tampons.

"I don't think I'll need a whole box." I took it anyway.

"That's what you say now." She smirked. "Go on." I stared at Laney in her short, frayed jean shorts and tight white tank top. Her legs were all tan, as was her face. And, of course, *her* hair was the perfect shade of blond, without the Sun-In. If I looked like Laney, using a tampon would definitely be easier. I know that sounds crazy, but I'm convinced everything in life would be easier if I looked like Laney. There's just something about my thick thighs and flabby belly that makes it all so much more challenging. Shallow, maybe, but it's true. Skinny people have it made.

"Fine, but *do not* come in." I gave her my sternest look. "Did you hear me?"

"Yeah, yeah. Just go." She seemed a little too eager to me. "Tell me when you're ready."

I walked into the bathroom, closed the door firmly, pulled my shorts and underwear down around my ankles, legs spread, and unwrapped one of the tampons. "I'm ready."

"Okay, so first you need to find the hole. With your finger."

"Gross."

"Kitty, come on. You can do this."

"Fine, okay." I searched the area. "Got it."

"Good. Now take the tip of the tampon and push it up there. *Gently.*"

"I really don't understand why I can't just wear a pad." I caught a glimpse of myself in Laney's full-length mirror. Can you imagine if I had to do this with my father? He'd be reading the instructions off the box. The thought of him even saying the word *vagina*, especially in reference to mine, is totally mortifying.

"Because it's like wearing a diaper. Are you pushing it in?"

"It won't go. Okay? It just won't go."

"It will. You're just tensing up. Try to relax."

"How am I supposed to relax with my legs spread open, trying to shove some random object up me?"

"If you can't put a tampon in, you can't have sex." I couldn't see Laney, but I suspected she had her hands on her hips.

"Well, clearly, I have some time to worry about that."

"Not as long as you think."

"No, not as long as *you* think. Having sex actually requires someone being interested in you first."

"Can't I just come in there?" The doorknob jiggled, and I started yanking my shorts up in a hurry.

"Laney, if you come in here, I will KILL you. Not everyone is comfortable prancing around naked."

"Touchy, touchy. Fine, I'm not coming in. Let's try this again. Relax this time."

Fifteen minutes and nine tampons later, it was in. I stepped out of the bathroom triumphant. "It feels weird."

"You'll get used to it." She hugged me tight. "I'm proud of you!" Even though we'd been friends for three years, Laney's spontaneous and frequent displays of affection still caught me by surprise.

"Thanks." I smiled.

"Don't be ridiculous." She stuck out her tongue and flopped onto her bed. "That's what best friends are for."

"Actually, I think that's what moms are for." I lay down next to her, our backs propped up by the nine thousand white and purple pillows stacked against her twin-sized headboard.

"Well, yeah. But we're more like sisters, so it's pretty much the same thing." I love that Laney calls me her sister, even though I never tell her that. Sometimes I wish she knew how much she means to me, without my having to say it. In three years she's never once asked about my mom, which—for

Laney—I know has been nearly impossible. I'm sure Mrs. Drake told her not to. That's the kind of person she is, always considering other people's feelings. But still, Laney rarely listens to her mom.

"I know. I guess I just wish . . ."

"Wish what?" Laney rolled toward me.

"That she was here sometimes." My eyes began to sting, and I pressed my fingers into the lids.

"Yeah." She rested her hand on my arm and rubbed it lightly, which only made me more emotional.

"It's not like she was a saint or anything." Tears began to creep into the corners of my eyes. "She was nothing like your mom, believe me."

"It doesn't matter. She was *your* mom."

"I know. But I hated her sometimes. I really hated her. It was like she was embarrassed by me because I wasn't beautiful and charming like she was." Unwillingly, I started crying, which I hoped wouldn't freak Laney out because I never cry, not if I can help it. "And you know what?"

"What?" Impressively, Laney remained calm. Not a word I'd typically use to describe her.

"That day. The day she died. We were in the supermarket, just before she got hit, and she was telling me that I couldn't have a cookie, because little girls with chubby thighs like mine didn't need cookies. So I called her Mommy Dearest. And do you know what she did?" My breathing was fitfully rhythmic, as I tried to stifle more tears.

"What?" Laney looked like she was about to cry, which provoked my reluctant sobs.

"She slapped me. In the *face*. In front of everyone." I'd never told anyone this before, not even my dad. I was so ashamed. What if he blamed me for what happened? "Then she grabbed me by the arm and dragged me out of the store.

I screamed, 'I hate you!' And she stalked off. That's why I was walking behind her. She didn't even want to talk to me and refused to be near me." I wiped my nose with the side of my arm, hiccupping in an attempt to catch my breath.

"That's awful." Laney pulled a tissue from the white lacy box on her nightstand and started wiping away my tears and blotting around my nose. "You didn't deserve that, no matter what you said."

"I'll never forget it. Right before the car hit her, she was so angry with me."

"I'm so sorry for you." Laney tilted her head downward. "But I'm not sorry about one thing." She looked at me again.

"What?"

"Well, if you'd been walking next to her, you could have been hit by the car too. And that would have ruined my life." I laughed through my tears. Leave it to Laney to make my mom's death about her.

"You'd never have known what you were missing."

"Maybe, but I know my life is better because of you." She smiled, still rubbing my arm.

"Thanks." I sniffled. I'm sure my face was all messed up. I'm not an attractive crier like Laney, who looks like Julia Roberts in *Pretty Woman* when she cries—tears gracefully cascading down her cheeks without all the smeared snot and red blotches.

"It's natural to miss your mom, Kitty, even if your relationship wasn't perfect."

"I know." I blew my nose, which sounded like an elephant.

"You never talk about her. It must be hard to keep it all inside."

"Sometimes. I just don't want to burden anyone with my stupid stuff, ya know?"

"It's not stupid, Kitty."

"I know, but my dad is so happy now. And I don't want to bring it all back up. He doesn't even talk about her any-more. It's like she never existed."

"Maybe he thinks you don't want to talk about her. That's kind of what I've always thought. Otherwise I would have asked sooner."

"I'm sure you're right. My dad has a lot to deal with at work and with being a single parent and all."

"That's why you have me." She thought for a second. "Maybe you had to lose a mom to gain a sister. I know it's not the same, but still."

"Maybe."

"You can talk to me anytime. I know I'm usually chatter-ing away, but you have to tell me to shut up and give you a chance."

"Okay, shut up." I laughed again.

"Good! I'm listening."

"I'm okay. It just hits me sometimes."

"Of course."

"Thank you."

"For what?"

"For being the best sister ever." This time, I hugged her.

I don't understand how Laney falls asleep so quickly. One second she's talking a mile a minute about whom she should date this year (yes, she actually has a choice) and the next she's snoring so loud I can barely think, which is rare. Lu-ella told me I suffer from insomnia because my brain won't shut down. That sounds about right.

I got up as quietly as possible, not that anything can wake Laney, and tiptoed downstairs for a drink of water. I noticed a dim light on in the living room, next to the kitchen, and turned back around. I really didn't want to bump into Mr. Drake, especially not in my nightshirt.

"Hey, Kitty. It's just me." Grant leaned his face under the table lamp so I could see him.

"Oh, hey." I stopped mid-stairs, not knowing whether to turn around again or head back to Laney's room as planned.

"Come down." Grant waved me toward him. I'm always surprised when he wants to talk to me or hang out with me. I guess I'm lucky to be Laney's friend; otherwise someone like Grant would never give me the time of day. I'm nowhere near as cool as he is. He can have any girl he wants at school, not that he *wants* me. Obviously. He sees me like a second little sister. Anyway, supposing I did like Grant, he'd never like me back. Plus Laney is superpossessive about him, even though she doesn't actually like hanging out with him.

"Looks interesting." I pointed at the TV and sat down on the opposite end of the couch, stretching my nightshirt over my knees.

"*Coach*. It's a rad show. You should watch sometime." I'd seen it. It wasn't that rad, but I was still happy to watch with Grant.

"Laney's sleeping." I stated the obvious, because that's what I do around boys, apparently even Grant. I say things there's no reason to say just to fill empty space.

"I gathered." He smiled, revealing a dimple at the center of each cheek, and then got a serious look on his face. "You shouldn't let her push you around."

"She doesn't push me around." I was instantly defensive.

"Kitty." He tipped his head, and his wavy dark blond hair fell to one side. He was just as tan as Laney and it looked really good. I imagined what it would be like to kiss him for a brief moment, and then shook the thought from my mind. "Laney pushes everyone around. The more you let her, the more she does it. You haven't noticed?"

"I guess." I glanced down at my feet. Laney had painted my toes a bright pink and the polish was already chipping. I resisted the urge to pick at it.

"I'm not trying to make you feel bad. I just know how she can be, and I think you should stand up to her a little more."

"Maybe." I didn't want to fight with Grant, especially since he was kind of right, but I also felt the need to stand up for Laney. "She's a really awesome friend to me, even if she is a little bossy."

"I'll take your word for it." He got up and walked toward the open kitchen. "Want something to eat? I'm kind of hungry."

"Sure."

"Soda?" He called across the room. I wanted to shush him, but it was his house, so I just nodded.

"Here." He handed me a Coke and sat next to me on the couch. "I didn't mean to insult you. We're friends too. Right?"

"Yeah." I'd never thought of it that way.

"Good." He smiled, revealing the dimples again. I felt a blush creep up my neck and spread across my face like a contagious rash. Thank God it was dark. I'd never had a male friend. "Wanna watch? I think Coach Fox is gonna lead the Screaming Eagles to victory."

"Okay."

I'm not sure how long we sat there, arms resting next to one another's, sharing a big bowl of buttery popcorn. All I know is that when Laney found us asleep on the couch the next morning, she didn't look happy.

Present Day

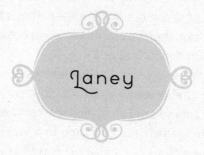

Laney

Laney peeked out her bedroom window at the maudlin sky with its dense, murky clouds dipping so low you could almost touch them. The backyard appeared muddy and slick from an aggressive overnight drizzle, and the gathering clouds threatened to downpour without warning. She cracked the window just enough to inhale a quick gust of cool air, letting it fill her lungs and infuse those parts of her body that still felt betrayed by the early arousal. It was a typical November morning in Manchester—chilly, damp, at times depressing. But today held promise, dismal weather notwithstanding.

At two o'clock she was scheduled to meet Luella Hancock's lawyer for the reading of Luella's will. Even the thought of it gave her a swift jolt of energy. She'd spent the week since receiving the lawyer's letter mourning Luella's passing. It had hit her harder than she'd expected and certainly harder than Rick would have imagined. He'd known Luella only peripherally, and while he understood Laney's history with her—long days spent swimming in her pool during the summer season, high teas on brisk fall afternoons, and hours devoted to erecting tall snow sculptures in her expansive backyard come wintertime—perhaps he didn't get that their relationship was infinitely more complex, in light of one common denominator: Kitty.

Over the past few years, Laney had barely seen Luella at all, save for a chance meeting around town or at the supermarket. After Laney's father had died six years ago, her mother had moved from their family home to a smaller property down the street from her and Rick. It was only four miles from where she grew up, but somehow those four miles made all the difference. Each time Laney had bumped into Luella, looking every bit as exquisite as always in her tailored cashmere coats and mink stoles, Luella had invited her for an afternoon tea or to bring Gemma and her friends by for a swim. And Laney had always replied with an optimistic yes. Regretfully, her optimism hadn't translated into action—life always seemed to get in the way. And she and Luella had grown farther and farther apart over time.

When Laney had delivered the news of Luella's passing to her mom, Carol had been predictably surprised—it was a rare circumstance for information to flow from Laney to Carol. Typically, Carol was privy to this sort of hot-off-the-press item first, through the Manchester gossip mill. Later that day, her mom had called back, armed with the knowledge that Luella had passed away comfortably in her sleep, and they'd shared a collective sigh of relief.

If Laney was being honest, she and Luella had never been that close. Nothing like Luella and Kitty. They'd had a uniquely resilient bond that could, in some measure, be attributed to their mutual losses—Kitty's mother, Luella's husband, and the children Luella had never been able to conceive on her own. It had taken years for Laney to truly understand the fundamental role Luella had played in Kitty's life. She'd been more like a surrogate mother to her than the mysterious albeit munificent neighbor she'd been to Laney. Still, Luella had named Laney in her will, an act that afforded Laney endless satisfaction. If only Kitty knew.

Laney wandered into the bathroom and cranked the shower lever all the way to hot. She stripped off her nightgown and stepped into the torrid stream of water, allowing it to beat against her sore muscles. A quick shampoo and shave, and she was toweling off, then slipping into her most professional-looking outfit—charcoal gray wool slacks, which she'd scored at the Ralph Lauren outlet sale, a buttondown mahogany silk shirt she'd had for way too long but still felt so luxurious against her skin, and old black heels specifically suited for crappy weather. She swiped blush across her cheeks and dotted her lips with a pinkish gloss. There was no time to dry her massive heap of hair, so she just squirted a generous amount of gel in her hands and raked them through her tangle of messy, wet curls.

"Morning." Laney moseyed into the kitchen.

"You look nice." Rick kissed his wife on the lips and handed her a mug of coffee.

"You're my hero." She sat down at the kitchen table and poached a piece of bacon off his plate. Laney marveled at the fact that Rick's internal clock woke him naturally at six a.m. every morning and that he took great pleasure in jumping out of bed, sometimes going for a run, and often making the two of them very elaborate breakfasts, especially for the middle of the week.

"So today's the big day?" He sat down across from her,

placing a tomato and Swiss cheese omelet with three slices of crispy bacon in front of her. "Bon appétit."

"Thanks, but I'm not that hungry." Laney picked at the bacon.

"I don't believe it." He shook his head incredulously. "In fact, I don't think I've ever heard you say those words."

"Very funny." She coiled a section of hair around her middle finger. "Nervous excitement, I think."

"Listen, don't come back with less than a million. Okay?" He tried to lift a slice of bacon from Laney's plate, and she swatted at his hand. "What? I thought you weren't hungry. Not to mention that one of mine mysteriously disappeared."

"I don't even know if she left me money. For all I know, it could be a dress or a couch or something." Laney cut into the omelet. "Has Gem made an appearance yet?"

"No, but I heard T.I. blasting in her room earlier, so she's up." Rick wiped the corners of his mouth with his napkin, and Laney smiled. He'd never lost his boyish good looks. It was so unfair how men seemed to only get better with age. Rick's once full head of thick, dark brown hair was now punctuated with specks of white, and there were some perfunctory lines around his arrestingly clear blue eyes, but they only served to make him more handsome.

"What's T.I.?" That was another thing about Rick. He was shamelessly in touch with teenage pop culture and lingo. Sometimes it felt like he and Gemma were speaking a foreign language. And forget their e-mail exchanges with the LOLs and the LMAOs and the TTYLs. Now there was a T.I.?

"T.I. is a who. A he, actually."

"Silly me." She rolled her eyes dramatically. "Can I go by HM?"

"What's that?" Rick laughed.

"Hot Mama."

"If you'd like, but I prefer MILF."

Laney looked at him perplexed. "Go ahead, tell me."

"Mother I'd Like to Fuck."

"Shut up!" She slapped his arm. "Is that for real?"

"The realest." Rick wrapped his arms across his chest and puckered his lips in a gangster pose.

"It's official. You're too cool for me." Laney finished her omelet and stood to bring both of their plates to the sink.

"I guess you got it down." He motioned to her empty plate.

"I didn't want to insult the chef. I hear he's a badass."

"Oh, do you, now?" Rick crept up behind her and grabbed her around the waist, turning her toward him. "I've got to run, but I love you." He kissed her gently on the lips. "More than anything." He kissed her again. "And I'll see you tonight. Call me after the lawyer. I'm seriously curious on this one."

"Yeah, that makes two of us."

Panting, Laney burst through the front door of Newman, Brink & Oliver. Tina had given her a hard time about leaving Oasis, even though Laney had told her a week ago about the meeting and had sworn she'd be back within the hour. How long could it take to read a will? Still, Tina was Tina, and Laney knew she was afraid of running the salon without her. On her way out, she'd handed Tina a lined pad and red pen and said, "Write everything down on this. Appointments, phone messages, and any other issues or problems. I'll deal with it all when I get back." Tina had nodded like an obedient child. And Laney had reminded herself to ask about that raise she so deserved. Unless, of course, she was about to become a millionaire. It had crossed her mind. The delicious satisfaction of quitting her job at a time when Tina was most vulnerable—she'd just fired Annie, the new receptionist, along with two manicurists and three hairstylists.

"I'm here to see Richard Newman." Laney let her purse fall to the ground and pulled her hair off her neck. Despite the freezing and inclement weather, she was still perspiring. She'd had to sprint four blocks from the Donna Karan outlet parking lot, the only spot she could find in the vicinity. She'd driven by the law office twice, to discover that they had room for only seven cars, most likely the three lawyers, two secretaries, one receptionist, and one paralegal who worked there.

"In regard to?" The receptionist didn't bother looking up from her paperwork.

"Luella Hancock's will. I have a two o'clock appointment." Laney's erratic breathing tapered as she removed her damp winter coat. The rain hadn't let up all day, which just made everything more difficult.

"He's on a call. Take a seat. I'll let you know when he's ready to see you."

"Sure, thank you." Laney was somewhat relieved to have a moment to pull herself together, even though Tina would probably kill her if she was gone for more than fifty-nine minutes and fifty-nine seconds. She hung her coat on a hook by the door and sat down in the first empty chair. There was only one other woman waiting, seated on the other side of the small room. Laney hadn't noticed her at first, but she did now. It was impossible not to. The woman was impeccably turned out in crisp black slacks, a creamy cashmere sweater that hugged her slender frame, and heels so high they were practically stilts. Laney couldn't make out the woman's face, since it was buried in her iPhone, on which she was typing furiously, but she did notice her diamond studs— more like diamond rocks, really. Her black hair was fashioned into a stylish shoulder-length bob, and it sparkled much like her earrings. This woman couldn't be from Manchester. No one dressed like that in Manchester. Laney surveyed her own outfit and frowned. She'd felt a little glamorous all day in her favorite silk shirt, since she usually wore a uniform of old black pants and a plain white cotton button-down to work, but now she felt more like the dumpy stepsister.

She stared at the woman for a few minutes, wondering what it would take to look like her. She was dying to see her face and, even though she dreaded Tina's temper tantrums, she kind of hoped the woman would get called in first.

"Ladies, Mr. Newman will see you now," the receptionist yelped from behind her desk, without moving an inch. Laney stood up, as did the woman, who—for the first time—lifted her head. Laney looked directly at her, pausing for a moment to place the familiar face, and then it hit her, nearly knocking her back into her seat.

"Kitty?" Laney's heart punched at her chest and she felt slightly dizzy.

"Laney." Kitty smiled coolly, submitting to a perfunctory acknowledgment.

"Through the door, second office on the left, ladies." The receptionist pointed, oblivious to the standoff right before her eyes.

"I guess that's us." Kitty tucked her black lizard clutch under her arm and strutted through the door, holding it open for Laney, who followed like a robot, too shocked to say or do anything else.

"Come right in and sit down," Richard Newman announced, as soon as they appeared in his doorway. He was an older gentleman, very polished-looking in a navy suit, pinstriped shirt, and a red bowtie. Just what Laney would have expected in the way of Luella's lawyer. His office was small but neat, with a large wooden desk that took up almost the whole space and matching wooden shelves packed with law journals. A collection of diplomas and awards hung on the stark white walls, along with a few photos of his family—his wife, their kids, and their kids' kids. But Laney paid no attention to any of it.

Very quickly, her shock had spooled into a fiery ball of anger, which was now rankling in the pit of her stomach, ready to erupt. How *dare* Kitty come back after all these years? How *dare* she come back for the sole purpose of cashing in on Luella's death? The same Luella whom she hadn't bothered to visit for more than a decade. Fine. So she looked good. Amazing, actually. How had it not crossed her mind that Kitty could be here? And why hadn't she put on a little more makeup this morning? Not only did she have to sit right next to Kitty under a halogen lamp, but she had to do it looking like crap.

"Thank you for traveling all the way from New York, Kitty." Richard Newman smiled pleasantly.

"It's actually Katherine."

Laney snorted.

"My apologies. Is that your full name?"

"Yes." Katherine folded her hands in her lap and crossed her legs.

"Oh, really?" Laney couldn't quell her acidic tone, nor did she try to.

"It is now." Katherine nodded decisively.

"Is that a legal change?" Laney challenged.

"It might as well be. I've been going by Katherine for more than ten years."

"Whatever." Laney rolled her eyes and hugged her purse to her chest.

"Neither here nor there," he chimed in. "Shall we get on with it?"

"Yes, absolutely." Katherine motioned to the stack of papers in his hands.

"Right, then." Richard Newman launched into paragraphs of legalese, reciting them so enthusiastically, it was as if he were reading a toddler his favorite bedtime story. He detailed what money Luella had left to her beautiful church, St. Ignatius, what money she'd left to the very grateful town of Manchester for the construction of an elaborate park and playground, and so on, and so on. It appeared she'd thought of everyone and anyone who'd had an impact on her life. Vintage Luella.

"Excuse me," Laney interrupted as politely as she could, given the awkward context. "Would it be possible to get to the part about me? It's just that I have to get back to work."

"I suppose," he said, turning to Katherine for consent, and she nodded. "Well, ladies. It seems this is your lucky day." He cleared his throat, as if waiting for a drumroll. "Luella has left the two of you her home and everything in it."

"What?" Laney's mouth dropped open.

"That's right." A satisfied grin spread across his face. He'd undoubtedly been waiting months, possibly years, to drop this particular bomb. A bomb he'd most likely assumed would be met with unadulterated joy. Maybe even a standing ovation.

"What exactly does this mean?" Katherine appeared infuriatingly unruffled by the news, entitled almost.

"It means the house is yours, along with all of Luella's belongings."

"So we sell it?" Katherine arched one perfectly groomed eyebrow.

"If you want." He looked somewhat deflated. "Oh, I almost forgot. There's a bit more to this." He shuffled through another pile of papers. "Here it is. Yes, that's right. Per Luella's last wishes, the two of you will need to clean out the house; split up, sell, or donate her possessions as you see fit; and make sure the house is in tip-top shape should you want to put it on the market. Then and only then you can divide the money between yourselves." He studied both of them carefully.

"That's preposterous. I can't stay in Vermont to clean out and fix up a house." Katherine shook her head. "I'd be happy to pay someone to do it."

"Fine by me." Laney's jaw clenched. How *dare* she throw her money around, even if it did make things easier on both of them?

"Oh no. That won't be possible, I'm afraid." Richard Newman wagged his index finger back and forth. "Luella was quite clear in writing and when I spoke to her, on more than one occasion. She specifically wanted you ladies to do this together."

"Not possible." Katherine huffed.

"At least we agree on something," Laney confirmed.

"Maybe this will change your mind." He scribbled something on a notepad, mumbling numbers to himself at the same time. One final flick of his pen and he looked up again, smiling triumphantly. "The house is worth one-point-four million dollars. Along with Luella's belongings, that means each of you stands to walk away with well over a half million after taxes. Now, how does that sound?"

Neither Laney nor Katherine said a word. They both just stared straight ahead.

"This is good news, ladies. Great news, really." He narrowed his eyes and tapped his pen on his desk. "Luella said you were the best of friends."

"We used to be." Laney sniffed.

"Actually"—Katherine's voice softened just a little— "we used to be sisters."

Katherine

Katherine zigzagged through the narrow side streets of Manchester, strings of saltbox houses whizzing past in a slideshow of vibrant colors. She'd managed to preserve her composure throughout the entirety of the will reading, but it had taken a distinct brand of discipline. The variety she'd spent the last twelve years honing. It was obvious that Laney hadn't expected to see her. Katherine, on the other hand, had considered the possibility that Laney could turn up. It wasn't that anyone had eluded to it, certainly not her father or Hazel, but if there was one thing Katherine had learned over time: never let yourself be caught off guard. It went hand in hand with another of her dependable mantras: expect the worst; hope for the best. She'd been dubbed a pessimist on more than one occasion for her cynical posture. Still, she maintained that it was far better to be happily surprised than gravely disappointed.

The inheritance was one of those happy surprises. Unfortunately, it had been muddied by Laney's callous reception and then exacerbated when the lawyer had informed them of Luella's outlandish proviso. Was she expected to just drop everything and move to Vermont for the foreseeable future—to devote her days to sorting through and packing up Luella's belongings and then tidying up her house? And with Laney, no less. As she'd said in the lawyer's office, it was preposterous. There had to be an angle. Despite their infrequent communication of late, Luella had known all too well that Katherine had a very important and time-consuming career. She'd also been acutely aware of Katherine's longstanding estrangement from Laney. Was Luella's intent to reunite them under the guise of her legacy? It seemed an ambitious, if not insurmountable feat—not altogether surprising coming from Luella. Once she'd set her mind on something, the breadth of the challenge became insignificant. Either way, it was simply unfeasible for Katherine, and—from the sounds of it—for Laney too, if she had a full-time job.

Katherine pulled into the driveway of her old house, screeching to a stop, and stomped her way up the stone path and onto the splintering porch. Before she could knock, her father opened the door, a placid smile spread across his creased face.

"Kitty Kat! What a wonderful treat. Were we meant to expect you?"

"The house, Dad? Really?" Katherine's hands were fixed to her hips and her lips were taut.

"Kitty," he grimaced. "There was nothing I could do."

"Well, for starters, you could have told me. Warned me what I was walking into."

"Luella swore me to secrecy. Hazel too." He backed up to let her inside.

"I hate to point this out, Dad, but Luella is gone. I don't think she would have known the difference."

"Sorry, Kitty. I don't break promises to anyone—dead or alive—and certainly not Luella," he admonished, and she knew he was right.

"You might have at least mentioned that Laney was going to be there." Katherine followed her father into the kitchen and slumped into a seat at the table. She'd barely slept the night before, in anticipation of Luella's will reading, and her body was exhausted. More so than usual. "Let's just say it wasn't a joyous reunion."

"I'm sorry to hear that." He sat down across from her, straining to bend his knees.

"What's going on there, Dad?" Katherine motioned to her father's legs.

"You haven't noticed your old man got old?" He smiled affectionately, and Katherine's chest tightened. She was a deadbeat daughter, if there was such a thing. It'd been so long since she'd visited her own father that it was like one of those before-and-after segments you see on daytime talk shows, only the after was far worse than the before. It was hard to believe he was nearly seventy. There'd been a time in the not-so-distant past when Katherine had considered seventy seriously old. If she'd been reading the paper, for example, and it had said that Mr. So-and-So had died at the age of seventy-something, it hadn't jarred her in the least. There'd been no *Oh, how tragic* response. She'd just casually flipped the page. Now, in her mid-thirties, all of the sudden seventy seemed more like what she'd imagined fifty-five or sixty would be. Still, it was depressing to see that her father had slowed down. That simple tasks, like sitting down in a chair or moving across the room, didn't transpire as quickly or as fluidly.

"You're not old, Dad. Just stubborn."

"I could say the same."

"Yeah, well, you know. The whole apple-tree thing." Katherine sat upright. What was it about being home that instantly transformed her into a slouch? "Now can you please tell me what you know about this house thing with Laney?"

"Kitty?" Hazel called out, the thud of the front door punctuating the silence.

"Saved by the bell." Her dad smirked, hoisting himself up so he could help Hazel with the armful of groceries she was toting.

"I'm so glad you're here." Hazel smiled pleasantly and patted Katherine's hand—a gesture that might have seemed awkward from anyone else. But not Hazel. There could never be anything awkward about Hazel. Every motion she made and every word she spoke was one hundred percent genuine. "Did your father offer you something to drink or eat?"

"I'm fine. Thank you." Katherine watched as Hazel unpacked their groceries, handing every other item to her dad. They had a system. It was nice. She couldn't remember how her mom and dad had interacted, at least not when it came to tedious responsibilities like unpacking groceries or watering the plants, as Hazel was now doing. She couldn't even remember if they'd had any plants in their Bennington house. She did recall that her mother never appreciated "extra things to deal with," which was typically what she said when Katherine had asked her to do something mundane, such as pick up school supplies or buy something for the school bake sale. *Just what I need is an extra thing to deal with.* It was unlikely that Hazel had ever felt burdened by anything, let alone such modest requests. But, then again, Hazel wasn't a frustrated housewife who'd felt robbed of her dreams. Hazel loved being a mother and a significant other. In her mind, those were her jobs.

"Actually, you look a bit pale, dear. Are you feeling okay?" Hazel touched her palm to Katherine's forehead. "Might be a little fever."

"I'm fine," Katherine insisted.

"How about a snack? I made some vegetable tarts this morning with you in mind. Very healthy." Hazel went to the refrigerator and pulled out a Tupperware container filled with neat stacks of tarts separated by individual pieces of wax paper. "I'll just warm these up. A cup of tea?"

"That would be great." Katherine relented. Domesticity was like breathing for Hazel. She couldn't live without it.

"Milk and sugar?" The toaster oven beeped, and Hazel slid her hand into a lime green pot holder that had been hanging on a hook next to the stove, while Katherine's father filled the teapot with water.

"No, thank you."

"Here you go, dear." Hazel placed a small scalloped white plate with four perfectly formed vegetable tarts in front of Katherine. "Now, let me see about that tea."

Katherine bit into one of the tarts, and a torrent of flavors erupted in her mouth. "These are amazing." She'd skipped breakfast and lunch, so just this once allowed herself the treat.

"Thank you. They're one of your father's favorites."

"I can see why." Katherine allowed herself one more and then one more after that. "These may be the best things I've ever eaten." She wasn't even exaggerating in order to stroke Hazel's nonexistent ego. This woman was talented.

"Oh, don't be silly. They're a cinch. I can give you the recipe if you'd like." Katherine nodded with her mouth full, even though they both knew she'd have no use for this recipe or any other.

"Kitty, Hazel's right. You really don't look yourself. You

sure you're feeling all right?" Katherine's dad sat back down at the table, eyeing the last tart.

"Go on, Dad." She pushed the plate toward him.

"If you insist." He grinned like a Cheshire cat.

"You know, I am feeling a little off. Maybe I should get back to the hotel." She stood up and nearly lost her footing. Her father stood immediately to steady her.

"You're not going anywhere." He was still holding her arms. "Why don't you go up to your room and lie down?"

"Dad, that's ridiculous. I can make it the few miles to the Equinox." Actually, she wasn't entirely sure.

"I'm not letting you drive, Kitty." This time she didn't argue. Maybe she could use ten minutes to lie down and then she'd be on her way. "Do you need me to help you up the stairs?"

"No, I'm fine."

"I'll walk her up, Joe. I've got your tea, dear."

"I'm really okay. You can even watch me go." She smiled and took the mug of tea from Hazel. "I still want more details on this house thing, Dad. You're not getting off that easy."

"Yeah, yeah." He waved his hand in the air.

"I'll be back down in a little bit." She started up the stairs slowly.

"Take all the time you need, Kitty Kat." He tipped his head downward, mumbling, "This is still your home."

Katherine opened the door to her old bedroom and closed it behind her. She stood, motionless, her eyes darting from corner to corner. Nothing had changed. Not one single thing. It was creepy, actually, like someone had pressed PAUSE twelve years ago and never returned. The walls were still the same pale pink, though the paint was chipping in the corners and a thin, jagged crack punctuated the center of the smooth white ceiling. Her grandmother's rickety wooden rocking chair sat to the right of her bed, which was unruffled and draped in the same white comforter covered in small pink flowers threaded by sprouting green stems. Flanking the bed were the identical white nightstands, which she and her father had purchased at an estate sale down the street about two weeks after they'd moved in. They'd been in perfect condition at the time. Now they were worn but still served their purpose as home to her pink-and-white lamps, which matched the pattern of her comforter. She moved toward the bed and climbed on top, laying her head on the mound of pillows. She remembered coming home one day, after having slept over at Laney's, begging her dad for more pillows so her bed could look just like her best friend's.

Katherine's muscles ached and her eyes were heavy, but she strained to keep them open, wanting to savor every last detail of a time that she could barely recollect. Who was the girl who'd lived in this room? Who'd slept in this bed every night for nearly a decade? She was a stranger now, so much so that Katherine felt, in a way, that she were interloping. Unable to keep her eyes open any longer, she finally let her body relax. *Just a quick catnap*, she thought, as she drifted in and out of consciousness, consumed by memories that hardly felt like her own.

When Katherine awoke, the room was pitch-black, save for her old Smurfette night-light glowing above her dresser. Even though the curtains were drawn, she knew it was no longer daytime. The teacup on her nightstand had been replaced by a glass of water and another plate of vegetable tarts—Hazel's handiwork, no doubt. She could barely make out her purse on the rocking chair as she stumbled across the room to retrieve her iPhone so she could see what time it was. She carried her purse back to the bed, feeling her way in the dark, and rummaged through her bag for her phone. The clock read five thirteen a.m. She'd slept nearly thirteen hours, which was unheard-of, given her persistent insomnia. She also noticed the ninety-three e-mails that had accumulated in what was undeniably the longest period of time she'd ever abandoned her in-box. Instinctively, she started scanning through them, deleting the junk mail and all of the annoying mass e-mails sent by her staff, to which everyone insisted on not only replying to all, but also on copying her. Their justification was keeping her in the loop, though she suspected it was more like self-preservation; if they included her, then they weren't entirely culpable if anything went awry. She put her phone down and let her mind wander again, to a time when she was definitely less cynical.

She'd lost her virginity in this room. In this bed. She'd been seventeen at the time. He'd said it was only his third time, but she didn't care. All she'd cared about was him. There'd been nothing awkward about it, not how Laney had told her it would be. She'd trusted him more than she'd trusted herself. And she'd been unable to keep her hands off every part of his body. Katherine inhaled deeply, half expecting to smell him—that familiarly intoxicating aroma of Drakkar Noir steeped in undertones of adolescent perspiration. But that was the one thing missing. It was all there: the bed, the rocking chair, the nightstands, even Smurfette. Everything except him.

She crept over to the window, using her phone as a makeshift flashlight, and peeked around the blinds at Luella's house, faintly illuminated by three tall streetlamps. Katherine couldn't shake the uneasy feeling that things were in motion—out of her control—with little indication of how'd they'd end up. Seeing Laney again had felt like home in a way she hadn't anticipated. And while Laney was obviously still very angry, Katherine had to wonder if there was even the remote possibility of a second chance at forgiveness.

Impulsively, she picked up her phone, searched for Laney's name—the lawyer had insisted they exchange cell numbers, despite their reluctance—and typed out a text message.

> **Can we meet tomorrow to talk about this house stuff?**

Almost instantly, her phone whirred in response.

> **Guess you're up too. Meet me at the Falcon Bar at your hotel. 6pm. I can't stay long.**

Katherine smiled. At least it was a start.

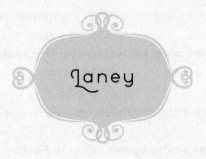

Laney

"Get you somethin' to drink, doll?" The waitress hovered over Laney's left shoulder, smacking her gum rhythmically.

"I'll take a glass of white wine, please." Laney didn't look up. Her focus remained strictly on the entrance to the Falcon Bar. The last thing she needed was to be caught off guard again.

"Pinot or Chardonnay?"

"Chardonnay, thank you." What she really wanted was a cold, dark, frothy beer, but Kitty—or Katherine, whatever her name was—would probably scoff at her for being so predictably plebian. She checked her watch. It was nearly six, and she was prepared to be annoyed if Kitty showed up even a minute late. Was her time more valuable than other people's? She'd certainly implied as much in the lawyer's office.

Laney was still reeling from the entire experience. She'd gone back to work directly after and had been unable to concentrate on anything, which had irritated Tina. Of course, Laney hadn't divulged a single detail about her meeting. Although it had been tempting, for once, to be the one bragging rather than listening to Tina go on and on and on about the many luxuries life afforded her. Still, she knew better than to give Tina any more information than she absolutely needed. She'd made that mistake once before, when she'd told Tina about a specific coat at Ralph Lauren she'd had her eyes on for Rick's Christmas gift. When Laney had gone to the store later that day to make her purchase, the saleswoman had informed her that another woman—fitting Tina's description to a T—had already bought the last one. She hadn't bothered asking Tina about it, but she had learned her lesson. God knows what Tina would do if she found out that Laney was about to come into a large sum of money. She'd probably try to sabotage it in some way, for fear that Laney would up and quit. Unfortunately, while five hundred thousand dollars was a lot of money—more than Laney had ever imagined she'd have access to—it was not enough for her to kick back and live off for the next sixty years.

When she'd told Rick, he'd been shocked at first, unable to believe that she wasn't screwing with him. *This is life changing,* he'd said. *This will put Gemma through college and more.* Then she'd explained the stipulation. *Who cares?* had been his response. *We're talking about a heap—no, a shit-fucking-load—of money.* That had made her anxious and a little resentful. *I care,* she'd insisted. *I'm the one who has to work with the bitch.* They'd gone back and forth for the better part of an hour. In typical fashion, Rick had tried to be sympathetic, even helpful, suggesting ways she and Kitty could work out their differences. Then came the kicker of all kickers, when he'd actually said, *Perhaps it's time to forgive and forget.*

This had sent Laney into a tailspin. How dare he insinuate that it was that simple! Kitty had betrayed her at a time in her life when she'd needed her more than ever. She'd abandoned their friendship in order to pursue her own selfish needs. Worst of all, she'd never, at least not sincerely, attempted to apologize or right her wrong, not that Laney would have been receptive to it. Still, no real attempt had been made, and that was all that mattered to her.

After Laney's rant, Rick had apologized, though it had seemed hollow, more like an effort to placate her than a legitimate expression of remorse. He didn't understand. No one understood. How many times had her own mother told her to call Kitty? Or to write her an e-mail. *If you don't mend this fence, you'll regret it.* She'd heard it so often she wanted to punch someone. If anyone had fence mending to do, it was Kitty. Kitty with her fancy clothing and her fancy high heels and her fancy attitude. Why was it that the one time something truly amazing happened, Kitty had to sabotage it by being so integral to the equation that Laney had to depend on her, the very last thing she wanted to do?

"Here ya go, doll." The waitress returned with her glass of wine, and Laney drank half of it in one sizeable gulp. "That kinda day, huh?" She blew a bubble and let the gum smack against her face, lapping up the stringy pieces with her pierced tongue.

"Something like that." Laney checked her watch again. Seven past six. The nerve. The absolute fucking nerve. She picked a straw out of the canister on the table and pulled off the paper, folding it methodically as small as she could and then letting it spread like an accordion. The Falcon Bar at the Equinox belied the overall mien of the hotel—it was more seedy than sophisticated, with dim lighting veiling sticky, dark wooden tables adorned with uniform caddies bearing old sugar packets and outdated maple syrup. An old-fashioned bar extended across one side of the room, lit by two multicolored stained-glass lamps hanging from rusty chain links. And a shabby pool table occupied the far corner for those townies who wanted to cue up while paying top dollar for a pint, just so they could say they'd thrown a few back in the company of the affluent tourists who swooped in and out of Manchester in their Mercedes SUVs and Bogner ski suits.

"All right, doll. Holler if you need a refill." The waitress continued to the next table, where an older couple who'd mistakenly wandered in, thinking the establishment would reflect the rest of the property, were surveying their surroundings dubiously.

Laney looked at her watch again. Six ten. Enough was enough. She wasn't going to sit around, wasting her time waiting on Kitty. Gemma would be home from her after-school activities by now, and there'd be plenty of homework for Laney to supervise, not to mention that she was responsible for dinner tonight, since Rick was out with the boys. She swallowed the rest of her wine and signaled to the waitress for a check, rifling through her purse for her wallet. If Kitty still wanted to meet, she'd have to apologize first and then work her busy schedule around Laney's. How disrespectful could someone be?

"Thanks, doll. You have a good night, now." The waitress set the check on the table and winked. Laney slapped a ten-dollar bill down, cursing under her breath that she could have had a decent bottle at home for the same amount, slung her purse over her shoulder, and turned to walk out the door, to find Kitty standing right in front of her.

"Going somewhere?" Katherine smiled smugly.

"You're late." Laney didn't return the smile, smug or otherwise. "My time is valuable too, you know."

"Of course it is." Katherine motioned toward the table, and Laney sat back down. "I apologize. I was on a conference call I couldn't escape."

"Whatever." Laney let her purse drop to the floor. "As I said, I can't stay long, so should we figure this out?"

"Thought you were leavin', doll." The waitress reemerged.

"Guess not."

"Anything else for you and your friend here?"

"She's not my friend." Laney smiled tightly, and Katherine rolled her eyes.

"All righty, then. You nonfriends want anything to drink or eat?"

"I'd like an iced tea, please. No sugar and just a little ice." Katherine nodded definitively.

"I'll have another Chardonnay." Laney wasn't usually much of a drinker, but the first glass had gone down too easily and her body was still clenched in torment.

"Comin' right up."

"So, how are you?" Katherine folded her hands on the table in front of her, predictably composed in a periwinkle cashmere wrap sweater and the same spangled diamond studs she'd been wearing at the lawyer's office. Laney had considered wearing her own diamond studs, the ones Rick had bought her for Valentine's Day. She saved them for special occasions, not that this qualified as anything special. Still, if Kitty's hadn't been three times the size and clearly her everyday earrings, Laney might have broken them out in an attempt to impress her. So much for that.

"I'm fine." Laney wasn't interested in small talk and she intended to make that evident from the get-go.

"And your family?"

"Fine."

"You have a daughter, right?"

"Yes, Gemma." Laney knew full well that Kitty knew full well she had a daughter. They may not have spoken in twelve years, but Kitty was still tied to Manchester, albeit loosely, through her father.

"Pretty name." Katherine smiled again, and Laney studied her face for a brief moment. It was remarkable, really. Kitty was barely visible behind Katherine's radiant skin, glaring white teeth, and expertly applied makeup. If not for her piercing green eyes, Laney may not have recognized her. She knew, courtesy of the Manchester gossip mill—her mom, Luella, and Laney's dad—that Kitty was extremely successful in the cosmetics industry and that she was unmarried, but beyond that Laney had learned nothing more. She'd once tried to Google Kitty after a late night out with Rick, having returned home in a martini-induced haze. But the one thing she'd been unaware of, the key to Kitty's anonymity online, had been her name change. There'd been only one Kitty Hill who'd surfaced and she was a high school sophomore living in Hawaii.

"Thank you."

"And you and Rick?"

"Still together."

"Unbelievable," Katherine mused.

"Well, I guess some people honor their relationship commitments," Laney snipped.

"I guess so." Katherine took Laney's prickliness in stride, which only served to annoy Laney even more. "And you're working?"

"Yes, I run Oasis, the spa in town."

"Excellent. You own it?"

"No, I run it." If only she owned it. Laney had thought about it more than a few times: all the things she'd change for the better, not to mention she'd treat her staff with respect and give them bonuses at Christmastime, unlike Tina.

"Still, that's a big job."

"Don't patronize me, Kitty."

"I'm not." She shook her head coolly.

"Fine. Whatever." Laney scanned the room for the waitress. "Where the hell are our drinks?"

"And your parents? How are they?"

"My mom is fine. My father passed away six years ago. But you knew that."

"I'm so sorry. I believe I did hear something." *Something.* Laney's chest cinched tighter. Just a little something, her dead dad. Incredible that Kitty could sit here pretending that she didn't know or that, perhaps, just maybe, in between a conference call and a business lunch someone had mentioned that Laney's fifty-five-year-old father—a man who had essentially helped raise Kitty—had suffered a massive heart attack, sinking to the kitchen floor in a quaking heap of agony and desperation while her mom had been right outside in their backyard. But who could really recall? "I should have written your mother a note."

"I'm sure that would have made everything better." Laney couldn't help herself, though her blatant insolence wasn't nearly as nourishing as she'd thought it would be.

"Well, I'm glad your mom is doing well. My dad and Hazel seem great. Have you met her?"

"Only briefly in passing." Laney was waiting. For her to bring him up. But Kitty was assiduously dodging the subject. She'd have to take matters into her own hands.

"Here ya go, dolls." The waitress reappeared. "One iced tea hold the sugar, light on the ice. One chilly Chardonnay."

"Thank you." They replied in unison.

Laney took a swig of liquid courage and went for it. "Don't you want to know about Grant?"

Katherine winced. "I suppose. How is he?"

"Oh, he's great. Fantastic, in fact." Laney smiled superficially. She'd rehearsed this bit of the conversation, knowing it would drive Kitty mad even if she managed to preserve her poised facade. "He's a very successful commercial real estate developer all over Vermont, and he's had an amazing girlfriend, Michelle, for years. She's practically a gourmet chef." It was mostly true, at least the part about Grant. Michelle was a sweet girl, perhaps not *amazing*, but certainly nice and easygoing, unlike Katherine. She was also a remarkable home cook, if not a gourmet chef. Maybe they hadn't been dating for *years*, more like a year or so, but whatever.

"So he's not married, huh?" Katherine smiled wryly, her rose-stained lips curling at the corners.

"He practically is. I'm sure they'll be engaged any day." Grant had never mentioned anything about proposing. "You know how it is these days. Marriage is just a piece of paper."

"Right, of course." Katherine nodded soberly, and Laney kicked herself for giving her even a glimmer of hope. Not that Kitty was still interested in Grant, but either way, Laney wanted to make sure she knew she couldn't have him.

"Look, I have to get home. Let's figure this house thing out and get on with it." Laney took another sip of wine.

"Fine by me."

"Do you have any suggestions?"

"I do." Katherine clasped her hands together, leaning her elbows on the table in front of her. "Obviously, I don't live here and I have a very hectic life and job in New York City," she started. "So I was thinking, what if you sort through

Luella's things. You can e-mail me on anything I can help with. And then I'll pay for someone to clean the house and find a Realtor to sell it. How does that sound?"

"So let me get this straight." Laney was gunning. "You want me to do all the work, and you'll just make a few calls and toss some money around?"

"Well, when you put it like that." Katherine mocked offense.

"How else is there to put it, Kitty? News flash: I'm not one of your employees."

"Well, do you have a better solution?"

"Yes, one where we're doing equal work. I can get some stuff done during the week, and you can come up on the weekends."

Katherine exhaled, outwardly exasperated, and tucked her slick black hair behind her ears. "Laney, I can't come to Manchester every weekend. My work is seven days a week, around the clock."

"Well, then, we'd better get started while you're still here. I'll ask for a few days off next week. Thanksgiving is a slow time at the spa." She regretted it as soon as she'd said it. Tina would flip out. She didn't like it when Laney left for a few hours, much less three days off at the last minute. "Are you planning to stay through the holiday?"

"I am." Katherine stirred her untouched iced tea. "So you want to work together?"

"I didn't say that."

"Okay."

"It's a big house."

"Fine. But we'll never get through it all in a week." Katherine folded her arms across her lean torso.

"We'll cross that bridge." Laney was pleased with herself. She'd taken control of the conversation, which Kitty likely hadn't expected.

"Whatever you say." Katherine's cell phone buzzed, and she answered instinctively. "Hi, Brooke. Okay, I see. No, that's not okay. No, it's not. Tell Derek he's going to have to answer to me. I don't give a shit. Exactly. Brooke, hold on." She stood up suddenly, causing the waitress to scuttle over. "Please charge this to room six twenty." Katherine turned to Laney. "I'll meet you at Luella's tomorrow morning. Eight a.m." She lifted the phone back to her ear, swiveled on her four-inch heels, and walked away.

And once again Laney was caught off guard.

June 1993

Kitty

It may seem unusual, but my idea of a good time does not involve hanging out with the obnoxious, not to mention immature, boys in our class. Unfortunately, it's all Laney ever wants to do these days, especially since she started dating Roger King. He's going to be a senior like Grant, except they're not really friends. Roger plays football, and Grant's on the lacrosse team. Even though he fits in with the jocks, Grant prefers his student-council friends, which means he and Roger are in completely different groups. Roger's group is more the burping-contest, chest-bumping, fling-boogers-at-the-teacher kind of crowd. Grant's friends are much cooler, at least in my opinion. They know how to open a book not involving pictures of naked women. Laney doesn't date Grant's friends for a few reasons. One, Grant would flip out. Two, Grant would flip out. And three, Laney doesn't usually fall for the intellectual type. She's more about brawn than brains. I, on the other hand, would completely go for one of Grant's friends if any of them would look twice at me, which they don't, because I see them all the time at Laney's house. I'm Grant's little sister's friend as far as they're concerned.

Anyway, this whole Roger thing has been kind of a bummer. I know it sounds selfish. I mean, obviously I want Laney to be happy, but ever since she had a falling-out with Lisa at Karen Mann's sweet sixteen, we haven't been hanging out with her or Meg anymore. Honestly, I can live without having Lisa around. In five years, we've never really bonded. Lisa, like Laney, is completely melodramatic and enjoys nothing more than having all eyes on her. I guess at some point there were only so many eyes to go around. I'm sorry that Meg and I can't stay friends, but that's how it works when you're sixteen. There are sides. Team Laney. And Team Lisa. Sadly, Meg and I were recruited by opposing captains. So now it's just me and Laney. And Roger.

It's not like Laney's had any shortage of boyfriends over the years. But there's something different about this Roger thing. It's like she's addicted to him. All she talks about is Roger this and Roger that. Roger has the most field goals. Roger's the most popular guy in the senior class. Roger has the biggest muscles. Roger has the biggest . . . I told her I did *not* want to know that. She lost her virginity to him three weeks after they started dating. She said it hurt, I guess because he has the biggest . . . She also said he yelled *touchdown* when things were finished on his end. Laney thought it was sexy. I didn't tell her I thought it was the cheesiest, most pathetic thing I'd ever heard. Mainly because that would have made me sound jealous, which she already thinks I am. As it happens, I haven't kissed a boy yet. That's right. I'm sixteen and never been kissed. There have been a couple of opportunities, but I just don't see the point in letting some sweaty, pimply, fidgety idiot play tonsil hockey in my mouth. And I'm certainly not about to let anyone take my clothing off until we've been dating for months, maybe even a year. So, essentially, I'm destined to be a virgin forever, which I think I'm fine with.

Today, Roger brought his friend Dan to Luella's pool to hang out. According to Laney, Dan is here to kiss me. I wonder if Dan knows. I also wonder if he knows he won't be getting anywhere near me, seeing as he's a bit of a Roger clone. Same spiky blond hair; same sunburned, beefy body; same stupid grin; same empty head. I'm sure I couldn't count on both hands how many mouths his tongue has explored. I told Laney that under no circumstances is she to leave me alone with Dan. She just smiled deviously and said, "Whatever you say, Moody McPrudy." Charming, huh?

Yet here I am, sitting on the edge of Luella's pool, in a blue bikini, dipping my feet in the water while Laney, Roger, and Dan do cannonballs off the diving board to see who can make the biggest splash. Laney has no shot, since she's ninety pounds of skin and bones, but the boys seem to enjoy watching her lose her bikini top. Every. Single. Time. Somehow it never gets old.

"Come on, Kitty! Do one jump!" Laney called from the tip of the diving board, wriggling her body in her teeny-tiny sparkly gold bikini.

"No, thanks. I'm good here." I waved her on. Splash. And the top was off. She shrieked for the hundredth time and swam to retrieve it, continuing on to my side of the pool.

"If you sit over here, you're never going to get to know Dan." She whispered it, as if the whole thing was a massive secret.

"That's kind of the idea." I tilted my face up to the sun and closed my eyes.

"Kitty, don't be such a dork. He likes you."

"He does not." I looked down at her, chin deep in the water, her blond hair slicked back off her forehead.

"Yes, he *does*," she insisted.

"How is that possible? We haven't said more than two words to each other." Come to think of it, words are probably not the key to Dan's heart.

"Well, he thinks you're hot."

"He thinks anything in a bikini is hot, maybe with the exception of Roger." I do have to hand it to Laney. She's been diligent in helping me improve my appearance. She took me to a great hair salon in town to get a pretty, fashionable cut that grazes my shoulder blades and looks all bouncy, like the woman whipping her head around for no reason in the Pantene commercials. They even put in a few reddish highlights for free. Laney talked them into it. She also taught me how to do my makeup, even though she does it better, and I always leave it to her when we have a party to go to. And she went through my whole closet with me before school this year. We dumped all the "heinous" stuff, as she put it, and then we raided some old boxes of my mom's clothing my dad had packed away when we made the move from Bennington five years ago. Turns out my mom had some amazing stuff, and most of it fits me now that I've shed some of the baby fat, except the tighter tops, because my boobs are bigger than hers were. I've definitely had more interest from some guys at school and around town, but still, they're not what I'm looking for. Sometimes I wish Laney could understand that and get off my back.

"Would you stop? Do you want to be eighty and yet to be kissed?"

"I'm okay with that."

"You are not."

"Fine. I'll find a great guy when I'm seventy-nine."

"You're infuriating." Laney looked back at Roger, who was about to do a flip off the diving board. "Listen. Roger wants to go back to my house. My parents are in Boston for the whole day, and the house is empty."

"Where's Grant?"

"I don't know. Around, I guess. But he doesn't care what I do."

"Or who."

"Very funny." She slapped me on the leg.

"That's fine. I'll stay here. I told Luella I'd help her make a pie for her dinner guests tonight."

"Okay, well, I'm leaving Dan with you."

"No, you are not!"

"Kitty, he came with Roger, and I can't very well ask him to sit in my house while we go upstairs." She hoisted herself out of the pool and sat next to me.

"You're getting me wet." I moved over. "Can't he just hang out with Grant?"

"Grant hates Dan."

Go figure.

"I'm sure he doesn't *hate* him. They're not even friends."

"He thinks he's stupid or something. I don't know. Can you please just give Dan a chance? If you don't like him, just let him stay here and swim."

"Fine."

"Thank you!" She wrapped her soaking-wet body around my very dry body and planted a soggy kiss on my cheek. "You're the best!"

"You're WET! Get off me." I shoved her playfully. "Do you have . . ." I raised one eyebrow at her.

"Condoms? It's okay to say the word, Kitty." She rolled her eyes. "Roger has them."

"Good old Rog."

"I really don't see what you have against him."

"Nothing."

"Well, you're not very nice to him."

"Would you get out of here before I change my mind?" The last thing I needed was to explain Roger's shortcomings to Laney. I really don't like to lie to her. Part of our best-friend pact is total honesty, no matter what. Like when one of us doesn't look good in an outfit, we always tell each other. Of course, it's rare that Laney doesn't look good, actually great, in something. Thank God she's still intent on fleeing to New York City after college, so she won't end up marrying this guy.

"Okay, we're going. I owe you one!" Laney grabbed her white Keds and gold hoop earrings from next to her lounge chair and shimmied over to the other side of the pool where Roger was tossing a football with Dan. I watched her drape herself on him and whisper something in his ear. Then I heard him summon Dan with one word: "Dude." Moments later, Laney and Roger were hand in hand, ducking through the bushes to Laney's house, and I was left alone with Dan the Man. Awesome.

Before I knew it, he was walking toward me. I got up and retreated to one of Luella's lounge chairs. His idea of a laugh is probably throwing girls in the pool. And I'm so not that girl.

"Whassup?" He sat next to me. Apparently, the five other empty chairs weren't calling to him.

"Not much." I folded my hands in my lap.

"You wanna swim?"

"No, thanks."

"Yeah, that's cool." I think three words is his max.

"Do you want something to drink?" Any excuse to get away.

"Nah." *Crap.* He put his hand on my thigh. *Double crap.* So much for small talk.

"Something to eat?" He actually paused to think on this one, and I took the opportunity to slide over, forcing his hand to fall onto the chair.

"Nah." He placed it back on my leg. "You're kinda hot." My whole body tensed, and I wasn't sure whether to run or laugh in his face. Clearly, these were his moves. Not that I know anything about moves, but I'm pretty sure there are better ones than his. I looked at Dan. He was actually passably attractive, and it should be said that most of the girls in the junior class would jump at the chance to hook up with him. Probably why he didn't need better moves. Unfortunately for Dan, I'm not most of the girls. And there would be no jumping.

"Thank you." Really, what does one say to that? Obviously, I could just let him kiss me. Get it over with. But I'd prefer my first kiss not be a matter of getting it over with. Though this is Dan Perry, and while he isn't the star quarterback, like Roger, he is still a really good football player, about to be a senior, and one of the most popular guys in the whole school. Maybe it's crazy not to let it happen. It would certainly improve my cool factor.

"Sure." He moved closer again and wrapped his left arm around my waist, pulling me against his rib cage. The word *awkward* didn't even begin to describe it. He leaned over and kissed my shoulder and then my neck. I sat frozen, praying he would stop or that Luella would come outside. I turned my face toward his to tell him I wasn't really interested, but before I could say anything, his mouth was pressed against mine and his tongue was stabbing at my pursed lips in an effort to pry them open. I tried to speak, but that only gave him the chance to thrust his tongue down my throat and slobber all over the outside of my mouth and even a little on my cheeks. Before long, his hands were on the outside of my bathing suit, smooshing my boobs.

"Actually, that's enough." I tried to move away, but the back of the chair was up against mine.

"Come on. We're just getting started." His hand was traveling down my stomach.

"Seriously, stop." I was firm but not panicked. It's not like we were trapped in a closet or something.

"I'm all worked up." He took my hand and tried to get me to stroke his penis, which was hard against his wet swim trunks.

"No." I jerked my hand away and attempted to stand up. He pushed me back down with his palms on my shoulders.

"Don't leave me hanging, Katie."

"Kitty." *Seriously?*

"Sorry, yeah." He tried to kiss me again.

"It's enough, really." I was struggling to get him off me. I knew I could scream at any moment and Luella would come rushing out, probably hit Dan over the head with a pie pan, but I really didn't want to cause a scene unless absolutely necessary. Still, he was freakishly strong.

"Hey, asshole! You want to get the hell off her?" Dan jumped back and we both turned around, startled. Grant was marching toward us, red in the face.

"What the fuck, dude?" Dan stood up, and I moved away immediately.

"I said, get the hell off her. Got it?" Grant was as tall as Dan, but not as big otherwise, and I estimated he might lose in a physical fight.

"What's it to you?" Dan got in his face, and Grant didn't back down. Not even a little. My heart was beating a mile a minute. Laney would kill me if anything bad happened.

"Just get out of here, man."

"Whatever." Dan grabbed his T-shirt off one of the chairs. "She's a cold bitch anyway." Grant started to say something, and I shook my head at him vigorously. I just wanted Dan to leave, which he did, stalking off toward Laney's house. I really hoped he wouldn't make a big deal of it.

"You okay?" Grant turned toward me after making sure Dan was really gone.

"Yeah, I'm fine. He's a meathead." My heart was still beating triple time and my knees were all wobbly.

"Where the hell is Laney?" He looked pissed.

"She's at your house with Roger."

"Fabulous. That guy's such a dick."

"I know."

"You should tell her."

"Me? Why don't you tell her?"

"Believe me, I have. You think she listens to a thing I say?"

"Yeah, that's true."

"Here." He picked a towel off the table and wrapped it around me, holding it there until I could feel his breath on the back of my neck. "You're too good for him, Kitty." I didn't say anything.

"Oh, hello, Grant." Luella opened the sliding door, wearing a gauzy white dress that—against her bronzed skin—made her look like a movie star. He moved away from me, and the towel dropped.

"Sorry." I grabbed it and wrapped it around me again.

"Ready to make that pie, darling?" Luella smiled regally. "You're welcome to join us, Grant."

"That's okay. I have a game in an hour."

"Suit yourself."

"I'm gonna run. I'll, uh, see you later, Kitty."

"Yeah, bye. And, um, thank you."

"Sure." He ran back toward his house.

"Pie time?" I turned to Luella.

"Kitty Hill." She grinned knowingly.

"What?"

"I'd say that boy fancies you."

Present Day

Katherine

She'd spent most of the night tossing and turning, unable to impede her mind from sprinting through the past. The sprinting part was habitual for Katherine. It was the way she lived her life, always moving at warp speed, from dawn until dusk and then continuing into the wee hours. But it was typically work, work, work. And then more work. Nothing personal about it. This was different, more stressful in a way. She'd be lying if she said she hadn't thought of Laney or Grant in the past twelve years. There had definitely been times when one memory or another had been triggered by something unexpected, but she hadn't dwelled on it. As far as she'd been concerned, the past was the past, and whether it had ended well or not, it simply wasn't her life anymore.

How could she explain to Laney—a woman who'd rarely left the town where she was born and bred, save for an infrequent vacation—that she was no longer that awkward girl who'd grown up two houses down? She was someone important now. Someone people listened to in board meetings. Someone they cowered from in the hallways. And someone they whispered about when she exited the ladies' room.

Once Katherine had returned to Vermont and been abruptly reunited with Laney, she'd expected Grant's name would surface eventually. And it was pretty clear from their conversation at the Falcon Bar that Laney had been waiting for the opportunity to bring him up. But did she have to be so visibly pleased with herself? Perhaps Laney did have good reason to be upset with her. She'd give her that. It wasn't like she'd been entirely innocent herself, though. There'd been a window of repentance all those years ago. It had been a small window, admittedly, but Laney hadn't been willing to open it even a crack. The light breeze that had been Katherine's remorse had been stifled. After that, she'd given up, justifying her own behavior every which way possible. The pain had been profound at first; for months she'd wavered on her decision. She'd gone from a college senior with a part-time internship to help pay off her student loans to a round-the-clock, entry-level workhorse for a titanic cosmetics conglomerate. Sometimes two weeks went by, one day disappearing into the next, without her having time to think about the world she'd left behind, much less sleep more than two or three hours a night. Other times, one hour at her desk felt like a life sentence, and she'd allow herself, even if for a fleeting moment, to consider exchanging the bright future everyone said she had for a train ticket back to Vermont. Back to her father, Laney, and Luella. But mostly back to Grant. Then a stack of papers would hit her desk like a wakeup call, and she'd push these reminiscences farther and farther into the comfort of obscurity.

Katherine parked her rental car in Luella's driveway, took a deep breath, and let herself out. She was uncharacteristically dressed down in tailored, dark-wash blue jeans and another of her many cashmere sweaters, this one a muted oatmeal shade. She'd gone light on the makeup, left her jewelry in the safe at the hotel, and had even worn flat ballet slippers. So what if they were Prada? Seeing as Laney's animosity had been palpable, to say the least, during their last two encounters, Katherine had decided to give her as little fodder as possible now that they were going to be working together, or at least in the same vicinity, for the better part of a week. She walked up the stone path toward the front door. *How many times,* she mused, *have I walked up this very path?* Now, though, the stones were cracked, even broken in half in a couple places. And the abundant landscaping was no longer. Once upon a time, Luella had been famous for her extensive and meticulously maintained gardens. Her front lawn had been bursting with pink peonies, yellow tulips, purple roses, white chrysanthemums, red coral bells, and, Katherine's personal favorite, the pink and red bleeding hearts with their long, arching stems and heart-shaped blooms.

She fished the key the lawyer had given her from her purse and turned it in the lock, which was corroded, as was the gold-plated doorbell. She had to force the door open, pushing it in with the side of her body. If the decrepit facade was any indication of the shape of the interior, she and Laney were in trouble. But, really, how bad could it be? Luella had always been a stickler for perfection, one of the many things Katherine had absorbed from her mentor. Immediately, she had her answer. It wasn't bad. It was a disaster. The air was thick with dust, and papers and trinkets were strewn about as if a tornado had gutted the interior. Some of the furniture was stained and tattered. And

Luella's vast chandelier with its rainstorm of crystals, which had once presided over the marble entrance hall, was now splayed on the floor in the center of what could only be described as mass chaos. Katherine swallowed a lump in her throat and, sidestepping all the crap, made her way from room to room on the first floor, unable to digest the enormity of the situation. Had Luella lived this way in her last days? When she'd finally had the chance to grill her father about Luella's death and the unique stipulations in her will, he'd divulged only scant details, swearing up and down that he didn't know any more. She, he'd said, had been found resting peacefully in her bed that day by a friend who checked in on her regularly. Clearly, Luella had fired her housekeeper long before that. He'd also confirmed what Katherine had already presumed, that Luella had opted to be cremated. There was no way, Katherine knew, that Luella would allow her physical beauty to decompose in a coffin underground for however long it took to go from flesh and bones to worm food. She knew because she wouldn't either.

Katherine half expected Luella to appear from around the corner, as she often did, keeping the girls on their toes. She was desperate to see her one last time, to tell her how she'd changed her life, how'd she set her on the right path to becoming the woman she was today—for what that was worth. Now she was also desperate to ask her what had happened. How had her once-immaculate home, which had gleamed from corner to corner, disintegrated into such disarray? Had she gone mad? The lawyer had indicated repeatedly that Luella was of sound mind until the very end. Perhaps he'd seen the condition of the house and had felt compelled to explain the unexplainable in advance.

"Holy shit."

Katherine jumped, startled by the company. She turned

around to find Laney standing in front of her, with the same staggering expression she'd donned only moments earlier.

"I know." Katherine watched Laney take it all in. She was still as beautiful as always without a trace of makeup or a brush run through her tangle of blond curls. There was a time when Katherine had been desperate for those curls, cursing her genetics for the heavy black mop that hung flaccidly atop her head.

"This is a complete shit storm." Laney picked up a dirty, crumpled piece of paper, holding it out in front of her between her thumb and forefinger, and then dropped it back onto the floor. "What the fuck happened?" She tiptoed around the chandelier in her faded carpenter jeans, white Converse sneakers, and gray UVM hoodie.

"I have no idea, but we certainly have our work cut out for us." Katherine crossed her arms. "We need a plan of attack."

"Rick said he can help with anything that needs fixing and a fresh paint job." Laney glanced at Katherine. "He's a contractor."

"That's convenient." Katherine followed Laney into the kitchen, where they'd spent countless hours playing cards and partaking in Luella's extravagant high teas. "I think we need to deal with getting all this crap organized. We'll throw out whatever's junk, and then I'd suggest we devote one room to gathering everything we want to sell or donate. Probably the foyer, since it's closest to the door."

"I know a woman who can organize an estate sale for us."

"Great. Then we can hire a cleaning service and get Rick in here to fix up and paint. And we'll be done." Katherine clapped her hands, rubbing them together like she was ready to dive in.

"You make it sound easy." Laney opened the refrigerator

and slammed it shut. "Holy fuck. I think something died in there." She wriggled her whole body. "Blah."

"Well, I wouldn't say it's going to be easy, but at least we know what we have to do. Deal with the crap, and leave the rest of the work to the professionals. Obviously, we'll need to hire a Realtor when all's said and done, so we can sell this place." Katherine smiled. "I hope the next people love this house the way we did."

"Yeah, me too." Laney met Katherine's gaze for a moment and then looked away. "I have garbage bags in my car."

"Excellent. Let's pick a place to start." Katherine was pleasantly surprised to find that Laney wasn't nearly as prickly as she had been the last two times they'd been together.

"I'll take the kitchen."

"Should we just do it together?" Katherine suggested optimistically.

"No, you can pick another room." Laney didn't give it a second thought.

"Seriously?"

"Yes, seriously."

"It'll be so much more efficient if we conquer each room together."

"Maybe so, but I told you I don't want to work with you."

"This is so ridiculous." Katherine rolled her eyes. "We're two grown adults."

"It's not ridiculous to me." Laney shrugged.

"Stop being immature." Katherine regretted the words as soon as they escaped her lips.

"*Immature?*" Laney's hands were on her hips. "Excuse me, Kitty, but we're not best friends anymore. We're not even friends. We're in this situation and that's fine, but it doesn't mean we're going to bond."

"I'm not saying we have to bond. I'm just saying we could

try to work together peacefully in the name of getting things done as quickly as possible."

"I said no." Laney was firm.

"Fine. Whatever. I'll take the living room to start. But I'm only here for a week, so I hope we can get it done."

"I hope so too."

The next eight hours flew by in a whirlwind of surveying, organizing, and tidying. Katherine and Laney worked separately, calling out to each other sporadically with a question about a document or trinket or piece of furniture—whether or not it was worth keeping. On the two occasions Katherine had gone into the kitchen to check on things, Laney had just ignored her until finally looking up and hostilely barking, "What?"

Fortunately, neither the kitchen nor the living room held many of Luella's personal items, so it was easy enough to weed through things without too much sentiment. Eventually, Katherine knew, they'd come to Luella's den and her bedroom, the two places reserved for special items such as family photos, books, significant pieces of jewelry, and her many gowns and furs. Katherine wasn't looking forward to it, and she hoped, as unlikely as it may be, that Laney would come around by then, at least enough to join forces in space, if not conversation. At some point during the middle of the day, Laney had gone out to pick up lunch. She had yelled out only, "I'm heading out for a sandwich" to Katherine, not offering to grab anything for her, not that she'd have eaten a sandwich. Laney was making her point loud and clear and, frankly, Katherine was getting a little irritated by the whole production. Normally she didn't care if people didn't like her; God knows there were plenty. But with Laney it irked her. Why hadn't time softened her even a little? Surely she'd had more pressing things to do than sit around and simmer about Katherine for over a decade. More than that, though, Katherine still couldn't understand why Laney felt like she'd been the only one wronged. Hadn't *she* really been the selfish one, trying to hold Katherine back to satisfy her own needs? If Laney's attitude didn't improve, Katherine wasn't sure how long she'd be able to remain the nice guy. Under normal circumstances, she wouldn't tolerate this behavior from anyone.

"You made a lot of headway." Laney appeared in the doorway to the living room. "The kitchen is pretty much empty too." She still had a scowl on her face, though her fists were no longer balled in Katherine's presence.

"Two rooms down, fourteen to go, if you count bathrooms." Katherine exhaled, standing up and dusting herself off before Luella's doorbell sounded its familiar chime. "I wonder who that could be."

"I wonder." Laney grinned mischievously and practically skipped through the foyer to answer it. Katherine followed, ready to call it a day and head back to the Equinox for a long, hot bubble bath.

"Who is it?" she asked, as soon as Laney had cracked the front door.

"Hey, I know I'm early. My last job went faster than I thought." Katherine had only to hear his voice to know. If there had been an escape route, she would have taken it, but there was nothing she could do now except stand there, paralyzed by panic, her mouth and hands quivering involuntarily.

"No worries. We're just finishing up." Laney smiled giddily and gave her brother a hug, closing the door behind him. Katherine cleared her throat unwittingly, and Grant turned around, an expression of profound shock on his face.

"Kitty. Wow, uh, you . . ."

"Um, hi." Katherine scratched at nothing on the back of her neck and then wiped nothing off her jeans. She licked her parched lips and bit the lower one.

"Uh, this is . . ."

"Awkward. Sorry. I didn't know you were coming."

"Yeah, I didn't know . . ."

"Oh, did I forget to mention it?" Laney feigned innocence, and Grant shot her a dirty look.

"I'd say so." Katherine smiled uncomfortably.

"He's going to help us sell the house when we're done. I told you he's in real estate," Laney declared a little defensively. Katherine nodded.

Grant looked good. Unbelievable, actually. He was still tall and slender, but his once-boyish physique had transformed into a strong and substantial man's body. His dirty blond hair had darkened to a rich chestnut, setting off his incisive blue eyes. And she even noticed a five o'clock shadow, which really suited him. Of all the times she'd imagined bumping into Grant over the years, and there had certainly been a few despite it being completely improbable, the one thing she had not imagined was looking like a slob. Katherine straightened her posture and regained what little composure she had left. "I have to get going."

"So soon?" Laney was enjoying this a little too much.

"Yes. I'll be here tomorrow at eight. It was nice to see you, Grant." Katherine maneuvered around them, slipping out the door and running to her car as quickly as she could.

As soon as she'd driven out of sight, she parked on the side of the road and hunched her torso over the wheel. "Pull it together, Katherine. Pull your fucking self together."

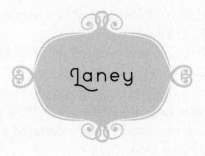

Laney

Laney woke up as pissed off as she'd gone to bed. She'd arrived home the night before to find an already disappointed Rick. Grant had laid into her after Kitty left and had then, apparently, called her house for a second round, only to get Rick on the other end of the line. "I'd be fucking furious too," Rick had said as soon as she'd walked through the door, craving his sympathy, not his judgment. This had set Laney off, mainly because—as she'd tried to explain to Grant—she'd asked him to meet her at Luella's house *after* work, when she thought Kitty would be long gone. How was she supposed to know that he'd be able to leave two hours earlier than usual? Fine, so she could have mentioned that Kitty was in town, that she was tied into the whole home-inheritance debacle, but honestly, she had yet to craft a delicate way of bringing it up. And now she was being punished for not just blurting it out like an insensitive sister.

Of course, Rick took Grant's side. Whenever she had a disagreement with Grant, Rick always thought that Grant was the reasonable one and Laney was the drama queen, blowing things out of proportion or manipulating the facts to her benefit. "Whether you meant for it to happen that way or not, Grant said you seemed pretty pleased with yourself," Rick had admonished. "So sue me!" Laney had retorted, stomping off to their bedroom. She hadn't resurfaced to eat dinner or to watch their usual Saturday-night shows. And when Rick had come to bed around midnight, she'd pretended to be asleep, even when he'd kissed her on her cheek and whispered, "I love you." They never, ever went to bed angry. She blamed Kitty.

To add insult to injury, she'd received a text message from Tina saying she absolutely needed her to come to work in the morning for a couple of hours. Apparently, there'd been some mix-up with a nail polish order, and Tina was desperate to get it sorted out on a Sunday. In an ideal world, Tina would have Laney working seven days a week, but when Tina bought Oasis, Laney had been firm that she could only work every other Saturday and never on Sunday. Tina had bristled at the notion, but Laney had held strong. That said, she couldn't count the number of Sundays Tina had begged her to come in for at least part of the day. In those cases, Laney had, to her long-term detriment, not held strong. The worst part about having to go in to work was that she'd had to text Kitty saying she couldn't meet her at Luella's until eleven, which probably gave her a rise. But Kitty had written back just one word: *fine*.

Laney wondered if Kitty was mad at her. Not that she cared. Kitty had definitely been ruffled by Grant's impromptu visit. She'd been all fidgety, and the look of sheer humiliation on her face had been priceless. Initially Laney had felt a little bad about it, until she'd taken so much heat from Grant and Rick. They'd both defended Kitty, which she could understand coming from Rick, but Grant? It didn't make sense. If anyone should understand her position, it was Grant. In fact, one might argue he'd been victimized by Kitty even worse than she had.

She hadn't bothered to wake Rick on her way out. He'd been sleeping so peacefully at seven forty-five, which was unheard of for him. Plus she was still annoyed. By eight, Laney was at Oasis, getting everything back in order. One day out of the spa and it was like a tornado had hit. Tornado Tina. By nine, Tina had arrived, and shortly thereafter customers began flowing in. Laney was busy buzzing around the place, making sure everyone was happy and that all was running smoothly. Tina was manning the front desk, the least labor-intensive of all the jobs, and things were humming along. Until *she* walked in.

"Hello. I'm here for my nine thirty massage."

"Name, please?"

"Katherine Hill." Laney spun around to witness Tina smiling as politely as she'd ever seen her, appraising Katherine's existence from head to toe.

"Wait. Oh, my God! Are you *the* Katherine Hill? Yes! Yes you are!" Tina was convulsing with excitement, awe, and envy—a veritable kiss-ass cocktail.

"Well, I'm not sure I'm *the* anyone, but I am Katherine Hill." She nodded modestly.

"Oh don't you be humble! I see you in all the society magazines. You know George Clooney! I saw you in *Vogue* together!" Tina was blushing like a schoolgirl.

"George is a friend." Katherine smiled demurely, and Laney rolled her eyes. She felt like sticking her finger down her throat, but managed to stifle the impulse.

"And you're the head of that huge cosmetics company!" Laney watched Tina groping through her empty head for the name.

"Blend." Katherine let her off the hook.

"Yes, Blend!" Tina punched the air with her bony fist.

"Though I don't see any of our products around here." Katherine craned her neck in either direction, spotting Laney out of the corner of her eye.

"That's because they're too expensive for a small spa like Oasis," Laney countered defensively, walking over toward the front desk, where Tina was still quaking with admiration. Laney hadn't known that Blend was the big cosmetics company where Katherine worked, but she was quite familiar with their overpriced merchandise.

"Oh no, no, no. I'm sure that's not the case. We'll work something out, Ms. Hill."

"Actually, I suspect Laney is right," Katherine acknowledged, and Tina's buglike eyes looked like they were going to launch out of their sockets.

"You two *know* each other?"

"For twenty-three years."

"How come you never told me you were friends with *Katherine Hill*?" Tina regarded Laney urgently, as if she'd withheld access to the Hope Diamond.

"Because I'm not." Laney tightened her lips and widened her eyes.

"She's just kidding." Katherine laughed, and Laney's mouth remained taut. If Tina hadn't been so obviously enamored with Kitty, she'd have engaged in her childish game of back-and-forth. *No, we are not friends.* Maybe she'd have stuck her tongue out for good measure and recited a verse of "I'm Rubber, and You're Glue."

"Well, any friend of Laney's is a friend of mine." Tina

tittered. "Now let's get you set for that massage. I'll even throw in an extra half hour."

"Thank you, but that won't be necessary. I'm meeting an old friend at eleven."

"Oh, I see." Tina was thwarted but not discouraged. "You'll have to come back, then!"

"Absolutely," Katherine offered graciously, as Tina led her toward the back of the spa. "I'll see you later, Laney." Katherine waved, and Laney recoiled. She'd never hear the end of it from Tina.

By the time she got to Luella's house at noon, Katherine's car was already parked in front, and Laney was stewing. Throughout the entirety of Katherine's one-hour massage, Tina had shadowed Laney around Oasis, peppering her with questions about their friendship. *How do you know each other? Are you good friends? Did you ever go to New York City to visit her? Did you ever go to any fancy parties? Or meet George Clooney? Maybe you could take me sometime?* And, *Why, in God's name, have you never mentioned Katherine before?* Laney had answered her litany of queries in as much detail as possible, irritated by the teeny-tiny, eensy-weensy bit of satisfaction it gave her to have something Tina coveted, even if it was the last thing Laney herself wanted—to be associated with Katherine.

Laney had managed to avoid Katherine postmassage, for fear she'd lose her breakfast watching the spectacle of Tina's sycophantic behavior a second time around. Now she had no choice but to face her. She pushed in Luella's front door, making a mental note to ask Rick to fix it, and stalked into the entrance hall.

"Hello?"

"In the living room," Katherine called out.

"Didn't you finish this room?" Laney stood in the doorway.

"Yup. But I just moved everything we decided to keep from the kitchen into here. I figured if we put it all in the foyer it would make it hard to get in and out. Not to mention we still have to do something with that chandelier. So, this is now our estate-sale room. What next?" Laney was impressed, though didn't indicate as much. She hadn't taken Katherine for much of a physical laborer, but somehow, slight frame and all, she'd managed.

"You did this yourself?" Laney looked around at the kitchen table, chairs, and some other pretty large pieces of furniture surrounding the living room couch, coffee table, end tables, and armoires.

"My dad stopped by to help me. You just missed him." Katherine's hands were on her hips, and her cheeks were flushed. Laney stared at her old friend's face for a moment. With scarcely a trace of makeup, Katherine was effortlessly graceful, her smooth, creamy, unlined skin radiating an undeniable physical beauty. "There's nothing much in the powder room. So it's just the dining room, and then we can move upstairs to the bedrooms and Luella's den."

"I can start upstairs if you want to take the dining room."

"Fine, but leave Luella's bedroom and den for now. I want to go through that stuff too." Laney noticed she didn't say together. Maybe she'd finally taken the hint.

"Okay." Laney turned to head upstairs. "Oh, and do me a favor. Don't come to my place of work without letting me know first." She hated having to call Oasis her place of work when clearly *my spa* would sound so much more impressive and be so much more gratifying. Katherine didn't look up from a box she was taping shut. "*Hello?*"

"I heard you. Let's not talk about letting each other know

things ahead of time, okay?" Katherine's face was serious. "We're here to work."

Three hours passed without a word between them. Predictably, the upstairs wasn't in much better shape than the downstairs, and Laney had her work cut out for her in the first of four guest bedrooms. It was hard to understand why Luella had needed so many extra bedrooms. At one time, she and her husband had lived there, but as long as Laney had known her she'd been a widow in a house fit for a family of at least six. She did like to entertain. Laney remembered countless times when she and Kitty had helped Luella prepare for a lavish dinner party, setting the long, mahogany dining-room table with luxurious silken linens, luminous fine china, crystal stemware, and silverware so heavy you'd break a toe if it dropped on your foot. Still, Laney was pretty sure Luella wasn't one for sleepover guests. She cherished her privacy too much.

Laney could hear Katherine clanking around downstairs, most likely packing all of said china, stemware, and silverware into boxes so that they could sell it off to people who wouldn't love it the way Luella had. There was no one who delighted in aesthetic beauty the way she had—both people and things. On any old Saturday in the summer, Luella could be found with a full face of makeup, expertly applied, and an ensemble so artfully coordinated she looked as if she'd stepped off the pages of a high-fashion magazine. Obviously, it had rubbed off on Kitty.

She sighed, looking around the room at what was left. It had been a long day already and a long evening prior, battling it out with her husband and brother. There was one more drawer to go and then she'd have to carry all the boxes down to the living room, which Katherine had declared home base. She scooted over to the other side of the dresser and tugged at the handle, which fell off in her hand.

"Shit." *One more thing for Rick to fix.*

The drawer was packed mostly with junk, which she dumped into the large black garbage bag she'd been gradually filling. Underneath an empty wooden picture frame, Laney noticed a familiar small, pink linen scrapbook, which she unearthed, pulling the white ribbon bow to open it. The first page read "Happy Birthday Luella" in shimmery gold marker. Kitty had penned it with her impeccable handwriting. Laney flipped to the next page, where there were photos of the two of them with their arms around each other, and one where Laney was kissing Kitty on the cheek, she in a red string bikini and Kitty wearing her shorts and a T-shirt to conceal a plain black bathing suit. Another showed them making stupid faces at the camera. They'd asked Grant to be their personal photographer for a week so they could give Luella the photo album for her birthday. And when they had, Luella had been so visibly honored, they'd sworn they'd seen her eyes well up with tears—a definite first, since Luella's poker face was about as polished as Madonna's voguing.

Laney stared at the photos, trying to find the resemblance between Kitty and Katherine, and even her old self and her grown-up self. The girls in the picture had been fun, lighthearted, unknowing as to what the future would bring. They'd loved each other so purely.

"How's it going?" Katherine came into the room, her formerly pristine white sweater blemished with dirt.

"Look at this." She motioned to Katherine, who knelt down beside her.

"Oh, my God." Katherine grimaced. "Those were some serious thighs."

"Look how happy we were." Laney continued flipping through the pages. Almost every shot was of them at Luella's pool, swimming, frolicking, or just being silly—whatever it was twelve-year-olds did.

"I know."

"You were so ridiculous with your shorts and T-shirt in every single photo." Laney pointed at the album.

"I was a pork chop."

"You were not!"

"I was. And you were a string bean. We made a lovely meal."

They both laughed.

"You were always so insecure about how you looked. I never understood it." Laney shook her head.

"That's because you looked the way you looked."

"God, it's so crazy to think that was us." Laney turned the page to a close-up of Katherine. "You were pretty back then too, Kitty. Just different."

"You look exactly the same."

"What?!"

"You do, seriously. Still skinny and gorgeous."

"Thanks."

"Listen, Laney, I know . . ."

"Don't."

"I just want to tell you . . ."

"Seriously, Kitty. It was a different lifetime." Laney snapped the album shut. "We're not those girls anymore." She stood up abruptly. "I have to get home to Gemma. I'll see you tomorrow."

May 1994

Kitty

"**A**re you ready?" Laney was bouncing up and down on her bed with a long rectangular box in her hands, which quite clearly she had covered in Santa Claus wrapping paper, despite the fact that my birthday is at the end of May.

"I'm ready. Would you sit down already? You're making me nervous." It's hard not to be seduced by Laney's infectious enthusiasm.

"Shut your eyes." She plopped onto her butt, holding the gift in her lap.

"Okay." I closed them halfway.

"They're not shut." She folded her arms across her chest and made a pouty face. "Put your hands out."

"Fine." I closed my eyes for real this time and extended my arms in front of me, palms facing up.

"Here you go." She placed the present in my hands. "You can open them now."

"Thanks!" I looked down. "Wait. Why was I closing my eyes?"

"It's part of the fun." She sighed dramatically. "You're so suspicious sometimes. Go on. Open it."

I tore at the paper to find an Absolut Vodka box. "You're giving me liquor? I don't even drink." I'm probably one of the only juniors in our class who doesn't. I just don't see the point of being out of control.

"Would you look at it more closely?" Laney was bursting with excitement. She'd only been talking about this gift for the better part of a month, dropping little hints here and there.

I examined the box. Laney had very carefully and creatively replaced the word *vodka* with *best friends*, so it read, "Absolut Best Friends." "Cool!"

"That's not it. Take the bottle out. Jeez, it's like giving a gift to a chimp."

"Shut up! I'm getting there." I freed the bottle from inside the box. "Oh, my God!" Laney had done the same thing on the front of the bottle, and she'd also affixed a list of ingredients on the back with adjectives describing our friendship: *loving*, *caring*, *kind*, *trustworthy*, *fun*, and on and on. She'd printed it in the neatest of handwriting, which I know must have taken a great deal of time and precision on her part. Inside the bottle were little pieces of colored construction paper and glitter, lending to its festive appearance.

"Empty it out. Don't worry about the glitter."

I dumped the pieces of paper and glitter onto her pristine white bedspread. "Your mom is going to kill us."

"Okay, now open each piece of paper."

"Mrs. Kotler?" I read the first one aloud. Mrs. Kotler was our ninth-grade math teacher.

"Keep going."

"Annie's sweet sixteen?" The night Laney dumped a
Coke on Mike Tanner's head because he'd tried to grope her
on the dance floor, and I had to run interference while she
escaped to the ladies' room. I looked up at Laney, who was
grinning from ear to ear.

"They're all of our memories from the last six years!"

"Oh, my God, Lane. I love it!" I hugged her tightly. I may
have even gotten a little teary eyed.

"I spent, like, forever on it. I think my dad was pissed
when I emptied out the vodka, but my mom told him it was
for a worthy cause."

"This is really amazing. Thank you so much."

"Yeah, well, I wanted to get you diamond earrings, but,
you know, what with the budget and all . . ."

"This is way better."

"You think?"

"Absolutely!" I laughed at my own joke. "Get it?"

"What?"

"*Absolut*ely." Sometimes Laney is a little slow on the
uptake.

"Oh, ha ha. You're a crack-up.

"Okay, so it's your birthday. Your choice for movie night."
She jumped off the bed and darted over to her closet in her
white cotton short shorts with little red hearts and matching camisole. Laney just got the "Rachel" haircut from *Friends*,
with all the layers, so now she's straightening her crazy
curls with a flat iron every day, and it looks really good. I
definitely couldn't pull it off. "I've got your favorite snacks
too. Sourdough pretzels, Cool Ranch Doritos, and Reese's
Peanut Butter Cups, the big ones."

"Wow, you really thought of everything." Friday nights
are always movie night at Laney's house, which typically
means Laney picks the movie and then conks out twenty

minutes in, leaving me to suffer through the entirety of something we've already watched ten thousand times, like *Thelma and Louise*. Laney thinks she's Louise, only rather than driving off a cliff, she plans to escape to New York City. "I'll go with *Beaches*."

"Ugh, sooooooo depressing."

"Don't worry. You won't make it to the depressing part. Plus it's a touching story about the depths of friendship. Kind of apropos. Don't you think?"

"I have no idea what that means. Sorry, genius."

"*Apropos* means 'fitting.' Like, it's so fitting for two best friends to be watching a movie about two best friends."

"Whatever you say." She opened the bag of Doritos and stuffed a handful in her mouth. "Want some?"

"How could you possibly be eating right now?" Laney's mom went all out for my birthday, cooking my favorites— fried chicken, mashed potatoes, and sautéed mushrooms. She even baked me a two-layer, all-chocolate birthday cake with a big pink 17 on it.

"I'm a growing girl," Laney declared, her mouth over- flowing with chips.

"Actually, you're not, which is completely maddening. Those babies go right to my thighs." I squeezed a hunk of my very unattractive leg fat. "See that? Cool Ranch Doritos."

"Oh, stop. Come on, let's watch." Laney was already un- der the covers, and patted the place beside her. By traditional standards, we're probably too old and too big to be sleeping in a twin-sized bed together, but we don't care. I climbed under next to her.

And sure enough, by the time Hillary Whitney and C. C. Bloom were meeting under the Atlantic City Boardwalk, Laney was snoring away.

"Lane?" I whispered, to make sure she was sleeping. She

didn't reply. "I'm going downstairs." After dinner, Grant had suggested meeting in the living room once Laney was out, so we could talk and probably watch one of his stupid shows. We do that from time to time, whenever he's not out with the guys. I just like being around him, even if it does make me anxious.

I tiptoed down the Drakes' creaky stairwell to find Grant waiting for me under a wool blanket, with a bowl of chips and two sodas.

"Hey, come on in." I was wearing the new purple silk pajamas my dad had given me for my birthday, with the hope that Grant would want to hang out. Stupid, I know. Grant is pretty much a god among men, while I'm a mere peon. He's so cute and so smart, and I don't know. He's kind of perfect. If I didn't know better or if I were prettier, I'd actually think he was interested. Luella is convinced he has the "hots" for me, but Luella is—for lack of a better way to put it—old. She doesn't get the fact that guys like Grant simply don't have the "hots" for girls like me, especially ones they consider a little sister.

"What are we watching?"

"*Saturday Night Live.*" He peeled the blanket back for me to get under, which I'm sure made my face all hot and red. "Madonna is on."

"Cool." I actually like *Saturday Night Live*, and, anyway, it's a drastic improvement from the cop shows and legal dramas he usually picks. Sometimes we talk about current events, like the fact that Nelson Mandela just became South Africa's first black president. Grant's very smart. Not that Laney is stupid, but she's not exactly into knowing what's going on in the world. At all. I'm not even sure she knows who Nelson Mandela is.

"Want some?" He held the bowl of Ruffles in front of me. If nothing else, this family can eat.

"No, thanks. I'm stuffed from your mom's birthday dinner." He put the bowl down on the glass coffee table.

"So, uh, speaking of your birthday."

"Yeah?" I looked at Grant, who suddenly seemed a little nervous. "Is everything okay?"

"Oh, yeah, yeah. Everything's fine." He moved the throw pillow on the couch to reveal a small, neatly wrapped gold box. "I got you something."

"You got *me* something?" A chill went up my spine and my heartbeat commenced its stampede.

"Well, it's your birthday. Isn't it?" He smiled, flashing the dimples that make my knees weak. "Open it."

I took the box and stripped off its gold skin. My hands were shaking a little, and I really hoped he didn't notice. "What is it?" Why do people ask stupid things like that when they're opening a gift? I have no idea. I can only cite complete and utter apprehension coupled with steep joy at the fact that a boy—and not just any boy—was giving me a birthday gift. One he'd presumably selected all by himself, since Laney definitely would have told me. I lifted the lid.

"Do you like it?" He was watching me expectantly.

"Oh, my God, Grant." There nestled in the little black box was a delicate silver chain with a silver, cursive "K" dangling from it. "It's beautiful."

"Are you sure? You can exchange it for something else if it's not your taste. The lady at Mancini's said initials are really in now. It's like the kind from Tiffany, she said. Whatever that means."

"You got this at Mancini's?" Mancini's is only the fanciest jewelry store in Manchester.

"Yeah, my friend's cousin works there. She helped me out too."

"I just can't believe . . ." I was literally speechless staring at the necklace. No one's ever gotten me anything like it. My dad isn't one for frills, and there certainly aren't any other boys lining up, proffering jewelry.

"Do you want me to help you put it on?" He still looked nervous, which was making me even more nervous than I usually am, which is a lot.

"Sure. Yeah." I turned around and lifted my hair off my neck, praying it wasn't sweaty. He fumbled a little to get it hooked. "So, do you get all your girlfriends—I mean, friends that are girls—necklaces for their birthdays?"

"No, I don't." He looked down, fidgeting with his hands. "Listen, Kitty. Speaking of that, I have to tell you something. I've been waiting a long time, and I just, well, I don't know. Maybe because of Laney . . ."

"What is it?" I nodded eagerly.

"I really like you."

"I like you too," I blurted.

"No, I mean . . ." He leaned forward, cupping my cheeks in his hands, and placed the gentlest kiss on my lips. "I want to be with you. I want us to be together."

I must have been in shock, because all I remember thinking is, *This is not happening to me. Things like this do not happen to me.* And then we were kissing again, this time with tongue.

"What about Laney?" I pulled back suddenly. "She's going to kill me. And you." Not that I really cared in the moment. All I wanted, yearned for, were his lips back on mine.

"Don't worry about Laney. I'll take care of her." He moved in to kiss me again.

For hours, we sat on the Drakes' couch, unable to get enough of each other, until the dim light of day was peering through the curtains and it was time to return to bed with Laney.

The following morning I wasn't even exhausted, despite

the fact that I'd gotten no sleep at all. If I hadn't stayed awake, I would have thought the whole thing was a dream. I wanted to see him again as soon as possible, but not this morning. What if Laney realized something was up before Grant had a chance to tell her? I was legitimately scared to see her reaction and was hoping he planned to break the news while I was not around.

"Lane?" I whispered.

"What?" she croaked, yanking the bedspread over her head.

"I've gotta go. I told my dad I'd have breakfast with him." It was a lie, which made me feel guilty, especially since Laney's birthday gift, listing *trustworthy* as one of the main ingredients in our friendship, was taunting me from on top of the dresser. It was really more of a white lie, though, which I justified by telling myself it was in her best interest.

"Okay. Call me later." Thank God she let me off easy. I got dressed as quickly as possible, grabbing my stuff in a hurry and making sure Grant's necklace was safely tucked in the inside pocket of my overnight bag, where I'd put it when I returned to Laney's room in the wee hours of the morning. I couldn't exactly let her see it.

Somehow I made it out the front door without waking anyone. I was bursting to talk about what had happened. Normally, I would have woken Laney, who would have been cranky about it at first but then thrilled to hear every last detail. Obviously, in this particular situation, that was not an option. Nor was my dad, who'd probably take the opportunity to lecture me on birth control, a sermon I'd succeeded in avoiding up to this point, most likely because my dad figured I wasn't cool enough to be having sex. Still true. Instinctively, I turned in the opposite direction of my house, toward Luella's. It was early, but I knew she'd be up. I walked up her stone path and rang the bell.

"Hello, darling." She appeared within seconds, looking like Grace Kelly at eight a.m., in a long orange linen dress that hugged her slender but shapely figure. "To what do I owe the honor at this hour?"

"He kissed me!" I announced, still standing on her porch.

"Who kissed you?" She ushered me inside, as if the paparazzi might be camped out in the bushes, waiting to catch wind of the big news. "Breaking Story: Grant Kissed Kitty!"

"Grant." I fished through my bag for the necklace. "And he gave me this." I held it up like an Olympic gold medal, even though it was silver.

"Well, now, that's lovely. And it's about time, I'd say." She smiled and pecked me on the cheek. "Happy birthday, darling. Come in for a little breakfast."

I followed Luella into the kitchen, where a plate of croissants was laid out on the table, as if she'd been expecting me. It seems like Luella is always expecting me, which I've never acknowledged is a pretty nice way to feel.

"I just can't believe it."

"Can't believe what?" She sat down across from me.

"That he likes me."

"As well he should. You're a beautiful, very intelligent young woman."

"I don't know." I took a croissant.

"Well, I do. You just need a little more confidence, that's all. Grant's a smart boy. He sees what everyone else sees."

"Not the other guys at school."

"Well, I can't speak for them. But I'd say they'll regret it one day."

"Doubtful."

"Nonsense." She paused, as if she were trying to figure out what to say next. "So, how was it?"

"How was what?" My whole body was still quivering

with adrenaline; it was hard to concentrate on anything other than the way his lips had felt on mine.

"The kiss. How was the kiss?" Luella didn't make eye contact. She just busied herself by tidying things on the kitchen table, which didn't appear to need tidying.

"Good, I guess." Honestly, I hadn't thought about the good or bad of it, and I don't exactly have a point of reference, unless you count Dan. Which I do not. Grant probably could have licked my face clean like a puppy dog and I'd still be in seventh heaven. Then it occurred to me: what if *he* didn't like the way I kissed? *Shit.* "I mean, I hope Grant thought so." It wasn't my typical course of conversation with Luella. Sure, we'd talked about plenty of personal things before, my personal things—like fights I'd had with my dad or even disagreements I'd had with Laney. Sometimes it was easier to confide in Luella than it was in either of them. With Laney, it could be challenging to keep her focused on anything but herself or what was going on at that very moment, in that it applied to her. With my dad, it was mainly about him being, simply put, a man. Luella had a way of listening without judging, and also understanding when I needed help and when I just needed her to hear me and, if necessary, console me without offering her two cents.

"Well, was it . . ." she trailed off. It was uncharacteristic for Luella to be at a loss for words.

"Was it what?"

"Brief?"

"Oh no, it went on for a while." She considered this.

"Well, then, sounds like a good start, my dear." She reached her hand across the table and patted my arm affectionately. Then she stood up and walked over to the drawer next to the oven. "Now I've got a little something for the birthday girl too. I've been waiting for the right time to give these to you." Luella handed me a jewelry box the same size as the one Grant had given me.

"Thank you so much."

"Don't thank me until you open it." Here eyes twinkled with anticipation.

There was no wrapping paper, so I just lifted the lid to find the most stunning pair of emerald studs I'd ever seen. "Oh, my God, Luella. These are gorgeous. They must have been a fortune."

"Not at all." She smiled.

"What?" I lifted them out of the box carefully.

"Those earrings, which are your birthstone, by the way, were mine. And my mother's before that. I guess you could say they were free."

"Luella." My eyes filled with tears. "I can't take these."

"Nonsense. My mother told me to save them for when I have a daughter one day." Her voice cracked. "And you're the closest thing I have, Kitty."

"I don't know what to say."

"Don't say anything, darling. Just wear them in good health and pass them down to your own daughter one day."

I stood up and walked toward her, catching her off guard with a proper hug, the kind where she couldn't just pat my shoulder and let go. "I love you, Luella."

"I love you too, darling. I'm so very proud of you." She squeezed me back. "And I'm happy to see Grant's finally appreciating what a smart, beautiful woman you've become. You have such a bright future ahead of you, Kitty. Only good things to come."

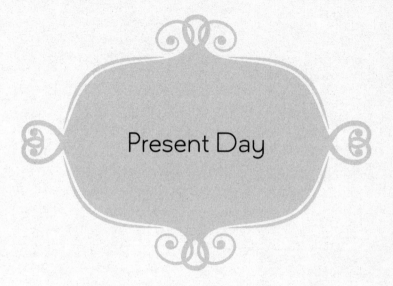

Present Day

Katherine

Day three at Luella's house had been a whirlwind—pandemonium, her father had called it. Katherine and Laney had made a last-minute decision to call in the estate-sale lady early, so she could start assessing the pieces of furniture, china, stemware, table linens, and other trinkets that had been in good enough condition to salvage for a high-end estate sale. They'd also hired a moving company—more like a friend of a friend of Rick's who'd materialized with a pack of burly men and two enormous trucks. When Katherine had asked about a contract, in the event of damages, they'd all had a hearty chuckle at her expense. "We'll get it all there in one piece, sweetheart," the leader of the pack had assured her, and she'd smiled stiffly. The idea, which Katherine had concocted on her way back to the Equinox, was to get as much stuff out of the house and into storage as they could so that the cleaners could come in and start on the first floor while Katherine and Laney proceeded to pack up the rooms upstairs. She'd called Laney and, to Katherine's surprise, Laney had agreed wholeheartedly, without any resistance. She'd even offered to find the movers—thus Rick's friend of a friend.

All day long it had been people running around the house, asking questions, needing answers, wanting to know what went where and who was supposed to do what. Katherine was in her element, at the same time fielding anxious pleas from Brooke back in New York. After all, it was a Monday in the "real world," as Katherine had heard herself repeating over and over every time someone raised an eyebrow at her phone ringing *again. If only they knew this is nothing compared to my usual pace,* she'd thought. Katherine suspected that Jane, her boss, had asked everyone at the office to give her as much space as possible while she was out; the phone wasn't ringing as often as it normally would, despite the fact that all of the other people working around her seemed to be burdened by the frequency. After the sixth consecutive call, one of the movers had said, "Boy, oh, boy, lady. You must be someone important" within earshot of Laney, which had afforded Katherine a jolt of self-satisfaction.

By five p.m. everyone had been exhausted, but the house did look—and smell—drastically better. It had taken seven of them—five big men, Katherine, and Laney—to cover and move the crystal chandelier, which had been the last piece of furniture. Now, arriving on day four, Katherine felt a profound sense of relief and accomplishment in finding a barren first floor, with only dust mites to dance atop the hardwood surface. They still had three guest bedrooms, which they hoped to knock out today, thereby leaving only Luella's den and bedroom, the most arduous, mentally and physically, of all the rooms in the house. Luella's closet alone could take a week. Last night in bed, Katherine's head had been spinning, conjuring every blouse, skirt, dress, scarf, shoe box, and belt they'd have to catalog, not to mention her jewelry. It was daunting, certainly, but it was also the only thing she could focus on if she wanted to avoid thinking about Grant. She'd dreamt about him again, as she had the two nights prior. She'd tried desperately to will herself not to. She'd long been a firm believer that if you told yourself you were going to dream about something, then you wouldn't. In the same way, she told herself that if she thought she was going to fall down a flight of stairs, then she wouldn't. Some strange combination of Murphy's Law and Katherine's own neuroses. Unfortunately, this time it hadn't worked.

All three dreams had been a version of the original, the one she'd had that first night after being abruptly reunited with Grant at Luella's house. She was a teenager living back in her father's house, only her mother was there. She looked just the same, with her bright red lips and bright red nails, except she couldn't find her way around the house. It was as if she'd never died, never been hit by the car on that fateful day, yet this wasn't her house and she knew it. She was frustrated by this, as so often she was by things, and Katherine was showing her where everything was. Then Grant and Laney showed up. Her mother didn't know Laney at all, and Laney couldn't see her mother; only Grant could. In turn, Katherine's mother loved Grant. She was fawning all over him, which annoyed Katherine, and she kept being pulled in two different directions—wanting to help her mom and trying to keep Grant away from her. Then suddenly the dream had switched locations, as dreams tend to do, to Luella's house. Grant and Laney were there too, but Katherine's mom was gone, and when she'd asked Luella about it, everyone in the room had gone silent, like she was going mad. Then she and Laney and Grant had gone out in Luella's backyard like it was any other day. Grant had wrapped his arms around her from the back and started kissing her neck. Right up until the alarm went off.

Katherine figured there was some deep-rooted psychological analysis to explain the overlapping layers of her dream, but she wasn't as much fixated on that as she was on the intense pangs of desire that having Grant's arms around her again had reawakened. Even if they were only his dream arms. It had taken her a few minutes to snap out of the blissful miasma and prepare herself for round four at Luella's house. Due to the frenzied nature of the previous day, Katherine and Laney hadn't been forced to interact for more than a few harried seconds at a time, nor had there been the awkward predicament of it being just the two of them. In light of both of these circumstances, Laney hadn't had the opportunity to snarl at Katherine or give her the cold shoulder, a marked improvement even if it had been conditional.

Laney was already upstairs in the second of Luella's four guest bedrooms when Katherine arrived, so she set her purse by the door and climbed the spiral staircase to join her.

"You're here early." Laney jumped up, startled by the company.

"Yeah, I needed to get out of my house." Laney pointed at overflowing piles of papers, blankets, and ski clothing on the other side of the room. "That's all the stuff from the dresser they took yesterday. You can start going through it."

"Okay." Katherine didn't make any mention of the fact that Laney was allowing her to work in the same vicinity as her. She just did as she was told, smiling inwardly at the irony. When was the last time anyone had told her what to do? "Seeing the first floor cleaned out was a total relief." Katherine sat down on the cushy white carpet and crossed her legs Indian style.

"It does look good." Laney was moody, Katherine noticed, but, for once, it seemed her ire wasn't directed at Katherine.

"Everything okay?" Katherine didn't look directly at her. She kept her head down while folding ski hats into a neat stack.

"It's fine." Laney closed the top of a full box of ski gloves and socks and stretched a piece of packing tape across the top. "I think all this stuff can go to Goodwill."

"Definitely," Katherine agreed.

"I can take it this week." Laney set the box to the side. "Fuck!"

"What?"

"I cut my fucking finger on the tape dispenser." She held up her index finger to reveal a small speck of blood. "This just isn't my fucking day."

"Feel free to vent if you want," Katherine stated plainly. "Don't worry, I won't think it means you actually like me."

"It's not a big deal. It's just Gemma. She's going through a bratty stage."

"How old is she?"

"Twelve."

"Right." Katherine scolded herself silently. Of course she was twelve—the same age as the number of years since Katherine had left Vermont. "So she's basically a teenager. That must be a nightmare."

"She's always been a really good kid, and all the sudden, out of nowhere, I'm like persona non grata. She's completely obsessed with this ridiculous friend of hers, Casey, who's gorgeous and rich beyond belief. If Casey has it, she wants it, and, unfortunately, I'm not in the business of buying my twelve-year-old three-hundred-dollar boots. Of course, she doesn't seem to hate Rick. Oh no. He's still a god to her. It's just me. I'm the bitch. I'm always the bitch."

"I know how you feel." Katherine smirked. "Not about the teenager daughter. Just the bitch part."

"And what's even more annoying is that I can never get a word in edgewise, because she's either on the phone, on Facebook, on Tweeter . . ."

"Twitter."

"Right. Or she's got those stupid headphones on, listening to TMI or TB—whatever that idiot rapper's called. Do you know he went to *prison*?"

"T.I."

"That's the one!" Laney's cell phone rang, intruding on her rant. "Shit. It's Tina." Katherine nodded. She certainly wasn't one to judge an incoming work call. "Hi, Tina. What's up? Right . . . Okay . . . I know. Yes, that's terrible. We'll find someone else . . . Tina, I can't. I really . . . Fine, okay. But just for two hours. Okay, I'll see you soon." Laney ended the call and threw her phone across the room, skimming Katherine's head by a few measly inches.

"Jesus!" Katherine shrieked.

"Sorry. I'm just SO FUCKING FRUSTRATED!"

"What's going on?"

"I need to go in to work for a couple of hours." Laney grabbed her camel-colored Uggs and yanked them onto her feet. "God forbid I should take a few days off during the slowest week of the year."

"Why don't you just tell Tina you're busy and that you can't come in?"

"Ha! You don't know Tina. She doesn't take no for an answer. And even if she did, she'd be calling me every three minutes to ask me something. Shocker of all shockers, another receptionist quit, because Tina verbally abuses them, and now I need to save the day. Yet again." Laney was all worked up, huffing and puffing as she got herself together.

"That's not right." Katherine had met Tina only once, but she knew her type—catty, bossy, and know-it-all, while incompetent and useless at the same time.

"What else is new?"

"Well, it's no big deal for me. I'll be here powering through. Whenever you get back, you get back. Don't worry."

"Thanks." Laney didn't smile, but she did seem genuinely grateful for the easy pass. "I'll be back before noon." She slung her monogrammed Coach purse over her shoulder and rushed out the door.

For the next hour, Katherine packed box after box amid the eerie silence. She thought about calling her dad to come over, but it was easier and more efficient to get things done on her own. Just as she was finishing up, she heard a ringing from nearby. It wasn't her cell, and Luella's lines had long been disconnected. She scanned the room and spotted Laney's phone, which was sticking out from under the curtains, where she had thrown it. Katherine crawled over and picked it up. The screen read: "Manchester MS." Katherine ignored it. Until five minutes later it rang again. And then again two minutes after that. Same caller all three times.

"Hello?"

"Mrs. Marten?" It was strange to hear Laney called that. She would always be Laney Drake to Katherine.

"No, sorry. This is her friend Katherine Hill. Laney had to run in to work and she left her phone behind. Can I help with something?"

"I'm afraid her daughter Gemma needs to be picked up from school *immediately*. We can't reach Mr. Marten either." The woman's voice was firm and schoolmarmlike.

"I guess I can try to reach her at work. Is everything okay?"

"Yes, Gemma is fine. She was caught smoking in the girls' bathroom, and we have a no-tolerance policy."

"Of course." Katherine tried to think quickly. She could definitely track Laney down at Oasis, but that would only make Laney's life more difficult than Tina was already making it. "Would it be okay if I come pick her up?"

There was a brief silence.

"Does Gemma know you well?"

"Yes, yes, of course." Katherine went out on a limb. Surely Laney had told Gemma about her, especially now with Luella's house and all. "I'm an old friend of the family, and I went to Manchester Middle School and the high school. Go, Maple Leafs! I'll be with Gemma's mom in an hour."

The woman thought for a moment, likely contemplating whether Katherine was really a family friend or a serial kidnapper. "I suppose I can make an exception, since I can't reach her parents."

"Excellent. Just tell her that Kitty is on the way."

It took Katherine less than ten minutes to arrive at Manchester Middle School, which was on the same campus as Manchester High School, both of which she, Laney, and Grant had attended. It was a strange blast from the past, driving through the familiar entrance with its green wooden sign etched with the school's name and a big red maple leaf—their mascot, if you could really call it that. The campus looked pretty much the same, save for a few new benches and one extra building called the Bartley Science Center, after Sam Bartley, who'd been killed in a freak skiing accident six years earlier. Katherine's father had sent her the clipping from the local newspaper. Apparently, Sam had been skiing down a blue slope with a few friends, well below his double-black-diamond capabilities, when a skier at the top of the mountain had fallen, thereby launching his ski through the air and into Sam's back, slicing his body like a machete. According to the article, it had been a grisly scene. Shortly thereafter, Sam's family had raised money for the new science center to be dedicated in his name.

Katherine pulled up to the front door of the middle school and waited until she saw Laney walking toward her. Only it wasn't Laney. It was the Laney she remembered. Gemma bounced toward the car with the same hair, practically the same face, and the same lean body as her mother. It was like traveling back in time, so much so that Katherine's immediate instinct was to start gossiping about what had happened in gym class that day.

"Katherine?" Gemma's face lit up—again, in the same exact way Laney's used to—as she opened the passenger's-side door.

"Gemma, hi! It's so nice to finally meet you." Katherine surveyed Gemma's outfit—skinny jeans, black leather jacket, knee-skimming black leather boots. She looked directly off the streets of Greenwich Village, only about five years older than she actually was. "I'm your mom's old friend Kitty." She couldn't remember the last time she'd introduced herself that way—even though Gemma clearly knew her by Katherine.

"I know who you are." She slid into the seat. "You're, like, superfamous!"

"Hardly." Katherine laughed unassumingly. "And I know your mom didn't tell you that."

"No, my mom doesn't talk to me about you at all. Mainly she just complains to my dad." Gemma's blue eyes sparkled at Katherine, who suddenly felt like Cameron Diaz.

"That's nice," Katherine replied sarcastically.

"But I looked you up online. You're, like, the head of

Blend. I love their makeup. And you go to all those fancy parties in New York City with all of the celebs."

"Something like that." *Kids these days and the Internet,* Katherine thought. In her day, unless you were a big movie or TV star, twelve-year-olds definitely did not know who you were or whom you partied with.

"I didn't even know until now that you used to be my mom's best friend. That's so cool."

"I'm glad you think so." Katherine drove down Main Street.

"I know you and my mom are fighting. She can be so unreasonable sometimes."

"I wouldn't say we're fighting," Katherine hedged. "We just have some things to work out."

"She said she hated you."

"Is that so?"

"When you first got here."

"Well, I'll have to work on that."

"I hope you stay. My mom could use a best friend."

"Oh yeah?" Katherine smiled. It was like talking to a pre-teen Laney, except Gemma was much more poised. "I live in New York City, so I can't stay, but I hope I get to spend some time with you and your mom while I'm here."

"Me too. I overheard my mom tell Dad that Uncle Grant used to be your boyfriend. Is that true?"

"It is."

"Why would he give *you* up for Michelle? I mean, she's nice, but . . ."

"That's not exactly how it happened." Katherine turned onto her old street.

"How did it happen?"

"I think it's best we leave that one alone." Katherine stopped in front of Luella's house. "Here we are."

"My mom's here." Gemma motioned to Laney's black Volvo. "She's going to be really pissed."

"I don't blame her. Smoking is a terrible habit, and getting caught is even worse."

"I know."

"Do you? Do you know that smoking ruins your skin and makes you less pretty?"

"Really?"

"Oh yeah. No one in the beauty industry smokes. You get lots of lines on your face and your teeth turn yellow."

"Oh."

"Come on, let's go inside."

"I like your bag." Gemma fixated on Katherine's Louis Vuitton checkered tote.

"Thank you." Katherine stepped out of the car, and Gemma followed her up the path to Luella's. "Have you ever been here?"

"Nope."

"Too bad. It used to be gorgeous." Katherine pushed the door in hard to find Laney standing in the middle of the entranceway floor, with her arms crossed and a scowl on her face.

"What the hell is going on here?"

Gemma cowered behind Katherine.

"You left your cell phone and the school called, so I went to pick Gemma up."

"And you didn't think to call me at work? We both know you know where I work. Right?" Laney glared at Katherine.

"Yes, I do. But I didn't want to bother you. I thought you had enough on your hands, so I did you a favor."

"A favor?" Laney huffed, tapping her boot on the hardwood floor, which was echoing throughout the cavernous space.

"Yes, a favor."

"Okay, well, why don't you let me deal with my own child?" Laney marched toward them. "Gemma, let's go home."

"Can't I stay with you guys?"

"No."

"I can help. Katherine and I were just getting to know each other!"

"Kitty. Her name is Kitty."

"*Please*, Mom."

"I said no, Gemma. Girls who get in trouble for smoking in the bathroom do not get to hang out. Got it?"

Gemma hung her head. "I'm never going to do it again."

"I've heard that before."

"Katherine told me smoking makes you ugly."

"Did she, now? Well, we've had quite enough help from Kitty today, so let's go."

"But . . ."

"No *but*s. Move." Laney pointed toward the door, walking past Katherine but not bothering to make eye contact. "I'll be back in twenty minutes."

Katherine waved her hand in the air. "Looking forward to it."

August 1994

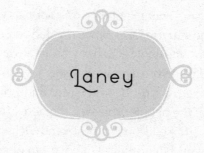

Laney

Every summer for as long as I can remember, my parents have rented a vacation home on Nantucket for the last week of August. They both used to go there with their own families when they were kids—even though they didn't know each other. "Because your father is older than I am," my mom always points out whenever my dad tells the story. Even though he's only three years older. We've been renting the same house for ten years now in Tom Nevers East, right near the beach. My mom always makes sure people know we don't rent *on* the beach, just near it. "We don't want to give the impression we're fancy," she says. Why not? I say. Let people think we're fancy. So, anyway, we're *near* the beach, in your typical gray-and-white-shingle, Nantucket-style cottage with a really cool circular shell driveway and wraparound farmers' porch. My mom calls the décor English country—whatever that means. All I know is there's a lot of chintz and the house is big enough. The kitchen is pretty modern because the owners renovated it last year, and the whole first floor has cathedral ceilings and French doors, which, as my mom brags, gives it that airy feeling.

Usually I can't wait to get there. As soon as we arrive, my parents go the supermarket, since my dad refuses to lug the groceries from Vermont, which my mom always tries to negotiate the day before we leave—she says everything on Nantucket is *such* a rip-off. And Grant and I ride our bikes, or the bikes of the people who own the house, to Something Natural on Cliff Road for *the* best sandwiches in the existence of the world. Normally I'm not a fan of egg salad, but there's something in theirs that makes it simply divine. Also, their herb bread is to die for. We usually pick up as many loaves as we can fit in our bike baskets, because, as my father would say, "That bread vanishes into thin air as soon as it comes in the front door." Of course, when you eat four pieces of it for breakfast like he and Grant often do, that's bound to happen.

This is the first year either Grant or I have been able to bring a friend. In the past, my parents have insisted that it's the one week they get to spend with us without interruption, and despite some pretty extensive groveling on our parts, they've never given in. Obviously, Kitty is way more than a friend. She's more like part of the family, and now that she and Grant have been together for three months, she's even more a part of the family than ever. Don't even get me started on Grant and Kitty. I mean, I'm happy for them, but the whole thing is completely weird. I knew they were friends, and they are freakishly similar in a lot of ways, but it's not really ideal to have your best friend and brother be boyfriend and girlfriend, especially since they're so grossly in-your-face with their PDAs. And Kitty used to be totally anti-PDA. But he's always got his hands all over her, and she's always all googly-eyed over him. Grant can do no wrong in Kitty's eyes, which is completely infuriating, since he does so much wrong.

Oh, and have I mentioned that my parents are completely obsessed with the whole thing? They were shocked at first, as was I. I think they assumed that Grant and Kitty had more of a sister-brother kind of relationship than a romantic one. I kind of thought so too. But apparently not. And now my mom is practically planning their wedding. She even showed Kitty her wedding dress last week. Yes, I've seen it before. And it's hideous. She knows I'd rather get married in a garbage bag, but of course Kitty was all, "Oh, Carol. It's stunning." If she considers an all-lace turtleneck bodice with puffy sleeves and a taffeta skirt stunning, she can have it. When I get married, I want something strapless with beading and crystals. Like a princess.

"You better hang out with me this week." I leaned back on the railing and tilted my face toward the sun. There's no easier way to get a base tan for vacation than soaking in the rays on the one-hour ferry ride from Hyannis to Nantucket.

"For the millionth time, I'm going to hang out with you." Kitty lowered the brim of her wide straw hat. "Unless you die of skin cancer first."

"Kitty!" Sometimes she can be *so* dramatic.

"What?"

"That's a terrible thing to say." As if she hasn't been preaching the same thing for six years. Fortunately, I'm still alive and kicking. And tan. A lovely golden shade, thank you.

"*Well?*"

"*Well*, what?"

"The least you could do is wear sunblock."

"I am." I pulled a tube of Bain de Soleil out of my olive green LeSportsac as evidence.

"SPF four isn't sunblock."

"Then why do they sell it?"

"For idiots like you!" Kitty sat down on the bench in her preppy khaki shorts and red T-shirt. "How long are we on this thing? I'm feeling a little nauseous."

"Only an hour. My mom has ginger pills, if you want."

"I think I should be okay. As long as the boat doesn't bump around too much."

"What do you want to do when we get there?" I know I have at least one whole day of Kitty to myself. A bunch of Grant's friends are leaving for college tomorrow, so he wanted to stay back and say good-bye. He's probably having a party at our house. Fortunately, UVM doesn't start for a couple more weeks; otherwise Grant wouldn't have been able to come at all, which probably would have been more of a bummer for Kitty than for me.

"I don't know. It's up to you." She squinted up at me, looking a little pale.

"I say we bike ride to Something Natural for lunch and then hit the beach."

"You know I can't bike ride."

"Yes, you can. Your dad told me he taught you when you were little."

"He may have, but I forgot."

"You can't forget. There's actually a saying—'It's like riding a bike,' meaning 'Once you know, you know.'"

"I'm familiar with the expression, thanks. Unfortunately, I'm the person who it doesn't apply to."

"We can go out tonight in town if you want to."

"I don't know. We'll see. Maybe we'll wait until Grant gets here for that."

"What? Are you afraid he'll be mad if you talk to another guy?"

"No, I'm not afraid of anything with Grant."

"Spare me."

Forty minutes later—including one puke over the side of
the ferry by Kitty—we arrived on Nantucket, piled into our
rented Jeep, and drove to the house. While my parents un-
loaded the car, I showed Kitty around.

"This place is unbelievable." She finally took off that stupid straw hat and set it down on the yellow-and-white floral
sofa. "It's almost as nice as Luella's house."

"I know. I can't believe you've never been here before. I'm
so excited! We're going to have the most amazing week
ever." She followed me upstairs to where the three guest
bedrooms were. "This is my bedroom."

"Wow."

"This is Grant's, though I'm sure he wouldn't mind if you
take it, since it's next to mine." We walked farther down the
wide hallway, which boasted an array of framed and neatly
displayed black-and-white photos of the owners' extended
family on the periwinkle walls. "And this is your room."

"Wow again. It's perfect." Kitty dropped her pink
suitcase on the queen-sized bed with its nautical-themed
comforter.

"I can't believe you still have that suitcase after all these
years."

"I know. It's really stood the test of time."

"Let's get on our suits and go to the beach."

"Sounds like a plan!" Kitty opened her suitcase, and I
ran down the hall to do the same.

By the time we were changed and downstairs, my mom
and dad were ready to go to the supermarket.

"Anything special you girls would like to eat while we're here?" My mom was in her traditional full-blown, get-the-house-in-order mode. "I'm sure we'll be at the market every day if your brother's stomach has anything to do with it. But for now?"

"No, thank you." Kitty smiled politely. Six years, and she still acts like a first-time guest around my parents.

"Honey Nut Cheerios. Turkey. American cheese. Doritos. And mint chip ice cream."

"Anything else?" My dad laughed. He's grown a little gut recently, and ever since the doctor told him he had to cut back on the junk food, he likes to pick on how much crap Grant and I eat.

"That should do it. We're going to the beach."

"Do you want the chairs? I don't know where they are." My mom scoured the room aimlessly, like they'd be anywhere but in the garage, where they are every year when she asks the same question.

"No, we'll lie on our towels."

"What about the umbrella? The sun is so strong."

"We'll be fine, Mom. We're not ten anymore."

"To me you'll always be ten."

"Okay, we're going. See you later." I grabbed Kitty's hand and led her out the back door toward the beach.

"Thank you!" she called over her shoulder.

"It's just down this path." We hopped from hot stone to hot stone in our bare feet and bikinis. Of course, Kitty had to wear a cover-up, because she's Kitty. Honestly, she's not even chubby anymore, but she insists she is.

"Remind me why we need four towels?"

"One for lying on and the other for drying off. You don't want to get out of the water and wrap yourself in a sandy towel, do you?"

"Good point."

"I brought magazines too, and—wait. What's this?" I re-vealed a small bottle of vodka I'd lifted from the liquor cabinet.

"Laney!"

"What?"

"Where'd you get that?"

"From the house. No one will miss it, trust me."

"You're going to drink it straight?"

"No, silly. I'm going to mix it with this." I pulled another small bottle out of my bag. "Orange juice. That's why I got an extra at the gas station."

"Nice foresight."

"Why, thank you. I even brought an empty thermos in case my parents come down." I poured the vodka and juice into the thermos and shook it vigorously. "Swig?" I held my arm out toward Kitty and arched an eyebrow. Surprisingly, she swiped it and took a big gulp.

"Bleh! That tastes like shit."

"I know, but it does the trick." We laid out our towels and sat down with the thermos between us. "Magazine?" I fanned copies of *Glamour*, *Cosmopolitan*, and *YM* in front of her.

"*Glamour*." Kitty grabbed it, and I took a sip of orange-juice vodka.

"This does taste like shit. Needs more juice."

"Give me that." Kitty took another healthy mouthful.

"Living on the wild side, huh?" She rolled her eyes at me. "'How to Improve Your Sex Life in Eight Easy Steps.'" I read the headline off the cover of *Cosmo*. "I'll leave this for you, since I'm not having sex right now." I finally broke it off with Roger. Turns out he was a bit of a meathead.

"I'm sure it'll only be a matter of time." She smiled smugly.

"Shut up!" I swatted at her with my magazine.

"Well?"

"Fine. I might be in the market for a hard-bodied Nantucket gentleman."

"Of course." We both laughed.

"This is nice."

"I know. The beach is so gorgeous."

"No, I mean this. *Us.*"

"Are you going to kiss me?"

"F you. I meant we haven't done a lot of this lately. Just sit around and talk. You're always . . ."

"With Grant. I know."

"You said it, I didn't."

"Actually, you've said it a billion times."

"Right. I just miss my best friend sometimes."

"You see me every day!"

"I know, but it's not the same." I protruded my lower lip.

"Well, you'll have me all to yourself next year."

"True. But then I'll have to share you again when we get to UVM."

"You should probably be really nice to me, then."

"Can I give you pedicure when we get back?"

"Sounds like a good start."

After a few hours at the beach, Kitty and I spent the rest of the day eating and watching TV, until dinnertime. My parents had picked up four huge lobsters in town, and Kitty totally freaked when they killed them in the pot. She didn't know you could hear them screaming for their lives. My mom also made baked potatoes, salad, and cherry pie—it was enough for about ten people. "I'm not worried. Grant will eat the leftovers," she insisted. Apparently, Grant had called earlier and decided he couldn't live without Kitty for another second, so he's getting here tonight instead of tomorrow. Actually, he didn't say that, but I couldn't help but torment Kitty a little. She's so sensitive, especially when it comes to Grant.

By ten o'clock we were all exhausted—the Nantucket sun, ocean, and air will do that to you. My mom was trying to stay awake to make sure Grant arrived safely, but she could barely keep her eyes open. So Kitty and I told her we'd wait up in Kitty's room, as if she would possibly go to sleep without seeing Grant, who finally arrived just before midnight. As expected, they practically had sex in front of me the minute they saw each other. I mean, seriously? It hadn't even been a full twenty-four hours.

"That'll be my cue. Night, lovebirds." They barely detached their faces long enough to say good night in return. "Don't do anything I wouldn't do."

"That shouldn't be a challenge," Grant retorted as I was leaving.

I'm not sure why, but I stood outside the door, listening for a moment. Not something I've ever done before because, honestly, the thought of hearing Kitty and Grant go at it is so repulsive I'd rather eat worms. Anyway, I overheard him say he'd missed her, and she said the same in return. Barf. Then there was a short silence. Probably kissing. Double barf. And then it happened. He said, "Kitty, there's something I want to tell you." Another short silence. "I love you."

I didn't stick around to hear Kitty's reply, not that there was any question what it would be. I know I should have been happy for her. For them. Isn't that the way best friends and sisters are supposed to feel? But for some reason I wasn't. My heart hurt, and all I wanted to do, all I could do, was go to my room and cry.

Present Day

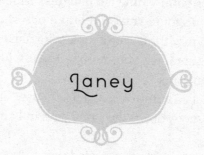

Laney

"I can't believe you made me get up this early on a vacation day," Gemma whined, rubbing her bloodshot eyes and slogging across the kitchen floor in her chocolate knee-high Uggs.

"Sorry, but girls who get caught smoking at school do not get the luxury of sleeping in." Laney spoke in a clipped tone while gathering her purse, car keys, and hulking winter jacket. "Maybe you shouldn't have stayed up talking to Casey until three in the morning."

"It's so unfair." Gemma slumped into a chair, crossed her arms on the kitchen table, and rested her head. "I'm exhausted."

"Come on. I don't want to be late." Laney tossed Gemma's coat in her direction. It fell at her feet. "I'm serious. Let's move."

"What am I doing again?" Gemma stood up reluctantly, taming her corkscrew curls with a gray wool hat.

"You're serving Thanksgiving meals to less-fortunate people at the Manchester Soup Kitchen."

"That sucks."

"I told you I don't like that word." Laney walked toward the front door, summoning her daughter with a wave of her free arm. "You shouldn't view this as a punishment. It's important to do nice things for people who don't have all that you have. I guarantee you, no one there will be wearing Uggs or Seven jeans."

"Can't I just go with you to Luella's house?" They trekked through the snow, down the stone path to Laney's car, and got in.

"No, you cannot." Laney started the ignition and "Eye of the Tiger" blared through the speakers.

"Can we *please* listen to something other than the eighties station?" Gemma reached for the satellite radio button. "I can help you and Katherine."

"Gemma, I said no. Dad will pick you up and drop you off at Luella's when you're done, but that's the extent of it. Got it?"

"Fine." She sighed, and they rode in silence for a few minutes. "Don't you want to be friends with Katherine?"

"We were friends at one time." Laney stopped at a red light.

"I know, but don't you want to be friends with her again?"

"It's not that simple, Gem."

"It seems like it is. I think she wants to be friends with you again."

"Did she say that?"

"Not exactly."

"Well, then."

"I don't know. You don't really have any friends, so I just wondered why you don't want to be friends with her. She seems really cool."

"Whether or not she's cool has nothing to do with it."

"Remember when I got in that huge fight with Ella?"

"Yes, your weeklong hibernation rings a bell." Gemma may have inherited her flair for the dramatic. "And I recall a few doors slamming as well."

"You told me I had to forgive and forget." Gemma smiled complacently.

"I think that was your father." It sounded way more like something Rick would say. Laney wasn't really one for forgiving or forgetting. She was more like the queen of holding a big, fat grudge.

"Nope, you said it, Mom."

"Well, this is different from you and Ella."

"How?"

"It just is. Trust me. Older, deeper wounds." Laney stopped in front of the Manchester Soup Kitchen. "Here we are. You go in that green door and ask for Martha. I'll wait here. Give me a sign when things are good, okay?"

"Okay."

"And remember to be waiting by the door for Dad at four. He'll call your phone when he's on the way, but he'll be in a rush. Give me a kiss." Laney cupped her hands on Gemma's flushed cheeks and pecked her on the nose. "I love you. Be good."

"I will." Gemma rolled her soft blue eyes. "Do me one favor, Mom?"

"What's that?"

"Give Katherine a little break. I think it'll make you relax. You're driving Dad and me crazy."

"Thanks!" Laney laughed. "Go. I'll see you later."

It was impossible to stay mad at Gemma, even though she could be completely infuriating at times. The bottom line was that compared to the Caseys of the world, Gemma was a good kid. If smoking in the girls' bathroom was her most serious offense, Laney could live with it. Sometimes, she just wanted to say, *Gemma, smoking in the bathroom* [or whatever it was she'd done] *is not a big deal in the grand scheme of life; I know this. However, since I'm your mom, I have no choice but to be upset and punish you.* But Laney knew that wasn't the best tactic with an almost teenager. You had to be firm and consistent, with no acknowledgment of the fact that you were once their age and had done far worse things.

Laney waited and watched until Gemma peeked her head out the green door and gave a thumbs-up. Then she turned her car around in the driveway and headed toward Luella's, replaying her conversation with Gemma in her head. No friends? Gemma thought she had no friends. What about Maxine and Joni, the hair colorists at Oasis? She'd gone out with them a few times for girls' night. Not for a while, but still, she'd call them friends. Kind of. And there was that mother at school she'd talked to on occasion, Allison. They'd even had coffee once. Honestly, who had time for friends? Between work, errands, and motherhood, there was little opportunity to gab on the telephone or meet up for a leisurely lunch. Forget dinner altogether. By the time she got home from work, it was all she could do to devour a bowl of pasta and help Gemma with her homework before collapsing from fatigue at ten o'clock. She couldn't imagine having more than one kid. How did those women do it and keep themselves so well groomed at the same time? It was no wonder Kitty looked like a model. She had no children to wear her down!

Laney pulled into Luella's driveway. Katherine's rental car was already parked in front. Maybe Gemma was right. Maybe she should give her a little break, if only to relieve some of her own stress. She got out of the car and hurried into the house. It was freezing outside. "It's gonna be a chilly T-Day!" the weatherman had announced on the morning's forecast, appearing a little too giddy about the single-digit temps, especially when he'd flapped his arms to mimic a turkey.

"Hello?" Laney called out once inside, peeling off her puffy black down coat. *Katherine would never be caught dead in this,* she thought, ascending the stairs toward Luella's bedroom. "Kitty?"

"In here." Laney heard Katherine's muffled voice and followed it to Luella's closet—one of four. She opened the sliding door and jumped back. "Holy fuck!"

"What?"

"You scared the shit out of me."

"Sorry, I called out. I thought you heard me."

"I did." Laney stood, immobilized, staring at Katherine wearing one of Luella's gowns. "It's just, I mean, I can't believe . . ."

"I know everything is fair game. I couldn't resist."

"It's not that. It's totally uncanny."

"What?"

"You look exactly like her. I literally thought I'd seen a ghost for a second there." Laney shook her head. "You have no idea how fast my heart is beating right now."

"Thanks, I think." Katherine started undressing. "Can you get this zipper for me?"

"Wow, I mean, seriously. With your hair pulled back like that." Laney unzipped the dress. "You should definitely take this. It looks amazing on you."

"It does fit well. With a few minor alterations . . ." Katherine regarded herself in the mirror. "Clearly, there's plenty to go around, but it's up to you."

"It's yours. It's not like I have any use for a gown like that, so you might as well." Laney peered over Katherine's shoulder in the mirror. "Listen. I owe you an apology."

"For what?" Katherine slithered out of the dress and back into her blue jeans and sweater.

"Yesterday. I know you were trying to help with Gemma. I was just in a really bad mood from dealing with Tina, and I'm also a little sensitive about things with Gemma at the moment. Playing bad cop all the time isn't fun."

"Apology accepted." Katherine smiled. "I think it's pretty natural for teenage girls to clash with their mothers. Or so I've heard. I guess that's one of the perks of not having a mom and not being one."

"I guess." Laney sifted through a rack of Luella's dresses. "Speaking of Gem, Rick's dropping her off here after her community service; she can help us out."

"Oh, great! I was hoping to spend some more time with her. And, actually, I wanted to ask your permission on something."

"Okay."

"So I know Gemma is really into makeup, specifically Blend. I got a big box of our new products sent to the hotel last night and I brought it with me. I thought maybe—only if it's okay with you—I could give some to Gemma. I was planning to send the stuff home with you today, but since she's coming here, any chance I can show her how to apply a less-is-more look that you'll both be happy with?"

"Um, sure. Yeah, that sounds fine." Laney certainly approved of the idea of Gemma looking age appropriate, but she wasn't entirely sure that rewarding her directly on the heels of getting caught smoking was the right thing to do. Though the soup kitchen really was her punishment, not that serving less-fortunate people a Thanksgiving meal should be viewed that way. Sometimes navigating the potholes of parenting could be so confusing. "On one condition."

"What's that?"

"You hook me up with some freebies too!"

"Deal."

"Oh, my God!" Laney pulled a floor-length white chiffon gown with intricate gold beading at the neckline and waist from Luella's closet. "Do you remember this?"

"How could I forget?"

"This gown is epic." Luella had worn it to the biggest and most glamorous gala she'd hosted at her home. Laney and Katherine had all but begged for invitations, but Luella had said it was strictly for grown-ups and that they'd be bored out of their minds. At the time, they'd been devastated and desperate for a piece of the action. So in lieu of attending, they'd borrowed a crappy pair of binoculars from Laney's father and watched—trading the binoculars back and forth for four hours—from Laney's bedroom window while they sipped sparkling apple cider. They were positive Luella had spotted them, but if she had, she'd never said a word about it.

"She was breathtaking."

"She literally glided across that dance floor. I can still picture it so vividly. And do you remember the shoes? Those gold shoes. They must have had ten-inch heels."

"Lest we forget the diamond necklace."

"It's probably all here somewhere. The lawyer said Luella didn't have a safety-deposit box."

"So strange." Katherine grabbed a shoe box from the top of the closet. "You'd think she'd want to protect all this stuff."

"I never told you, but I asked my mom about the house. You know, if she knew why it was in such disarray." Laney twirled around in front of the mirror, holding the dress up to herself. "She said Luella didn't let anyone come visit her for two years before she died, except one neighbor who checked in sporadically."

"That explains the uncleanliness, but what about all the papers and junk everywhere?"

"I don't know. Maybe she was going through things. Or bored being cooped up."

"It doesn't surprise me that she didn't want to see people. Or, more likely, that she didn't want people to see her. Luella was pretty vain."

"*Pretty* vain? She was completely vain. But can you blame her?"

"Definitely not." Katherine reached for another shoe box. "I'm dying to find the gold heels."

"I'm sure they're here somewhere. It doesn't look like she threw anything out." Laney stopped for a second. "You know, I always wanted to be her."

"And I always thought you would be."

"Ironically, you're the glamorous one now. Huh?" Laney tried not to sound bitter. She was channeling Gemma's advice and doing her best to give both Katherine and herself a break.

"I don't know about that."

"Yeah, you do. Luella would have been proud. She loved you more than anyone."

"She loved you too."

"It wasn't the same, Kitty, and you know it. She loved me, but just as the crazy little girl next door. You were like her daughter. You remind me so much of her now."

"Really?"

"Oh, absolutely."

"I'll take that as a compliment, especially coming from you. But I'm nothing like Luella." Katherine sat down on the floor of the closet with a pile of sweaters, separating them into neat, color-coordinated stacks. "Luella was wise and kindhearted. She was fair and philanthropic. She loved her community. And she loved this awkward girl from next door with no mother." Her eyes began to mist. "I am definitely nothing like Luella. She was one of a kind."

Laney watched Katherine folding sweaters fastidiously, her head bowed. For the first time, she saw Kitty. Just barely, but she was in there somewhere. Beneath the flawless makeup. Beneath the designer clothing. Beneath the cool demeanor. "Yes, she was."

There wasn't much else to say. Luella had been one of a kind, no doubt about it. She was the sort of person you could never truly appreciate in the moment, but years later, once she was gone, you wished you'd paid better attention, soaked in a little more of her . . . je ne sais quoi.

Katherine and Laney worked quietly and efficiently after that for the next few hours, stopping only for bathroom breaks and a quick bite to eat, courtesy of Hazel. They didn't converse about anything other than the items they were cataloging, save for an occasional and transitory reminiscence. Still, the mood was lighter, easier. Laney was hardly ready to forgive and she could never forget, no matter how hard she tried, but she had to admit it was a relief to let go, even if just a little.

"Mom!" Both Gemma's voice and the slam of the front door echoed throughout the house. "I'm here!"

"We're upstairs. Third door on the right when you get to the top." A series of thumps later, Gemma tumbled into the room, breathless and red-faced from the cold weather, and shucked off her coat and boots. "So, how was it?"

"It was good, actually. You wouldn't believe how nice the people were, and some of them don't have any place to live at all."

"I know, sweetheart. It's terrible." Laney beamed with

pride inside and out. Nothing was more gratifying than watching your child learn a lesson, especially one you'd orchestrated.

"Hi, Katherine." Gemma's face lit up.

"Hi, Gemma. I'm so happy to see you again." She looked to Laney for approval, and Laney nodded. "I know you and your mom have to get going pretty soon, but I have a little treat, if you're up for it."

"Sure!" Gemma's eyes brightened at the prospect of any treat Katherine could possibly offer.

"Excellent! Let's get started, then." Katherine had retrieved the box of makeup from her car in advance of Gemma's arrival, and she'd even set up a stool from Luella's bar by her bedroom window to achieve the best lighting. "First, you should open this." She patted the seat of the stool, where Gemma sat obediently, and handed her a nondescript big brown box.

Without missing a beat, she lifted the flaps to reveal what appeared to be a lifetime supply of Blend cosmetics. "Oh, my God! This is all for me?!"

"You got it!" Katherine grinned.

"Eh-hem."

"Oh, sorry. You have to share with your mom."

"No problem!" Gemma appraised every bottle, every brush, every compact, and every lip gloss like it was an Academy Award. "Thank you, Katherine!"

"That's not all." She checked back in with Laney, who gestured her approval again. "What say I give you a little lesson on how to apply some of this stuff? Like a mini makeover."

"Right here, right now?"

"Yup."

"That would be *amazing*." Gemma nodded eagerly. "Casey is going to be so jealous!"

"Well, that's the whole point. Isn't it?" Laney winked at Katherine, as she set about arranging the products she was going to use on Gemma's perfectly unmade-up face. If only she recognized how beautiful she was without any of it.

"Now let's start with a tinted foundation."

"What's that?"

"It's foundation that has a hint of bronzer in it. Evens out the skin tone while giving you a sun-kissed glow."

"Ooh."

"Exactly."

"Then we'll dab on some cheek stain, otherwise known as the modern-day girl's blush, a little brown eyeliner, and some clear mascara, and you should be good to go. It's all in the application—trust me. Less is always more."

"I like a smoky eye."

"Do you?"

"Uh-huh. And red lips."

"Well, that, my friend, goes against the first rule of makeup."

"It does?"

"Absolutely. You never want a dark eye and a dark lip."

"Oh, okay. How come?"

"It's too much. If you wear a dark eye, you want a nude gloss on your lips. If you want red lips, we go light on the eyes."

"Really?"

"Yup. Do you think I look okay?"

"Yeah, but you're gorgeous."

"That's what you think. Or perhaps I just know how to apply my makeup the right way."

"Thanks for the tip!"

"Anytime."

Laney sat quietly while Katherine did her handiwork,

sketching and coloring to highlight Gemma's finest features, which were all of them. She had to admit, Katherine was talented.

Twenty minutes later, Katherine stepped back to evaluate her progress. "Almost there." She moved close to Gemma's face again and then away, over and over, intermittently smudging and dabbing this spot or that. "Voilà! You, my dear, look like a supermodel. Go see for yourself."

Gemma hopped off the stool and ran into Luella's massive bathroom.

"You're good with her." Laney smiled.

"Believe it or not, it comes easily." Katherine started packing the makeup back into the box. "She reminds me so much of you at that age and the instant rapport we once had."

"Well, I applaud anyone who can have a civil conversation with a teenager, namely my teenager."

"Thanks."

"I love it!" Gemma shrieked from the bathroom, practically signaling Katherine's cell to ring.

"Hi, Brooke." Katherine sighed, lifting the phone to her ear while sealing the makeup box with duct tape. "I know. I'm sorry, but I have things to take care of here. Well, John will have to wait . . . oh, Christ, fine." She covered the mouthpiece with her hand and whispered to Laney. "I have to take this."

"Go ahead. I have to get my delightful daughter home anyway."

"So, I guess we're skipping tomorrow for Thanksgiving?"

"Yeah, I'm at my mom's all day. What about you?"

"My dad's. Hazel is doing her thing." Katherine put the phone back to her ear. "Brooke, I'll be a few more seconds and then I'm all yours."

"Listen, I know it's last-minute." Laney was whispering

too, though she wasn't sure why. "My mom made me swear to invite you for dessert or coffee—whatever—if you can make it. Obviously, you shouldn't feel obliged. I can see where it could be awkward, and you have your own plans . . ."

"I'd love to."

"Really?" Laney hadn't expected Katherine to say yes, certainly not so immediately. If she were being honest, she didn't really think it was the best idea, but her mom had been unrelenting. She'd yet to see Katherine and, despite her litany of questions, Laney hadn't been willing to talk about her at all. "You do know Grant and Michelle will be there."

"Sounds good." Katherine nodded decisively, smoothing her glossy black hair and slipping into an expensive-looking shearling coat. "I'll look forward to seeing the entire Drake clan."

"Great." Laney smiled stiffly. Whatever faint trace of Kitty had resurfaced, it was no longer discernable. Katherine had regained control.

The question was, Which one would show up to Thanksgiving dinner?

December 1994

Kitty

For about four and a half years after my mom died, I had this recurring dream. I never mentioned it to anyone, but it was always exactly the same. My mom would be sitting on the rocking chair in my bedroom in our old Bennington house, talking to me about life. She'd be racing through all the really important milestones at warp speed, like time was running out and she had to transfer all of her knowledge to me in a hurry.

I have the feeling my mom would have liked the opportunity to write a note. You know, to express her opinion one last time, have one final say, and possibly offer me some self-improvement advice before she died so suddenly. I don't know—maybe it's me who would have liked some motherly guidance in advance of losing her forever.

Anyway, I can't remember the specifics of the dream anymore, but lately I've been having it again, which I believe has been updated since I was eleven. I doubt I had sex on my mind back then. Now it's on my mind all the time because of Grant, so in the new version of my dream, my mom is explaining the birds and the bees and urging me to "be safe." I guess even my dream self didn't want to hear my mom use the word *condom*. Unfortunately, the whole thing is kind of past the point. I figured out the birds and the bees on my own. And how to be safe. Well, actually, Grant takes care of that part.

I will say that I definitely do not recommend commencing a relationship with someone less than four months before they leave for college. Obviously, I didn't give it much thought back then. That's what happens when you're in love. Yes, I am in love. There, I said it. At first I was completely against it. Saying it, that is. Which really annoyed Grant. I'm sorry; it's just that it's so . . . what's the word? *Syrupy. I'm in love with you* is tantamount to *I want to make love to you*. Sweet, sticky, and gooey. I might as well be on *General Hospital*.

Grant used the "L" word before I did, this past August when I was with the Drakes on Nantucket. I was kind of caught off guard, so I didn't say it back initially. This probably won't come as a surprise, but it was a first for me. That's right. Never been in that situation before. Apparently, prior to Grant, I was unlovable to the male sex, except for my dad, who doesn't count. I'm only seventeen, so it's not a big deal or anything. In fact, I'd venture a guess that this is the one social milestone I'm not behind on. I mean, really, how many girls lose their virginity to the second guy they've ever kissed? And how often is the second guy you've ever kissed the one to tell you he loves you? I'm not sure, but I don't think it's a high number. Leave it to me to make the one and only normal teenage experience I've had completely abnormal.

At any rate, now that Grant and I are *in love*, he's gone. It wasn't easy saying good-bye either. I cried for nine days. Not in front of Laney, because I think she's already a little thrown off by the whole thing, even though it's been seven months now. After Grant told me he loved me, I told her, and she acted really strange for the rest of the vacation and for a few weeks after that. No guy has ever told Laney he loves her. Well, at least not in a serious way. I'm pretty sure it bugs her that I did this one thing before she did. And the fact that it's with her brother just makes it that much more complicated. Once Grant left for school, things with Laney and me went back to normal. She still reverts to her weird behavior when he comes home on the weekends, but I can deal with that.

I suppose I'm lucky he didn't go far. University of Vermont is only a two-and-a-half-hour drive from Manchester— it's in Burlington, which is a very cool town. Grant's come home all but three weekends, which I survived by counting down the days on the UVM wall calendar he bought me, along with a sweatshirt, socks, and a mug. My dad really appreciated the mug.

It's going to be great when we're all at UVM together next year. Laney and I have both been accepted already. We applied early action, which means you find out if you got in before all of the regular applicants send their stuff in this coming January. I wasn't too worried about it. I've been getting pretty much straight A's since we moved to Manchester, and I scored a 1420 on my SATs, which was the second best in my whole class, next to Mark Chin, who got a 1590. Seriously, Mark? We were slightly more concerned for Laney, who doesn't pay any attention to homework and tests, though still manages to get mostly B's and a few C's. She did have the whole legacy thing going for her, since Grant is there and Mr. Drake and his brother went to UVM too. Laney only got 1100 on her SATs, which really isn't bad. She's not good with standardized tests and she even got to take it untimed, because she was diagnosed with a mild form of ADD. I could have told the doctor that.

I got my letter two days before Laney, so she was convinced the writing was on the wall and that she was destined to disgrace the Drake name by being rejected from her father's, uncle's, and soon-to-be her brother's beloved alma mater. She tried to convince me to wait to open my letter, but both my dad and Grant said that was absolutely ridiculous. I thought it would be a nice display of solidarity, since we are best friends and all, but—as my dad pointed out— since Laney is my best friend, she can't be upset with me for wanting to know. Turns out he was right. She was superexcited for me, if not biting her nails in anticipation of her own fate.

I'm kind of jealous because Laney went up to visit Grant this weekend. Her dad had some alumni reunion, so she joined him. I didn't say as much, but I would have liked to go with them. Unfortunately, Laney didn't extend an invitation, and Grant didn't mention it either. He did say he can't wait to see me when he comes home next weekend, though. So, back to the calendar.

Today I'm going over to Luella's. She called the house last night to ask if I'd like to come for lunch. *I want to talk* were her exact words, which was somewhat unnerving. I feel like whenever anyone says anything along those lines, it's never a good sign. Not in real life and definitely not on *General Hospital.* So here I am, standing at Luella's door, waiting for her to answer, so I can find out what it is she wants to talk about. Maybe she wants her emerald earrings back.

"Hello, darling. Come on in." Luella glided through her expansive foyer and into the kitchen, where she'd laid out a beautiful lunch of poached salmon with dill cream, her famous warm saffron potato salad, and hot mulled apple cider with cinnamon sticks. I wish I had her gift for making a meal look like a magazine spread lifted from the pages of *Elle Décor.*

"This looks delicious, Luella. You've outdone yourself, as always." I sat down at the kitchen table and spread a powder blue cloth napkin over my lap. I'd dressed up a little for the occasion in my mother's black crepe slacks and one of the few of her sweaters that fit me on top—a pale green cashmere shell with a matching cardigan that's snug across my chest. For whatever reason, going to Luella's house for lunch, if it isn't a pool day, feels much more formal than dining at anyone else's house. She'd probably drop dead on the spot if she knew that my dad and I put plastic containers directly on the dinner table. Like, if we buy coleslaw from the deli counter at Manchester Market to eat with our hamburgers, we don't bother transferring it to a serving bowl. Gauche, I know.

"Nonsense. Salmon is brain food. Keeps the mind sharp. And with all that college preparation, it can't hurt." She placed a small piece of fish on my plate, dolloped the dill cream on top, and spooned a conservative portion of potatoes next to it. Luella believes that moderation is the answer to most things. She claims she's never dieted a day in her life but has also never deprived herself of anything she's craved. She always says, *A piece of chocolate does not wide hips make. The whole bar, well, that's a different story.*

"Sounds good to me." I waited until her own plate was full and she'd sat down opposite me. One of the many things Luella has taught me is to mind my dining etiquette. Thank God, because my dad is relatively hopeless in that area. *Never begin eating until everyone at the table has been served.*

Always chew with your mouth completely closed. Smaller, outside fork for salad. Larger, inside fork for main course. Utensils rest on the plate together in between bites, not on the table. Soup bowl tilted away from you to scoop up that last drop. And so on. And so on. "You know I got into college already, though. So that kind of takes the pressure off."

"I did, yes." Luella furrowed her brow. "That's what I wanted to talk to you about." She lined her fork and knife up neatly on her plate, took a deep breath, and folded her creased hands on the table in front of her. "What would you think about going to New York City for school?"

"You mean instead of UVM?" Didn't she understand what already being accepted to college meant?

"Yes." She cleared her throat. "I'm sure you've heard of New York University—NYU the kids call it."

"Of course." Although I think everyone calls it NYU, not just the kids. Luella can be so old-fashioned sometimes.

"It's a highly esteemed university." She nodded meaningfully. "The kind of place that launches careers."

"Sure." I nodded back. I don't know much about NYU, but it seems like Luella does. And who am I to argue?

"A unique opportunity has presented itself, Kitty." She looked me directly in the eyes. "One of the board members at NYU is a dear friend. We spoke at great length about you yesterday, and she'd like to set up an interview."

"Oh, wow." I wasn't sure what to say. Did I mention I got into UVM already? I mean, I know early action isn't binding, but why would I bother applying elsewhere, especially someplace so far from home and from Grant?

"Do you understand what this could mean for you?"

"I think so."

"It could change your life, Kitty. New York City is a mecca for bright minds like yours. There are so many opportunities UVM won't afford you."

"Isn't it really expensive? You know, what with it being out of state and all?" I knew my dad was already working overtime to be able to pay for college. I'd offered to apply for financial aid, but he'd said he was going to try to get by without it. He too can be so old-fashioned.

"I took the liberty of speaking with your father before I approached you. He feels very buoyant about the prospect, Kitty."

"Okay." So she was really serious about this. It's no wonder my dad was eager to get me over here today. He kept asking what time lunch with Luella was, which is pretty uncharacteristic for him. "I don't know what to say."

"Say you'll at least think about it."

"I guess." Laney and Grant would kill me if they even knew I was considering Luella's offer, not that an interview meant I would get in.

"I know there's the issue of Grant."

"And Laney."

"Yes, of course." Luella thought for a moment. "Kitty, sometimes the best decisions we make are the most selfish."

"Okay." It seemed ironic coming from Luella, who, by all accounts, hadn't made a selfish decision in her entire life.

"Do you understand what I mean?"

"I think so."

"What I'm saying is that, while UVM might be the best school for Grant and Laney, it might not be the best school for you. And just because they want you to go there too doesn't mean you have to. If they love you like I know they do, they'll want what's best for you. Often, absence makes the heart grow fonder."

"That's true." Though absence from Grant hadn't made my heart grow any fonder yet. My heart was just about as fond as it could get, and what it most wanted was to be *with* Grant. All the time. Still, what if Luella was right? What if I could go to a school like NYU? I hadn't even considered applying anywhere but UVM, even though my guidance counselor had told me I had options. Now I was beginning to wonder why. Why had I not looked into NYU or even Harvard or Yale? Mark Chin was probably applying to all the Ivies. What if I passed up Luella's offer and regretted it forever? Or what if—like my mom—I couldn't make it in New York?

"You know I want what's best for you, Kitty. I love you very much, and while I know it's not my responsibility to guide you through life, I'd like to think my opinion carries at least a little weight."

"Of course it does." Luella had never led me astray; quite the opposite, in fact. "I'll give it some serious thought. I promise."

"That's all I can ask. Naturally, it would be my pleasure to help you." She commenced picking at her salmon. "Now, enough academic chitchat."

"Thank you. I really appreciate it, Luella." I closed my eyes for a quick second, visions of the Empire State Building, the Twin Towers, Times Square, and the Statue of Liberty cavorting in the darkness. "Can I ask one favor?"

"Anything for you, darling. Anything at all."

"Can we keep this between us for now?" Looking down, I pushed the potato salad around my plate. "You know, not say anything to Laney and Grant. At least not yet."

"That's sounds very wise, darling." She smiled. "Very wise indeed."

"I still can't believe it." I sat in our kitchen, poring over the glossy NYU admissions booklet spread open in my hands. Four students walking shoulder to shoulder—all different nationalities and all alarmingly academic looking—beamed up at me. Their smiles spelling it out one pearly white at a time: *If you enroll at NYU, you'll be as happy and smart and successful as we are.*

"I'm just so darn proud of you, Kitty Kat. Have I told you that?" My father looked like he might cry, for about the tenth time since my acceptance package arrived this morning. Apparently, the admissions office was so impressed by me and had one student suddenly back out, so a slot opened up practically by magic. I asked Luella if they have a waiting list for when this kind of thing happens, but she just waved her hand and said, "What's the difference? You're in."

"Only about a million times, Dad. Thank you."

"Well, I second that!" Luella walked into the room by way of the front door with a freshly baked cinnamon apple pie—my absolute favorite. "For you, my dear." She handed it to me, kissed my forehead, and sat down in the chair next to me, letting my father take her coat like the gentleman he is. "As I've always said, big things are going to happen for you. Oh, to be young again."

"Thank you. I'm actually really excited, if not a little nervous. I wouldn't be the first Hill woman to leave New York disappointed."

"Hey now, Kitty. Your mother would be very proud of you."

"Whatever you say, Dad."

"I want you to know how much she loved you. And she would have been *extremely* proud that you were accepted to one of the top schools in the country. She had high hopes for you."

"Now I just need to figure out how I'm going to tell Grant and Laney." The thorn in the side of my complete and utter enthusiasm, which I sensed that my dad and Luella were picking up on. Obviously, I'm not in love with the idea of being apart from Grant for pretty much five years, or being away from Laney, but I've come to realize it's a small piece of my life to compromise in pursuit of the bigger picture— at least that's what Luella told me.

"They will understand, darling." Luella nodded. I could tell she wasn't entirely convinced. "If they don't, then they're not real friends. But they will. I know they will."

"I agree with Luella on this one, Kitty Kat." As if there's anything he doesn't agree with her on.

"They might be upset at first. But they'll get over it. You kids have your whole lives ahead of you. And there will be holidays and summers. For God's sake, you get more time off from college than you're actually there." Luella's face was flushed. She was personally invested.

"You're right. I'm not looking forward to it is all I'm saying."

"You're an NYU girl now. You'll figure out the best way to tell them. I have all the confidence in the world in you." Luella put her hand on mine and smiled. And I watched the smallest but most meaningful tear trickle down her cheek.

Present Day

Katherine

Katherine opened her eyes slowly. The room was still menacingly dark, just the way she liked it. If there was so much as a hint of light insinuating its way through a fracture in the curtains, she couldn't sleep. Light and silence—they were her Kryptonite—coercing her to toss and turn restlessly, held hostage by her own anxieties. She stretched her arms above her head, yawning, and then rubbed her eyes until they adjusted to the obscurity. Sitting up, she wedged two fluffy white pillows behind her back, switched on the porcelain lamp beside her bed, and allowed her eyes to adjust again, only this time to the faint glow illuminating her spotless hotel room.

Katherine wasn't one of those people who could live any less tidily when displaced from her habitual surroundings. She required order wherever she was, and could often be found cleaning her hotel room, even if housekeeping was right down the hall. In fact, her very first order of business when arriving at a hotel or resort was to reorganize the room to best suit her needs, both aesthetic and practical. She'd move a garbage can from here to there, since hotel rooms never had enough garbage cans. Or she'd gather all of the property's promotional materials—local magazines, guidebooks, information on area activities and dining options—which they'd strategically positioned around the room in the hopes that guests would be enticed into an afternoon of, say, fly fishing or horseback riding, and she'd stick them in drawers or cabinets. Clutter was not an option.

A journalist from *Allure* magazine who'd once interviewed Katherine for a beauty feature had asked her, *Why is it that you're such a neat freak?* She'd been slightly taken aback by the off-topic inquiry, but—as per usual—had not let it unsettle her. Instead, she'd replied coolly, *When everything is in its place, my mind is free to think about the things it should be thinking about. Like running a major company.* It had been the truth then and it was still the truth some five years later. But today, unlike most days, Katherine didn't want to think about work. It was Thanksgiving, after all. One of the few days a year she gave herself a break, sort of.

It was also the first Thanksgiving in over a decade that she'd be spending with family. Year after year, her father and Hazel had invited her to join their party of two in Vermont. Hazel's own two daughters lived in California and, while they tried to visit as often as possible, with their combined brood of seven children—Thanksgiving was not one of those times. Often, with the best of intentions three months out, Katherine had told her dad she'd try to make it, but in the end she'd always manufactured an excuse, something to do with work, something she absolutely could not get out of. It was an easy fallback into the lazy lap of selfishness. Her father had become so accustomed to hearing it time and time again that there was no reason to blame it on anything else. Of course, she knew what they'd say, or at least think. *Work, work, work. All Katherine does is work.* And they were right. Except on Thanksgiving.

Really, she'd be sitting at home in her pajamas with Chinese takeout. Fine, so they were La Perla pajamas and the Chinese takeout was from Philippe, one of the Upper East Side's chicest, see-and-be-seen restaurants. Still, for Katherine it was as pedestrian as it got. Fried dumplings drenched in salty black liquid with sliced scallions bobbing about, a perfectly golden egg roll for dunking in thick, sweet duck sauce, and cold sesame noodles in all their tangy, peanut buttery glory. The order never changed. Sometimes she even dreamed about it the other 364 days of the year, when snacking on baby carrots and rice cakes was standard fare. The nice thing about Chinese restaurants, or restaurants in general, was that they didn't discriminate against those home alone, familyless by choice, giving thanks for greasy food on a holiday widely commemorated with loved ones. Loved ones who would gather around to feast on succulent turkey, fluffy stuffing, pungent cranberry sauce, velvety sweet potatoes, and creamy pumpkin pie, which they'd most likely spent the day preparing *together.* Katherine often felt vaguely sick after her indulgence—the calorie-laden food sitting heavily in her typically empty belly. But it was a good sick, if there was such a thing.

This year would be different, though. She was actually a little excited about dinner with her father and Hazel, if not uneasy about seeing Grant again and meeting his girlfriend, Michelle. Naturally, she'd tried to conjure what Michelle might look like. Would she be prettier than Katherine? Wasn't that the crux of what every ex-girlfriend, ex-fiancée,

or ex-wife cared about? It always came down to physical appearance. You never overheard two women gossiping about
how smart or funny so-and-so's ex was. No way, no how.
They might blather on about her bloated ankles, her frown
lines, or possibly her sagging breasts, but her sharp wit was
typically excluded from the chatter.

Katherine picked up the telephone next to the lamp on
her nightstand and pressed the room service button. "Yes,
hello. Can I please order half a grapefruit; one slice of whole-
grain toast, hold the butter; and a large pot of coffee? Black.
That'll be all, thank you."

After breakfast she'd hit the hotel gym, do a little pre-
binge workout, attend to any international e-mails that had
rolled in—the bulk of what she'd receive on Thanksgiving—
and then make her way over to her dad's house to help, or
rather watch, Hazel fabricate a spread so tantalizingly delicious even Katherine's willpower would have to surrender.
Next would come the moment of truth. Dessert at Carol
Drake's with Laney and Grant. And Michelle. Initially, when
Laney had extended the invitation, it had seemed like an
excellent idea. In fact, it had fortified Katherine in an unexpected way. Though now, on the day of, every time she thought
about it, her resolve weakened a little more. She was so different now. What if she showed up at Carol's house proffering
the store-bought pecan pie she'd picked up at the new bak-
ery in town and Carol didn't welcome her with the same
unconditional warmth she once had? Was it too much to ask
to waltz out of someone's life and then back in twelve years
later, as if no time had passed?

Dinner at her father's house had been everything she expected it to be and then some. Hazel had outdone herself,
not that Katherine knew what normal protocol was. She

simply couldn't imagine anything more elaborate for less than a party of ten, and she suspected that Hazel enjoyed impressing her as much as she enjoyed watching her eat. Hazel would have made a great Jewish mother, if only she wasn't Catholic. Katherine had eaten way too much, which, she told herself, was what people did on Thanksgiving. Sure, it was a holiday centered around giving thanks, but ultimately gorging yourself with food tended to be the main event. Hazel had not only roasted a twenty-pound bird, which she'd brined the night before, but she'd also prepared two kinds of stuffing—one with dried raisins and walnuts, and one without—plus mashed white and sweet potatoes, cranberry sauce, gravy, and garlicky Brussels sprouts. And to top it off, she'd baked her own loaf of crusty French bread and three pies: pecan, pumpkin, and apple. They'd been mildly disappointed when Katherine had said she couldn't stay for dessert, but her father had been delighted to hear that she was on her way to Carol's house, rather than back to her hotel to stare at her laptop for the rest of the night. Before she'd left, Katherine's father had hugged her tightly, unwilling to let go until she'd sworn up and down that she'd come by at least twice before returning to New York on Sunday. "I'll be here next weekend," she'd reminded him. And then he'd reminded her, "Last time you left, you didn't come back." *Touché.*

As soon as Katherine had closed the front door behind her, she couldn't wait to get over to Carol's, but now, standing at Carol's front door, she didn't feel quite as jovial. Katherine had never expected to see Carol living anywhere but at 309 Pine Street. Laney's mother had embodied that house—everything and everyone in it. They'd all worshipped her, even Laney, who throughout the bulk of her teen years had pretended to be rebellious.

Katherine hesitated before announcing her arrival. Silly, perhaps. She'd been family once. Practically. She should have been family permanently. But instead she was walking into a life that was no longer hers for the taking. A life that she'd never have been satisfied with. Or would she have been, if not for Luella? Maybe marrying Grant, remaining in Vermont, and popping out a few kids would have left her content, unaware of a world where running a company and attending star-studded galas was par for the course.

She willed herself to knock, and as soon as she did she could hear the pitter-patter of someone's feet scurrying toward her. She prayed it wasn't Grant.

"Kitty!" Carol flung open the door.

"Hi, Carol." She smiled instantly. That was what people did around Carol Drake.

"I can hardly believe my own eyes." She ushered Katherine inside and wrapped her frail arms around her. "Look at you. How gorgeous you are. And so skinny—my goodness. Do you ever eat?"

"Sometimes." Katherine laughed. "I've just made up for every diet I've ever been on at my dad's house. Hazel's cooking is something else."

"You're telling me?" Carol couldn't keep her eyes off Katherine. "She's beat me in seven straight Manchester pie contests. That woman should have her own Food Network show." *Not a bad idea*, Katherine thought. Though Hazel wouldn't enjoy that kind of glory. "Come in, come in. We've just finished dessert, but we saved pie for you."

"That's quite okay. I'm stuffed to the brim, and I have four pieces in the car that Hazel insisted I take." Katherine had already planned on giving them to the staff at Equinox. Tomorrow she'd be back to her stringent healthful eating, and also she felt sorry for people who had no choice but to work on Thanksgiving.

"Well, come sit down, then. Everyone's in the living room." Katherine followed Carol, who looked significantly older, no doubt the toll from losing Laney's dad, the love of her life. Outside of that, she was still the same Carol, albeit with a diminished spark. The spark she'd passed on to Laney. Only Carol's had always been a little purer. This was a woman who, until she lost her husband, had experienced no profound disappointments in life. She'd married the perfect man and had two great kids. The Drakes had always been comfortable. Certainly they'd been able to splurge on weeklong house rentals in Nantucket, which—looking back—must have cost a pretty penny even then.

Katherine shadowed Carol through the narrow hallway into the living room. The house was smaller than the one on Pine Street, but much of the furniture had made the move as well and, all in all, things looked similar, only on a reduced scale.

"Everyone, Kitty is here!" Carol announced, as if Angelina Jolie had just swooped in on their Thanksgiving celebration with Brad, Maddox, Shiloh, Zahara, Pax, Vivienne, and Knox in tow. Katherine felt her face boil and likely turn an unflattering shade of crimson as all eyes—Laney's, Grant's, Michelle's, Gemma's, Rick's, and four other unfamiliar adults'—focused on her.

"Hi, everyone." Katherine raised her hand and held it up for a minute.

"Isn't she stunning? Laney, you didn't tell me Kitty looked like a supermodel." She had taken extra care when getting ready earlier. Who wouldn't have? Her makeup was flawless—she'd touched it up in the car. And she was wearing a simple but figure-hugging black Diane von Furstenberg wrap dress. She looked good and she knew it. But now, with everyone staring at her, she felt like running for cover.

"Oh, please. Not at all," Katherine replied modestly, standing awkwardly in front of Carol's nine guests.

"Don't be shy, Kitty. You are a sight. Stunning, absolutely stunning."

"Leave her alone, Mom," Laney piped up, walking toward Katherine. "You'll give her a complex."

"Oh, sorry." Carol looked momentarily deflated, but rebounded quickly. "I have to get back to cleaning up. You'll introduce Kitty around?"

"Sure." Laney nodded at her mom and rolled her eyes at Katherine. "Sorry. She's just really excited to see you."

"It's fine. Your mom can do no wrong." Katherine let out a deep breath as people went back to their own conversations.

"Come on. You can meet everyone you don't already know." Laney walked Katherine around, introducing her to Carol's friend Andrea, Andrea's sister Joan, and to Michelle's parents, Jim and Marsha. Rick and Gemma seemed legitimately happy to see her, greeting her with bear hugs and making her promise to talk more later on. Gemma immediately pointed to her freshly made-up face—"Light eye, dark mouth," she declared, puckering her Racy Red lips. Then they came to Grant and Michelle. "Michelle, this is Kitty, or Katherine. We're not really sure what to call her."

"Katherine is fine." She extended her hand, and Michelle shook it limply. "It's so nice to finally meet you." Katherine smiled politely, outwardly pleased to make her acquaintance. Inside, her heart was hurtling violently. Michelle was pretty in the most basic way. Pale skin, long blond hair, light blue eyes. Every feature was symmetrical and unassuming. No crooked beak or pointy chin to speak of. But she wasn't beautiful.

"Nice to meet you too." Michelle smiled back and territorially rested her arm on Grant's knee, until he stood to hug Katherine.

"Hey, glad you could make it." His lips grazed her ear as he pulled away, sending a shiver down her spine.

"Me too."

"I'll show you around." Laney tugged at Katherine's arm. "This must be weird for you," she whispered as soon as they were out of earshot.

"Ya think?" Katherine watched out of the corner of her eye as Grant walked out onto the back porch alone. It had turned out to be an unseasonably warm day for November in Vermont, with a high temperature of 55 degrees.

"Go ahead." Laney motioned with her chin toward the porch.

"What?" Katherine feigned ignorance, which might have worked on anyone but Laney.

"Go talk to him. My brother. You know, the one you used to be madly in love with?"

"I don't know." Katherine shook her head.

"Don't be such a sissy."

"I feel like it's disrespectful to Michelle."

"I didn't say go fuck him. I said go talk to him. It has to happen sooner or later."

"Maybe." Katherine's stomach churned.

"Yes." Laney gave her a little shove. "I'll go in the kitchen and chat up Michelle, if that makes you feel better."

"Okay." Katherine inhaled and exhaled twice. "Thank you."

"Yeah, yeah." Laney waved her hand at Katherine and set off in the direction of the kitchen, while Katherine walked out onto the porch, where Grant was leaning against the railing, staring out into the darkness.

"Hey." She spoke softly and he turned around.

"Hey, stranger." He smiled, and Katherine had to stop her knees from buckling. "Running for the hills yet?"

"Not yet."

"It's good to see you." He came toward her, standing

only inches away. She wanted to reach out and touch his face, but she couldn't. Not anymore. "And my mom is right. You do look amazing."

"This old thing?" Katherine laughed nervously.

"It's not just the dress, Kitty. You're a different person."

"Am I?"

"It sure looks that way."

"Maybe on the outside." And the inside too, but for whatever reason, she didn't want Grant to know that, at least not any more than Laney had already told him.

"That all?"

"I don't know." She couldn't lie. Not to him. "So, how come you don't hate me?"

"Oh, I do." He laughed, raking his hands through his chestnut brown hair. "Or I did."

"And now?"

"Like you said, I don't know."

"I guess *sorry* won't cut it?" Katherine looked down at her Christian Louboutin heels, which seemed so frivolous now, standing on Carol's porch with him. The man she walked away from. The man who'd never done anything but adore her.

"I don't need an apology, Kitty. Life happens." He cleared his throat.

"Well, I am. Sorry." She lifted her head, meeting his penetrating blue eyes. "I never meant to hurt you."

"I know."

"Do you?"

"I do now."

"Michelle seems lovely." Katherine changed the subject, a reliable tactic whenever things were getting uncomfortable.

"She's great." He nodded. "She cooked everything tonight."

"And she's still cleaning up?"

"That's Michelle."

"Sounds like your mom."

"Funny, I never thought about that." He laughed again, revealing the dimples Katherine had once said she wanted to slice off and carry around in her backpack while they were apart. Cheesy, but true.

"Grant? Grant?" Carol's voice grew louder as she approached. "There you are. Oh, hi, Kitty." She looked a little embarrassed. "I hope I didn't interrupt."

"No, that's okay. I actually have to get back to my hotel anyway."

"So soon?" Carol frowned. "I've barely had a chance to talk to you. We have so much to catch up on!"

"I know, but I'll be here until Sunday. And then I'll be back next weekend. We still have a good bit of work to do at Luella's house."

"So Laney tells me. Well, you'll have to promise to visit again."

"I promise." *Oh, the irony,* Katherine thought. She'd spent the past twelve years avoiding seeing people. What was the point in getting together if you could pick up the phone or, better yet, send an e-mail? Now all anyone wanted to do was see her, see her, see her. And then see her some more.

"Grant, I need to borrow you. A light's gone out in the dining room."

"I'll be right there, Mom." Carol scurried off, and he turned back to Katherine. "That's my cue."

"Absolutely, go."

"Let's do this again, okay?"

"Oh, sure. That's fine."

"You said you'll be here until Sunday?"

"That's the plan."

"Good. My mom's not the only one who wants to catch up." Grant smiled, kissed her on the cheek, and headed back into the house, allowing Katherine to breathe.

Minutes later, she walked inside, looking around for Laney to say good-bye, but she found Carol instead.

"Are you all set, sweetheart? Sure I can't send you home with some pie?"

"Yes, I'm stuffed. Thank you." Katherine paused before speaking again. She knew she needed to say something and there was no right time. "Carol, I owe you an apology."

"Whatever for?" She looked instantly worried.

"I should have reached out to you when Andrew died. There's no excuse. He was such a wonderful man and always treated me like his own. The fact that I didn't even take the time to acknowledge his passing makes me, well, shameful."

"Oh, Kitty. Andrew adored you. He always said you were a fine example for our Laney." Carol dabbed the inner corners of her eyes with a hand towel she'd tucked into the pocket of her apron. "Don't even think about it. Life goes on. Right?"

"I guess so. I just wanted you to know how important he was to me, and that not calling you or even writing was wrong. I'm sorry."

"Nonsense. Now go get some beauty sleep. God knows it's been working!"

"Thank you." Katherine leaned in to hug Carol and spotted Grant across the room, staring directly at her. He winked and waved. She smiled and blushed. "I'll just go say good-bye to Laney and be on my way."

"I think I just saw her in the kitchen."

"Perfect." Or not. She was probably still with Michelle. Katherine reluctantly moved in that direction, pausing outside the kitchen door long enough to overhear a conversation that definitely wasn't meant for her ears.

"She's beautiful. Gorgeous, actually," Michelle bemoaned. "And that body? Come on."

"You hate her, don't you?" This was Laney.

"She seems nice enough. Gracious, they say. Right? Isn't that what people like her say?" *People like her.* Katherine didn't know whether to be flattered or stung.

"Don't worry. Kitty's a bigwig in New York City. She may be sentimental up here for a few days, but she doesn't want Grant." *Bigwig, huh?* "Remember, he dated Kitty, not Katherine." *Ouch.*

"Do you think he'd want her back? You know, if she didn't live in New York?"

"He loved her. A lot. And it was hard for him to get over her, but he did. He loves you now, Mich. Be secure in that."

Katherine crept away furtively. She couldn't go in and say good-bye. They'd both suspect, if not know, that she'd overheard them. Instead she made her way toward the front door, slipping out of Carol's new home as she'd slipped out of their lives so many years ago. As soon as she got to the car, instinctively she checked her phone. There was one voice mail.

> *Katherine, this is Jane. I'm sorry to do this, but I need you back in New York tomorrow. Call me. Oh, and Happy Thanksgiving.*

February 1997

Kitty

"I can't believe you came all the way to New York and we've been stuck inside the whole time," I lamented, snuggling up to Grant and nestling my head into the crook between his arm and naked torso. You really have to like the person you're sleeping with if you're going to share a twin-sized bed, which is what Grant and I have been doing for the past two nights in my hole-in-the-wall—albeit roommate-less—dorm room.

"Remind me what's wrong with that?" He pulled me on top of him with his strong arms and nipped at my earlobe, scattering soft kisses along my jawline and down the front of my neck, which he knows drives me crazy, in a good way.

"I really wanted to show you the city," I pouted, rolling off Grant and sitting up to face him. "I can't believe you've never been to the Empire State Building or the Statue of Liberty."

"Neither had you until last year." He tried to draw me back toward him, his eyes greedy with lust and clearly apathetic with regard to the Empire State Building. Or any other tourist attraction, for that matter.

"I know! It's disgraceful. And what about MoMA and the Met and the Natural History museum? I had an extensive itinerary typed out for us!" It's not that I don't enjoy spending the whole day and night in bed with Grant; it's just that I never get to show him any of the stuff I tell him about. As it turns out, New York is really awesome. There's an endless list of things to do, from museum exhibitions and sightseeing to amazing restaurants and Broadway shows. And, of course, there's Central Park, with its boundless possibilities. I'm not sure why I thought I wouldn't love it here.

"I guess Mother Nature had something else in mind." He grinned naughtily, and whatever angst I'd had over my well-laid plan began to melt away. Grant has that affect on me. He always has, but now that we don't get to see each other very often, his powers are even more potent.

For the past three years, Grant's been at UVM, and for two of those years I've been at NYU. It's been virtually impossible for him to visit me or for me to visit him on the weekends, since Burlington is way too far to travel for a weekend trip, and vice versa. Plus I have a job at the student center here on Saturdays, which I can't skip out on. Although yesterday Grant used his powers to convince me otherwise. It's the first time I've called in sick since I took the position the second week of my freshman year. Rolph, my boss, was definitely perturbed, considering it's been snowing hard for a day and a half, which means a lot of people are at the student center. But when Grant begged and pleaded and then unleashed his dimples on me, I finally caved—which, for the record, is very unlike me. Rolph told me I'm the most reliable, organized, and efficient employee he's overseen in his fourteen years of running the student center. He's probably rethinking those accolades now.

I just couldn't say no to Grant. He cut all of his classes on Friday to hitch a ride with a group of guys he doesn't even know, just because they were driving to New York and he wanted to spend forty-eight hours with me. He didn't even tell his parents or Laney, who think he's in Boston. Well, Laney may know better. She did call me on Friday after Grant was already here to grill me about what I was doing this weekend and what Grant was doing in Boston. It was a little hard to maintain my composure while Grant was peeling off my jeans, though somehow I managed. I don't know why he didn't just tell her he was coming here. I encouraged him to, but Grant insisted she'd be jealous and want to come with him, which is probably true. I really do hate lying to Laney, though this seemed like a harmless enough fib and for a worthwhile cause.

"Mother Nature sucks!" I lay back down, nuzzling Grant once again and inhaling the undertones of lavender in his signature cologne—Drakkar Noir—which he's been wearing since before we started dating. It's become an aphrodisiac for me, which can be dangerous, considering it's one of the most popular colognes on the market. Sometimes when I'm riding the subway I'll get a whiff of it and unknowingly migrate toward a random stranger merely so I can transport myself to moments like this, even if only between stops.

I can't lie. It's been challenging being away from Grant. I really struggled with it for the first few months of my freshman year. Sure, he'd already been at college for a year, but it was different when I was still in Manchester. For one, he was coming home every weekend and there was something about knowing he was close by, even if we weren't physically together. Does that make sense? It was like I knew I could get to him at a moment's notice if I needed to, even though I never did. Then, suddenly, my own first year arrived and I was on my own, in a new and entirely intimidating place, where I knew no one, and all at once that security was gone. Because that's what Grant is. He's my security blanket. And when your security blanket is ripped off like a bandage—in one swift motion—well, let's just say it stings. I can't tell you how many times I considered transferring to UVM. The only person I told was Luella, and she said that I couldn't give up on New York until I'd truly experienced it, and if I still wanted to move back after that, she'd support my decision 100 percent.

I wanted to heed Luella's advice and go out and live it up, take a great big, juicy bite out of the Big Apple. But I had no one to go out and live it up with, so instead I immersed myself in classes. Until I met Freya. She sat next to me in Biology 101 and instantly reminded me of Laney—not in appearance, but in personality. She was outgoing, possibly to a fault, and a little full of herself, with her wavy, thick brown hair that fell midway down her five-foot-eight statuesque dancer's body, and her doe-shaped hazel eyes hooded by eyelashes so long they flapped like butterfly wings. Freya was up for any adventure she could conjure. She told me she was from Connecticut, only about an hour or so out of Manhattan, and that she would be my personal tour guide as long as I could help her pass bio. Sounded like a good deal to me.

Freya lived up to her word and then some. Before long, my nights spent pining over Grant in my triple room with my two excruciatingly quiet Korean roommates were a thing of the past. If it was going on at NYU or in the surrounding city, Freya was there, and by association so was I. Phone calls with Grant—which had once been as frequent as three or four times a day—became more sporadic and, eventually, a day or two could pass without us being able to catch each other for more then a few abbreviated minutes— just long enough to remind us how much we loved each other and that we couldn't wait to see each other. I even stopped counting down the days on my UVM calendar. Yes, it's my third one.

"Really? I think Mother Nature knew exactly what she was doing." Grant kissed me tenderly on the lips, tracing the outline of my face with his index finger, and my whole body ached for him, even though he was still there.

"I don't want you to go." I kissed him back and he pulled me closer, until I could feel the rise and fall of his chest against mine.

"I don't want to go." He nibbled at my ear.

"I miss you so much when we're apart." My eyes burned, threatening to mist, and I squeezed them shut in protest.

"Let's not think about it. I'm here now." He lifted my tank top over my head to expose my bare breasts and began working his way down to my nipples—grazing, caressing, stroking.

"I know, but . . ."

"Shhh." He pressed his finger to my lips, trailing gentle kisses from my nipples to my navel and back up to my mouth, urgently exploring every inch of my body, until I couldn't hold back anymore.

Four hours later, I was alone. It never gets easier. Learning to exist separately is one thing, but the actual extrication it- self continues to be that special brand of tear-you-up-on-the- inside painful. Like when you lose your appetite and just want to lie in the dark alone, listening to cheesy eighties ballads. I felt a little sick and started calculating how long it would take to get to Bennington by bus the following weekend. Unfortunately, I knew the answer. Long. Too long. Not to mention that I'd lose my job.

Before I could become completely mired in self-pity, the phone rang. I sprang for it, despite being the only one in my single room, with the hopes that it would be Grant. Maybe he'd pulled over to call me from a gas station, unable to endure the six-hour drive without one more profession of love.

"How's my favorite girl?" Luella's voice came clearly and cleanly through the receiver.

"I'm okay. He left a few hours ago." I'd told Luella that Grant was coming. She knew she couldn't tell the Drakes, which she didn't appreciate, insisting repeatedly, "I will not get in the habit of fibbing for you kids." I swore it would only be this one time, so she relented, against her better judgment—her words, not mine. I thought about pointing out that we're not kids anymore, but seeing as I was asking her to lie, I figured it might not be the best approach.

"I get that it's hard, but you're really thriving there, so I hope you won't let it get you down for too long. Your father is so proud of you, Kitty; he tells everyone in town that his brilliant daughter goes to New York University in the big city. Your mother would have been very proud too."

"Maybe." Luella's always saying things like that about my mom, even though she never met her. I think she feels like it's her responsibility to make sure I don't hate a ghost. "She never seemed all that proud when she was alive, so let's not give her too much credit."

"Don't be silly, Kitty. I know for a fact that she loved you more than anything, and she's smiling down on you from heaven."

"Then why was she so critical of me all the time?"

"Sometimes people have a strange way of expressing

love." Luella cleared her throat, and I decided to leave it at that. I didn't have the wherewithal to combat even her standard defense of my dead mother. "Now let's talk about when I can come for my next visit. I was thinking mid-March, when the weather will be a bit nicer. Perhaps a walk around Central Park if it's a warm day."

"That sounds good. Remember, you promised to try one of the hot dogs from the cart." The mere thought of it made me giggle. Luella Hancock did not do street food.

"Yeah, yeah." I could picture her waving her hand dismissively in the air. "All right, then, my dear. I'll book my room at the St. Regis. And in the meantime, don't sulk all day long. You've got a whole city to explore right outside your door."

"I won't." *I might.* "Thanks, Luella. Love you."

"Love you too, dear."

I knew she was right. I also knew that by the time next weekend rolled around, the pit in my stomach would be replenished with whatever exploits Freya had in store for us post-Grant, as she likes to call it. In fact, in a few weeks, I may be wondering once again, even if only for an instant, what it would be like to kiss Ben, the unbelievably hot guy in my English lit class. Not that I'd ever act on it.

Ben could never be Grant. No one could ever be Grant. I just have to keep reminding myself.

November 1998

Laney

Kitty was supposed to come home last Friday. She has the week off, like I do and like the rest of the college students in the world, but she called Grant on Thursday to say she wouldn't be able to make it to Vermont until today. The day before Thanksgiving. Something about an internship. I guess her dad's struggling a bit with tuition and Kitty feels guilty—no surprise there—so she's trying to help out. Obviously, I can't blame her for that. I know how fortunate Grant and I are that our parents could pay for school without worrying, and that we didn't have to take on jobs in addition to all the class work we have. Or, rather, *had* in Grant's case. He's done. He graduated last May, and since then he's been working at our dad's shipping company until he figures out exactly what he wants to do, which, from the sounds of it, is not to join our father at the shipping company. I don't think my dad had any expectations of that happening, so no harm done. He's pretty content to have his son around for now, and when the time comes that he's ready to move on, my dad will be cool with that too.

I think Grant's just waiting for Kitty and me to graduate at the end of the year. Well, really, he's waiting for Kitty, but he knows that Kitty and I are going to move to New York, so—for once—Grant's life kind of hinges on my plans. I mean, *our* plans. Kitty's and mine, that is. Grant and I were not happy when Kitty decided to go to NYU instead of UVM. For one, she failed to mention that she'd applied—to either of us. She said it was a last-minute thing and that it all happened very quickly. She felt bad, I think, but she still left. I was angry for a while. For starters, NYU was not part of the master plan. Of course, Grant wasn't part of the master plan either, so I'm trying to be flexible.

I couldn't understand why she'd want to leave her best friend and her boyfriend, whom she's so obviously obsessed with, and move to a city she claimed she didn't even like in the first place. I've made the best of it for almost four years, as did Grant, but I know he was more upset than he admitted. At first they talked on the phone, like, a million times a day. They needed to know what the other one had eaten for breakfast, lunch, and dinner; which classes they'd attended that day; who their friends were; whether or not there were any cute guys or girls on their respective halls—like either of them had or would ever have eyes for anyone else. And, worst of all, they had this mushy-gushy language that they spoke. *I wuv you. I wuv you more. Well, I wuv you the most.* It was enough to send Grant's roommates packing after his first semester. For real.

By the middle of Grant's sophomore year, the phone calls had slowed down. He and Kitty talked maybe once a day, if not a few times a week. I could tell it bothered Grant and that he wondered what Kitty was doing, where she was doing it, and whom she was doing it with, but he kept it to himself, burying himself in his schoolwork and a few extracurricular activities, not one of which was dating other girls. Not that they weren't interested.

Kitty has come home for the usual breaks, most of them, at least. But it always seems like she's in a rush to get back to school for one thing or another. She actually likes New York, despite her initial resistance. She says she's learning the lay of the land so that by the time I get there, she can be my personal tour guide. From my perspective, it sounds like she's experiencing everything without me. She has this friend called Freya who lives down the hall and is from Connecticut, so she's spent a lot of time in New York and, apparently, she's acting as Kitty's personal tour guide. Whatever. If I have to hear about another off-off-off-off-off-Broadway show or Thai restaurant Freya took her to, I might lose my noodles.

Obviously, I'm still Kitty's best friend, but she has changed. Everyone's noticed it. Even my dad said something about it when she was home for fall break, and he's usually pretty clueless about stuff like that. She has this air of confidence about her that she never had before. And she's started dressing more sophisticated too. Instead of the baggy clothing she used to wear, all the sudden she's in slim-fitting jeans and flowery tops with turquoise jewelry. Must be Freya's influence. I know; the name's a little much. I made fun of it when Kitty first told me about her freshman year, but she got defensive, so I dropped it. Too bad for Freya that she's not part of our master plan.

In other news, I started dating someone two months ago: Rick. He's hot and smart—not the type I usually go for. The smart part, I mean. Oh, and he's good with his hands, in more ways than one. We met at the frozen yogurt dispenser in the cafeteria. It had broken down for about the millionth time since I got to UVM, and Rick was able to fix it in about four minutes flat. Even the kitchen staff was impressed. After that, he paid for my swirl yogurt with sprinkles and promptly asked for my number. I knew he'd call. A girl knows these things. And, sure enough, he did. Three days later. I kind of liked that he made me wait. College guys can be so desperate sometimes, and it's really unattractive if you ask me. Rick lives in Boston, but he said he might be able to sneak away after Thanksgiving and come to Vermont to meet Kitty.

Is he the one? Doubtful. I suppose he could be—in a universe where I could actually stay with one person for more than a few months. And in a universe where I wasn't twenty-one years old with my whole life ahead of me. I'm not like Kitty. She and Grant have already committed to spending the rest of their lives together, or at least that's what they tell each other and anyone else who will listen. We'll see.

Kitty's train got into the station at one o'clock today. I wanted to pick her up, but she said she needed to spend a little time with her dad first and that she'd be over here no later than two thirty, which is in fifteen minutes. Then I'll have her to myself for about three and a half hours before Grant comes home and steals her away. I'm so excited, I can barely contain myself. We have *so much* to catch up on. She barely knows anything about me and Rick. All we ever talk about, when Kitty actually has time to talk, is her new life in New York. Without me.

I curled up on the window seat by our front door, the same window seat where I sat waiting for Kitty to arrive in Manchester ten years ago. On the one hand, it's hard to believe it's been that long. On the other hand, I feel like Kitty and I have been best friends forever.

By two forty-five, there was no sight of Kitty, and I was

starting to get annoyed. I know she rarely gets to see her dad, but she rarely gets to see me either, and between the three of us—me, Grant, and Kitty's dad—it always seems like I'm the one that gets screwed. Just as I was about to go over and drag her from her house, I saw Kitty walking across our lawn. I jumped up and bolted to the door, flinging it open to find her standing there with a sheepish look on her face.

"Don't kill me. I know I'm late." She waited to see if I was pissed.

"I'll spare you this time. Get in here!" We did our little hugging, shrieking dance we always do whenever it's been too long since we've see each other. "You look great!" I held her at arm's length. "Did you lose weight?"

"Maybe a little. My dad asked the same thing." She tucked her hair, which was streaked with fresh auburn highlights, behind her ears. "I do a lot of walking in New York. It's not like here, where you have to drive everywhere."

"I know. I wasn't born yesterday." I narrowed my eyes at her. "Wait a minute. Are you tan?"

"I think so." A guilty expression hijacked her innocent face.

"What do you mean, 'I think so'?" I grabbed her hand and led her up to my room. Yes, I know we're twenty-one, but I can't help myself. I've missed Kitty so much. I've met some okay girls at UVM; no one like Kitty, though. Anyway, I've come to the conclusion that I'm not really a girls' girl. I get along better with guys. And Kitty.

"Freya took me to a tanning salon this week. She said I couldn't go home to my boyfriend looking like a corpse."

"Is that so?" Fine, so Freya was right. It's just a little ironic considering that Kitty has been on my ass for years about sun overexposure. I once nicknamed her SPF and called her that for an entire month.

"I know it's really bad for you. I only did six minutes. Freya tans every week. She has some frequent-tanner card and everything."

"Fancy Freya." I rolled my eyes and plopped onto my bed.

"Sorry." Kitty lay down across from me, our feet dangling off the side.

"Sorry what?" I propped my head up with my right hand, digging my elbow into a small throw pillow.

"I know you don't like Freya." Kitty pointed to one of the many other pillows stacked against my headboard and I tossed it to her.

"I don't even know her."

"Yeah, but it annoys you when I talk about her."

"No, it doesn't."

"Yes, it does, Laney. I know you."

"Sue me if I don't want to hear about Freya every five seconds."

"Don't worry; she'll never take your place." Kitty cocked her head and gave me a silly smile. For the first time, I noticed just how different she looks. It could be the tan or the auburn highlights—I didn't ask, but I can only assume this Freya chick had something to do with those too—or the fact that she's lost at least ten pounds, if not fifteen. Still, it seems like more than that. It's the whole way she carries herself and the way she speaks. So self-assured and grown-up. Don't get me wrong; Kitty has always been a fifty-year-old trapped in a younger body, with her impressive vocabulary and her overall mature-for-her-age disposition, but this is different. I can't put my finger on it.

"As if she could, even if she wanted to."

"Exactly." She kicked off her boots, and her face got serious all the sudden. "So, how's Grant doing?"

"Fine, I think. You'd know better than I would."

"Honestly, we don't get to talk that much." She knit her brow. "There's always so much going on and our schedules never seem to match up. If I'm coming, he's going. If I'm going, he's coming."

"I guess we can't all keep up with your busy life."

"Lane, come on. That's not what I'm saying."

"Whatever. I'm really busy too. There's so much to do at UVM and in Burlington. It's like I'm never even in my dorm room."

"Well, that's a good thing. Right?"

"Oh yeah. I mean, it's not *New York City*, but there's still tons of stuff going on."

"I wish Grant told me more. It's like I don't even know what he does every day."

"Well, as you say, it's hard to reach you, so . . ." I really did not want to talk about how busy Kitty's life in New York is anymore. "Wait a minute. You're not . . ."

"What?"

"Thinking about breaking up with Grant?"

"Oh, God, no!" Kitty perked up immediately. "I love Grant. It's just hard being away from each other for such long blocks of time. I miss him. A lot."

"He misses you too."

"I know. And sometimes . . ." she trailed off.

"Sometimes what?"

"I don't know. I feel like he thinks it's my fault." She sat up.

"Well, I mean, you did leave, but I think he's past that. Hey, the good news is, it'll all be over soon!" I clapped my hands together excitedly in an attempt to lift the mood.

"Yeah, I know. Six more months."

"What's six months when you have the rest of your lives to be together?"

"True." Kitty didn't seem convinced.

"Let's talk about something else. I don't need you all depressed about my brother when he's not even here yet."

"Good idea. What do you want to talk about?"

"Me, of course!" Kitty laughed. Finally.

"That's right. Hot new man, huh?"

"You could say that."

"Do tell." I could see Kitty was trying her best to indulge me, but it was obvious her mind was elsewhere. Probably thinking about Grant.

"Well, he's gorgeous. And smart."

"Really?"

"I know. Right?"

"Smart like he knows how to count to ten, or smart like he's going to graduate?" Kitty smiled irreverently.

"Like he's going to graduate. With a three-point-eight GPA, thank you very much."

"Wow!"

"Yup! I can date smart men too. Actually he's coming here Friday to meet you. I think I told you he lives in Boston."

"That's cool. I can't wait."

"Oh, and my mom invited you to dinner that night."

"I can't. I promised Luella."

"Boo! How about Saturday?"

"About that."

"What?" I knew exactly what she was going to say. The same thing she's said every other time she's been home on break for the past two years.

"I have to go back to New York on Saturday morning."

"Kitty!"

"I know. I know. I'm sorry."

"What is it this time?"

"Don't say it like that."

"Well?"

"I haven't had a chance to fill you in, but I got this new internship at a cosmetics company. Well, Luella got it for me. Her friend Jane owns it. They're going to pay me. Not much, but at least it's something, enough that I can give up my student-center job, which sucks, so that's a relief. Anyway, there's this event on Saturday night that Jane asked me to come help at, and since it's my first thing for her, I really can't say no."

"Wow, that's really great for you." *Don't worry about the rest of us.* "Have you told Grant yet?"

"No, I'm telling you first."

"Well, good luck with that."

"Thanks."

"We're still on for August, right?" Grant, Kitty, and I are all going back to Nantucket together for our final free week before we have to get jobs and actually become responsible adults. Okay, I guess Grant is already a responsible adult, as is Kitty. So before *I* become a responsible adult. "I may even ask Rick to come, if we're still together."

"We're still on. Definitely."

"The whole week?"

"The whole week."

"Pinkie swear?" I held out my right hand and she linked her smallest finger to mine.

"Pinkie swear."

"Excellent! Now let's go get something to eat. I'm starving."

Kitty laughed. "Good to know some things never change."

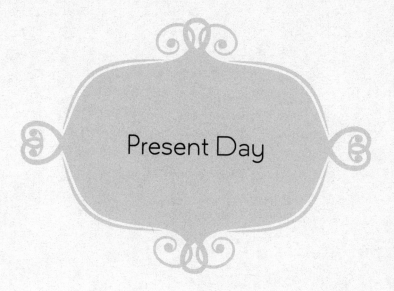

Present Day

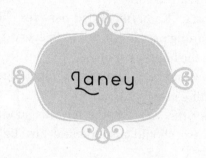

Laney

"I'm having flashbacks to college." Laney sat on the floor of Luella's closet, her legs crossed Indian style, while she divided Luella's jewelry, and, boy, was there a lot of it, first by category—earrings, bracelets, necklaces, and rings—and then by subcategory. Pearl, diamond, hoop, and chandelier earrings. Bangle, charm, gemstone, and cuff bracelets. Choker, pendant, beaded, and statement necklaces. Gold, silver, stacking, and diamond rings. There must have been at least a hundred of everything.

"I'm sorry. I wish there was something I could do about it." Katherine sat across from Laney, adeptly folding Luella's mass of silk scarves.

"I thought you ran the company. Can't you just say no?"

"I don't run the whole company. I run the largest department and oversee the others. I do have a boss, though, if only one. And she needs me to meet with some very important clients who were able to extend their visit from Hong Kong. I can't just say no to that."

"Yeah, sure." Laney held a diamond teardrop earring up to her left lobe and glanced at herself in the mirror. "You better come back this time."

"Don't worry." Katherine rolled her eyes. "By the way, I called the cleaning people. They'll be in every day this week to make sure the house is spotless."

"Great. Rick and his guys can start touching up the paint and fix anything else that's broken."

"Remember the door." Katherine was suddenly in boss mode. "And we should also replace any lightbulbs that are out."

"I'm sure you'll make a list before you go." Laney smirked. "When are you coming back?"

"I'm going to try to leave as early as I can on Friday, but I won't make it to the house until Saturday morning." Katherine placed her neat stack of scarves into one of the many open boxes. "Hand me those." She pointed to a pile of leather, chain-link, and suede belts, most boasting chunky designer buckles.

"That's fine. I think one more weekend should do it. And then we'll schedule the estate sale for the following weekend. Does that work?" Laney pushed the belts toward Katherine.

"I've already blocked out the next two weekends to come up here. I'll also plan to be around for the closing, once we have a buyer."

"I guess we can work out all the financial stuff after that."

"It'll take a little while, but it looks like we're going to survive it. All of it."

"Imagine that." Laney smiled reluctantly. Her feelings of

anger and resentment toward Katherine hadn't disappeared, but somewhere throughout the week they'd subsided. Perhaps she wasn't as bad as Laney had originally made her out to be. Sure, she was particular. Even the way she was handling the scarves and belts was enough to clue anyone in to her obsessive compulsivity. But there had been moments when Laney had seen a hint of Kitty, an expression she used to make, or something she would say that sounded more like something the old Kitty would say. And last night at her mom's house, there had been a very specific look on Kitty's face—one Laney had recognized instantly—when she'd first laid eyes on Grant.

It was so hard to understand why Grant wasn't more upset with her. When Kitty had left all those years ago, he'd been shattered, a shadow of his former self, sulking around for months on end, unwilling to talk about it with anyone. Laney hadn't even tried to comfort him. She'd been submerged in her own ire, coupled with the fear of what life was going to be like not only without Kitty, but with a baby on the way. Eventually, Grant had resurfaced from his yearlong funk, the fog lifting gradually month by month, and then day by day. The irony was that he'd never seemed terribly angry *at* Kitty. It had seemed more like he was angry with himself for having invested in their fairy tale to begin with.

Now, looking back, Laney realized that while she and Grant were cut from the same parental cloth, there couldn't be two more different siblings. For that reason, they'd had two very different ways of dealing with things. While Grant had dipped into a quiet depression of sorts, Laney had been consumed by a fierce rage. A fierce rage that had been directed solely at Kitty. And now that said rage had faded, there was nothing left but the vestiges of bitterness and resentment.

"Does this mean you've forgiven me?" Katherine regarded Laney dubiously.

"It's not that simple." Laney stood in front of the mirror, clasping a four-strand pearl choker around her neck. If Katherine expected them to be best friends again just because Laney was easing up, she had another think coming to her. Laney would tolerate Katherine for now, until she went back to New York for good. That was the extent of it.

"It would have been twelve years ago."

"What's that supposed to mean?" Laney whipped her head around.

"I'm just saying it's not like I didn't try to apologize."

"Really? I don't remember any apology."

"That's because you refused to take my calls."

"Oh, right. All two of them. Sorry, I was a little busy being furious and pregnant." Laney crossed her arms—her reflexive pissed-off pose—and the pearl choker fell to the floor.

"I remember." Katherine picked up the pearls and walked behind Laney, fastening them around her neck. She stared at her friend's reflection in the mirror. "They suit you. You should take them."

"What?" Laney sputtered, temporarily sidetracked by Katherine's abrupt change of topic and by the fact that she could no longer press her buttons as easily as she'd once been able to.

"The pearls. Do you want them or not?"

"I'm sure they're worth a fortune." Laney admired herself. They did suit her. "Half of which is your fortune."

"I don't mind." Katherine shrugged. "Seriously, they're yours. Just say the word."

"Maybe." Laney tilted her head to one side. "I don't even know what I'd wear them with."

Katherine turned and walked toward Luella's closet, rifling through one of the many racks until settling on a simple, sleeveless black shift dress. "Here, try this."

Laney held it up in front of her. "They do go well together."

"I'll be the judge of that. Let's see it on."

"I'm not trying it on," Laney protested.

"And why not?"

"I don't know."

"Come on. You know you want to," Katherine prodded.

"Fine. But only if you put on the white gown," Laney
challenged.

"Which one?"

"Don't play dumb with me. You know full well which
one." Of course Katherine had to know that Laney was re-
ferring to the white chiffon with the gold beading from the
most extravagant gala Luella had ever hosted; Laney could
still read Katherine's expressions, and she knew she had
fallen in love with it all over again.

"Okay." Katherine went back to the rack and retrieved it.

Both women changed, back-to-back—Laney's directive—
so they could turn around on the count of three for the big
reveal.

"Ready?" Laney was already a little giddy. "One, two,
three!" They pivoted to face each other. "Holy mother of
God!" She stared at Katherine wide-eyed. "You look like a
movie star."

"You think?" Katherine faced the mirror, appraising herself in the layers of flowing chiffon with delicate gold beading adorning the neckline and nipping her tiny waist. She
looked spectacular. There was no denying it.

"I'm not sure about this one." Laney stood next to Katherine, twisting from side to side.

"Wait a minute." Katherine glided back toward Luella's

closet, in the same fashion Luella had that enchanting evening; it was almost hypnotizing. "Put these on." She handed
Laney a pair of elbow-length black silk gloves and the highest pair of black peep-toe heels Laney had ever seen, much
less worn. "Now stand up straight." Katherine came behind
her, tugging the dress in this direction and that. "There you
go. All you need is sunglasses and a tiara."

"Yes, because I'm so very Audrey Hepburn." Laney
grabbed one of the permanent markers they'd been labeling
boxes with and held it up like a cigarette. "I don't think I'll
be eating breakfast at Tiffany's any time soon."

"You should definitely keep the necklace." Katherine
laughed a little. "I'm sure Gemma will like it, if nothing else."

"Oh yeah, sure. She can wear it when she's smoking in the
girls' bathroom." Laney rolled her eyes and focused on Katherine again. "Let's find the gold heels!" She walked back toward the stacks of shoe boxes they'd set aside and started
flipping lids. "Could this woman have owned any more
footwear?"

"Come here," Katherine called from a second, adjacent
closet. "*This* will look amazing on you." She held up a midnight blue, floor-length gown with a gold choker-inspired
halter neckline. "With your eyes, this is going to be perfect.
Put it on. But you have to take off the pearls." Laney scrunched
up her face. "I didn't say you have to give them back; just take
them off for the moment."

Laney snagged the dress and draped it across Luella's
bed, before opening one more shoe box. "Jackpot!" Katherine darted toward her, peering over Laney's shoulder like a
little kid.

"Oh yeah, those are the ones." Both women were breathless. "I almost don't want to touch them."

"Then I will." Laney extracted the gold brocade masterpieces from the box carefully, as if she were handling a new-born kitten, and then handed them to Katherine. "Go on."

Katherine sat down on Luella's bed and slipped each shoe on gingerly. She stood up again, making sure her posture was perfectly straight, and took a deep breath. "So?"

"Unbelievable. I feel like I'm standing next to Julia Roberts. And I'm her ugly cousin."

Katherine laughed aloud and then sucked her breath in. "Oh, apparently, no laughing in this dress. I might split it down the side. Jeez, Luella was skinny."

"Hard to believe anyone could be thinner than you."

"I could say the same."

"You *have* to take that dress, Kitty. It was made for you."

"Only if you take the Audrey Hepburn—gloves, pearls, heels, and all!" Katherine arched an eyebrow.

"Okay, you twisted my arm."

"Now let's see the midnight blue number on."

"You're relentless."

"Not the first time I've been told that."

"Shocking." Laney struggled to unclasp the pearl choker. "Can you help me out here?"

"I still can't believe Luella didn't put any of this jewelry in a safety-deposit box. It's like a thief's dream come true." Katherine unhooked the necklace in one fluid movement.

"I know. Can you imagine if she'd let us in here when we were kids?" Laney arranged the pearls carefully in their case, snapping them in securely.

"No. Though I probably wouldn't have appreciated it back then."

"True." Laney put the velvet case back in its place with the other pearl necklaces, took off the black shift dress and gloves, and stepped into the gown Katherine had selected for her. "Zip me up."

Katherine obliged. "Done." And then stepped back. "Oh yes. *That*, my friend, is the one," she practically squealed, clapping her hands together.

"It does look nice on me." Laney smiled, catching herself in the mirror at every angle. "Not as good as the white on you, but I'll take it. Thanks."

"You're welcome. Honestly, though, you'd look fantastic in any of them."

Laney took one last look in the mirror before Katherine unzipped her. "So, what happened to you last night? You skipped out without saying good-bye."

"Not exactly." Katherine undressed next to Laney, returning the gown to its garment bag and the shoes to their resting place. Then slipped back into her own clothes, and sat down again to start rolling belts. "I did come to find you in the kitchen, but you were engrossed in an interesting conversation with Michelle. One I didn't particularly think I should interrupt."

"Oh, that."

"Yeah, that."

"How much did you hear?"

"Something about me being sentimental while I'm here and then heading back to my bigwig job. And, of course, there was the fabulous bit about Grant loving Kitty, not Katherine."

"Right." Laney shifted from one foot to the other, squirming a little. Obviously, that conversation had not been intended for Katherine's ears, but Laney had nothing to hide. She hadn't said anything to Michelle she wouldn't have said directly to Katherine's face. "You can't blame Michelle for being wary."

"Well, as you said, I live in New York now, so she has nothing to worry about."

"Is that the only reason?"

"You tell me. You seem to have it all figured out. Apparently, I am not the woman Grant was once in love with."

"Well, are you?"

"In some ways, no."

"Okay, then. That was all I was saying."

"It doesn't mean I still don't have some of the same qualities." Katherine reached for a small black satin box and instinctively cracked the lid. "Oh. My. God. You have to see this!" She waved Laney over.

"Holy shit!" Laney knelt down next to Katherine, her mouth hanging open. "That's some fucking rock."

"More like a boulder." Katherine freed the hefty ruby ring from its slot and slipped it onto her left ring finger, even though she knew it wasn't Luella's engagement ring. *That* she'd worn every day, and it had most definitely been diamond. "The center stone can't be less than six carats. Seven, with the smaller rubies flanking it."

"Wowza!" Laney looked down at her own ring finger, which was still sporting the same one-carat diamond solitaire Rick had bought her when they were just kids. Twenty-two-year-old kids, but still. Rick had been working for another construction group at the time, well before starting his own company, and the pay had been negligible, to say the least, scarcely above minimum wage. Fortunately, Laney's parents had been able to take them in until they'd saved enough money to rent a small one-bedroom condo on the outskirts of town. Those first years had been dicey, with Laney unable to contribute a second income and Rick unable to offer much help with Gemma.

"Hey, at least you have a ring." Katherine slid the ruby off her finger, leaving it familiarly bare.

"You could have had one too." Laney bowed her head, instantly regretting that she might have said too much.

"From whom?" Katherine laughed.

"Grant." Laney's expression was stone-cold sober, and she watched as Katherine's sobered too.

"What do you mean?"

"Forget it. I shouldn't have said anything."

"Are you kidding? Now you have to tell me."

Laney took a deep breath through her nose and exhaled out her mouth. "He was going to propose."

Laney eyed Katherine attentively as the look on her face morphed from controlled confusion to uninhibited astonishment. She'd always assumed that somewhere, deep down, Katherine had known. But by the authenticity of her reaction, Laney gathered that was not the case. Not even a little.

"When?" Katherine shook her head incredulously.

"Before you left. He had the ring and everything." She paused. "I think he still does."

"I never . . . no one . . ." Katherine sat paralyzed, unable to formulate a cohesive sentence. And then she did something neither of them had expected. She started to cry.

August 1999

Kitty

t's been a strange week in Nantucket. When Laney first suggested these plans almost a year ago, it sounded like a revolutionary idea. Then she took it one step further and convinced my dad, the Drakes, and her boyfriend Rick's parents to kick in and rent us a small but clean house—a short bike ride from the beach—as our graduation gifts. Seven days of unadulterated sunshine, succulent lobsters, best friends, significant others, and cocktails from noon to night. The icing on the cake: not a single "real adult" in sight. Definitely a suitable springboard into an era promising work, responsibility, and financial independence. Our final free week, as we came to refer to it, became the light at the end of a long, convoluted tunnel congested with tests, papers, job applications, and, ultimately, packing up our lives of four years to dive head-, and empty wallets-, first into the big, bad world of uncertainty. Grant graduated last year, so

it wasn't quite the same for him, but he never had a last hoo-
rah and he, too, was planning to leave his father's shipping
company—eventually—and strike out on his own, so we
were all pretty excited.

As the vacation approached, I started feeling a little
stressed-out. None of my job applications had been met
with offers of employment, and while Jane said I could keep
my internship at Blend, the stipend wasn't nearly enough to
support myself in New York City, even with Laney as a
roommate. Of course, Laney didn't share my anxiety. For
one, her parents are able and willing to subsidize her rent,
bills, and lifestyle expenses to a certain extent. Same goes
for Grant, to a lesser extent. They're old-fashioned that way.
And then there's also the fact that Laney still thinks we can
move to Manhattan, find a "fab pad"—her words, not
mine—land well-paying, glamorous jobs, and live happily
ever after with the wave of her magic wand. It's a combination of ignorance and invincibility, for which Luella holds
the Drakes responsible. Fortunately, I do not live with my
head in the clouds, nor does my dad. He's firm in his convic-
tion that relocating to the city without a means of income is
not only a stupid plan, but also an unrealistic one at that.
Most likely because he saw what happened with my mom.
If he hadn't saved the day, she'd probably have had to move
back home to Iowa. Or she could have become a big-time
movie star, playing Tom Cruise's love interest in major motion pictures. It's really a toss-up.

Anyway, maybe it's got something to do with my stress
or the fact that Laney's been sick to her stomach the whole
week, puking daily, but the whole dynamic has been tense.
Rick, as it turns out, is everything Laney said he was—cute,
nice, and smart. I'd met him only once before, briefly, when
I was home for Thanksgiving break, but he really is great,

especially for Laney. Unfortunately, most of his time in Nantucket has been spent playing Florence Nightingale, and when he's not doing that, he and Grant are usually out on the deck, drinking beers and shooting the shit—whatever that entails. Laney has been somewhat grouchy. I can't blame her. Out of all of us, she was the one who romanticized the trip the most. And while Grant and I have had a lot of alone time together, it hasn't been exactly the way it used to be. I really can't explain why. He keeps saying how much I've changed, like it's a bad thing. I haven't mentioned as much, but I think *not* changing at all over the course of four years might be worse. Not that Grant needs to change. He's perfect the way he is. Sometimes I just feel like he doesn't fully understand me anymore. Even though we've been dating for what seems like forever, the times we have been able to spend together over school holidays haven't been enough to nourish the relationship. We've always had the summer months to get things back on track, although we haven't actually acknowledged that, but it's worked.

This final summer, though, things have been slightly, well, awkward, which I feel weird even saying. I mean, he's Grant. My Grant. When we were home and he was working every day, we'd see each other only in the evenings, and everything was fine. Being together all day, every day, is different. Honestly, he's getting on my nerves a little—mostly insignificant things like the way he consumes half a sandwich in one bite and then has to chew with his mouth slightly open in order to break the huge wad into digestible pieces.

There are also a few bigger things. Like the issue of moving to New York. Grant keeps insisting he wants to be together forever, more so than usual, but he refuses to commit to leaving his dad's company, which is inconveniently located in Vermont. I guess he's making good money and feels like he needs to save up, which is fine—great, actually. I keep telling him he has time to do that, since Laney and I aren't planning to leave until the fall, but every time I try to nail him down on a long-term plan, he changes the subject. It kind of feels like he doesn't want to go. Either that or he's just being wishy-washy. Come to think of it, Grant never really has an opinion on anything—what we're going to do, where we're going to eat, what show we should watch. He always defers to me. Always. I know that seems like a silly gripe. Like, who wouldn't want someone so affable? But, truthfully, I don't want to make every decision in our lives all the time. Also, he's pretty content doing nothing. Sometimes I think he could sit in front of the TV or lie by the pool indefinitely. I need to be going, doing, experiencing, and learning. I think that's part of what he means when he says I've changed.

So now here we are. It's Saturday, and I'm guessing this free week hasn't lived up to anyone's original projections. I have to go back to Manchester today, since Hazel is throwing a little birthday dinner for my dad. Laney, Grant, and Rick are going to stay the final night. Laney is committed to one healthy, or at least non-throwing-up, day on the beach. At first I was kind of disappointed that Grant couldn't come home with me for my dad's party, but he's got to close up the house, and it's his name on the rental car, since Rick is going back to Boston, where his family lives. I'm not entirely sure what's going to happen with Laney and Rick. It's obvious they're in love, but Laney hasn't mentioned inviting Rick to New York with us as of yet. I think she's afraid to admit, even to me, that she found someone she might actually want to be with in the long term. Naturally, Rick wasn't part of her master plan. Though—as she's reminded me repeatedly—neither was Grant.

"We have to go, or I'm going to miss my ferry," I called up the steps to where Grant was getting dressed. He insisted on taking the ferry ride with me to ensure that I catch the right bus from Hyannis back to Vermont.

"Do we have any more ginger ale?" Instead of Grant, Laney appeared at the top of the staircase, gripping the railing as she walked very slowly down the steps. Her typically sun-kissed skin was an unflattering shade of green, and I noticed that she was still wearing the same pink cotton robe she'd had on for the last two days. She's actually been a reasonably good sport about being sick, which is unlike her. I'd have been more than moderately grouchy in her shoes. That's the thing about Laney: every now and then she does surprise you, in a good way. Or it could be Rick's influence.

"Let me look." I opened the refrigerator, pulled a can from the top shelf, and then reached into the cabinet above the sink for a tall glass. I filled it with ice, tipped the soda in, and rushed over to help Laney to the couch. "Oh, sweetie. You really don't look good."

"Thanks." She smiled feebly and sat down, allowing me to prop some pillows behind her back so she could sip the ginger ale from an incline. "I don't know what this is, but it's a stubborn fucking bug. I'll tell you that."

"No kidding. I think you need to see a doctor." I leaned over the back of the couch to check the stairs, anxious for Grant to materialize. "I know you don't like doctors, but can we agree it's time?"

"Rick already found a guy who can see me today. Someone his dad knows who practices here in the summer." Laney's eyes were bloodshot and her blond curls were matted against her forehead, which was glistening with sweat.

"Good. I'm really glad to hear that." I pushed her hair out of her face. "I'll see you tomorrow, okay? Rest, relax, and know that I love you."

"You ready to go?" Grant emerged from behind us with my suitcase in tow.

"Ready as I'll ever be." I kissed Laney on the cheek and stood to leave, but she grabbed my arm with what little energy she had before I could walk away.

"As soon as I feel better, we're going to nail down our master plan, right?"

"You got it." I nodded definitively. We'd still have to find jobs and an apartment we could afford, but Laney wasn't in the mind-set for straight talk, not that she ever is. "Say good-bye to Rick for me. And tell him he has my stamp of approval, okay?"

"I will." She grinned faintly. "He'll like that."

Grant and I didn't talk much on the ferry ride, in part because I was feeling a little nauseous, but also because he knows I'm waiting for him to make a decision about New York, and every time he alludes to anything in the future—even something as simple as telling me he loves me—we end up bickering about his lack of dedication to the master plan. I'll say something like, "You have to make a choice one way or another." And he'll say something like, "I don't understand what the rush is. Why does this ridiculous master plan have to commence so soon?" And then I'll reply, "It's *not* ridiculous." Even though it kind of is. And then he'll say, "Well, it's not *my* master plan and it never was." I knew the whole thing was liable to rear its ugly head again at some point, so I figured it was better not to waste the beautiful ferry ride squabbling.

"This is me." I motioned toward the Greyhound bus,

from which I could already smell the faint stench of body odor and fast food emanating.

"I'll see you tomorrow, okay?" He held my face in the palms of his hands and looked at me with such pure adoration in his eyes, it made me feel guilty. "I love you, Kitty. More than anything."

"I love you too." I stood on my tippy toes to kiss him properly. "We'll figure everything out when you get home?" I couldn't help myself. The least he could do was commit to committing.

"Kitty," he sighed, and his hands dropped to his sides. "Do we have to do this now?"

"Do what?" I hated having to nag, but what choice did I have? My father didn't have a job ready and waiting for me, nor was he willing to support me, unemployed, indefinitely.

"You know what I'm talking about. I just want to have one moment with you where we're not planning everything out. Relax. No matter what happens, we're in it together. Forever. Okay?"

"I guess." I forced a smile, let him kiss me again, and boarded the bus.

Sunday morning after the party, I came downstairs around ten thirty—much later than I typically sleep—to find my dad practically bursting to tell me that Jane Sachs had called with a job offer, a full-time staff position at Blend with a real salary, albeit minimal, *and* health insurance. For whatever reason, the words *health insurance* are like liquid gold to most parents, my father included. Jane might as well have phoned to announce that Barbra Streisand was on her way to Manchester to marry him.

Job offer aside, apparently Jane charmed the pants off my dad, which isn't saying much, because Jane could charm the

pants off a plant. Fortunately, Hazel—who was still cleaning up from the birthday dinner—seemed to find the whole
thing adorable. In fact, when my dad recounted the entire
conversation, word for word and breath for breath, she
stood at the sink, giggling like a schoolgirl cooing over her
first crush. As expected, Hazel outdid herself last night. It
was a small group—just ten of us—me, my dad, Hazel, Luella, and three other couples they're friends with. Hazel
erected a long folding table in the backyard, draped it in a
gauzy gold cloth, and placed flickering votive candles down
the center, from one end to the other. She set out their fine
china—cream-colored plates with a hairline gold trim to
complement the linens—and heavy crystal wineglasses. The
feast itself was a stunning salute to all of my dad's favorite
dishes, anointed with Hazel's gourmet touch. There were
tarts and quiches, even pigs in blankets, which I'm pretty
sure are not standard fare at the dinners Luella normally
attends. For the main course, Hazel prepared a prime rib so
tender, you could cut it with a spoon. When it came time for
dessert, she revealed a four-tier birthday cake she'd baked
herself, with a homemade raspberry jam filling. Every guest
cleaned their plate, and we must have emptied a bottle of
wine per person. Thus the late-morning arousal.

As luck would have it, my dad, who was still beaming
from the spectacular evening—and, in small part, the conversation with Jane—had the smarts to tell her that I was
out for a run, rather than recovering from a hangover. Little
does Jane know, I do not run.

"You're going to call her back *immediately*, right?" He regarded me anxiously, proffering a Post-it note with a series
of numbers scribbled in his chicken-scratch handwriting.
"She said she needs to hear from you as soon as possible. I
think the job starts tomorrow."

"*What?*" Now I was really awake. "That can't be right. Obviously, she doesn't expect me to move to New York overnight." I shook my head disbelievingly. On the one hand, it sounded preposterous. On the other hand, it sounded exactly like what little I knew of Jane and, with that in mind, my body quivered in anticipation.

"Oh, and Luella called too. She said she wanted to see you as soon as you were up. I told her you were sleeping, if that's okay." I glanced at my dad, who was already beset with pride at the mere notion that someone in New York City had called to hire his daughter. His little Kitty Kat. And to offer health insurance.

"Yeah, that's fine. I'll just go get dressed." Honestly, I was still trying to process the news. "Do you think Luella knows about this?" After all, she had gotten me the internship in the first place. She and Jane were old friends, even though they didn't keep up with each other regularly.

"She didn't say."

"Okay, let me go talk to her and then I'll call Jane." Before he could protest, I added, "Don't worry, Dad. I'll be back within an hour."

Ten minutes later, I was sitting at Luella's kitchen table in front of a glass of chilled iced tea and a plate of blueberry scones.

"So?" She sat down across from me and pinched a crumb off one of the scones.

"I guess you know."

"If you're talking about the job offer, then yes." She nodded soberly.

"My dad said he thinks it would start tomorrow." I waited for a reaction to register on her face, but it didn't. "That's kind of fast. Don't you think?"

"I suppose." She filled her own glass with iced tea.

"I mean, I don't even have a place to live. And I haven't packed anything."

"Kitty, I have an apartment in Manhattan."

"Really?"

"I used to stay there when I went to the city for theater and such. I rented it out for years, but that was more of a headache than it was worth, so now it mainly sits there. You could live in it until you find a place of your own."

"That's a very generous offer, but you've done so much already. I couldn't impose anymore." *Not to mention that I can't move to New York by myself tomorrow!*

"Nonsense. It won't be forever. Just until you get on your feet. It would be my pleasure."

"What about Grant? And Laney?"

"What about them?"

"I'm supposed to move there with them in the fall, or at least Laney, once she has a job." Maybe this would finally be the kick in the pants Grant needed. "We were going to start figuring everything out this week."

"Then she'll follow you as soon as she's made arrangements, as will Grant."

"So you think I should consider going?"

"Do you really want to hear my opinion?" She arched an eyebrow.

"Yeah." *Not sure.*

"Yes, Kitty. I think you should go. It's a once-in-a-lifetime chance to work for Jane Sachs. She has the power to open doors for you that you never even knew existed. If you let this opportunity pass you by, someone else won't, and I worry you'll regret it." She cleared her throat. "Kitty, as you know, you are like a daughter to me, but you are not my daughter. You're an adult. You don't have to do this. You wanted my opinion, and now you have it. Go home and talk to your father. I suspect he'll give you the same advice."

Not surprisingly, Luella was right. My dad was equally adamant about my moving to New York and taking the job at Blend. After my chat with Jane, I have to say I was pretty convinced myself. She explained that it's an entry-level position in marketing, as an assistant to one of the executives—apparently his assistant's mother died suddenly, and she had to go back to California for an undetermined amount of time, so she e-mailed her resignation on Saturday morning, thereby opening up the slot for me. No, the irony of the abruptly dead mom was not lost on me. Jane also conveyed that while the pay isn't great to start and the hours will be long, that there's ample room to grow and climb the ladder of corporate success. "All in due time," she said, concluding with, "I have high hopes for you, Kitty. Very high hopes." Which sealed the deal. Now I just have to tell Laney and Grant. Laney first, since Grant is fly-fishing with his dad until early afternoon, and my dad said we have to leave no later than five p.m. if we're going to make it to New York with enough time to get me settled in, or as settled in as one can be with such little notice. The whole scenario is simultaneously exhilarating and terrifying, and I'm really not sure how Laney and Grant are going to react.

When I got to the Drakes' house, Carol directed me up to Laney's bedroom, where I found her tucked under the covers, her face still awash in an unflattering avocado hue. She sat up a little and tried to smile.

"Jesus Christ, you still look like crap." I stood at the foot of her bed for fear of contracting whatever she had. Normally, I'd have curled up next to her, but in light of recent developments, I couldn't risk getting sick. "I'd ask how you're feeling, but I think I know the answer." She nodded mutely. "So, I know this may not be the best time, but I have to tell you something. Good news, actually. I think."

"Okay," she croaked, looking dubious.

"I got a job." Her eyes widened. "In New York." And then narrowed. "It starts tomorrow."

"Yeah, right." She laughed. "Are you trying to kill me?"

"I'm serious. A full-time position opened up at the place I was interning. The pay isn't great, but it's enough for now. And I can stay at this apartment Luella apparently has on the Upper East Side. You know, until you can move and we can find a place together."

"I hate to burst your bubble, but I think it might have to wait."

So much for congratulations.

"What do you mean?"

"Well, it turns out I have a little news of my own."

"Okay . . ." I couldn't really imagine why Laney's news would affect my job, but Laney does tend to think that anything going on in her life indelibly impacts everyone else's.

"I'm not sick." She exhaled. "I'm pregnant."

"*What*?" Now was not the time for practical jokes, though from the solemn expression on her face, it didn't seem like she was kidding.

"Yup. Confirmed by the doctor in Nantucket. And about a dozen home tests."

"What are you going to do?" I couldn't think of anything else to say. Part of me knew I should go to her, hug her, hold her, tell her it was going to be okay, but all I could do was stand there in shock.

"I'm going to keep it."

"Are you serious?" She couldn't be. I mean, it's not that I like the idea of having an abortion, but I'm pretty sure—no, *certain*—that I would not want a baby out of wedlock at twenty-two years old. "What about the master plan?" It was probably a stupid thing to say.

"It'll just have to wait," she bristled. "Like, a year or so. Aren't you happy for me?"

"Of course." *Not really.* "Who else knows about this?"

"Rick, obviously, Grant, and my parents."

"And what do they think?"

"They think I need to be supported, not judged."

"I'm sorry, Lane. It's just a lot to take in." Then my mind turned back to my job. "So, what? Are you still going to move to New York? With the baby?"

"Probably. I'll have to stay here for at least a year so my mom can help with stuff. And Rick's going to move in until we can rent a place of our own. But I figure you and I can work it all out. Maybe you can get a job in Manchester in the meantime?"

"Lane, I already accepted the job in New York. I have to leave later today."

"Well, call them and tell them you changed your mind. Are you following here, Kitty? I'm going to have a baby."

"No, I know. It's just. I mean. This is a really big opportunity for me. I need a job badly, and positions like this don't open up every day. I can't put my whole life on hold."

"I'm not asking you to put your *whole* life on hold. I'm just asking you to delay it for a year. Maybe eighteen months."

"Don't you think you're being a little selfish?" Possibly another wrong thing to say, especially to someone with high levels of hormones pumping through her veins.

"Excuse me? You think *I'm* being selfish? Don't you think *you're* being selfish? It's always about you, Kitty."

"What's that supposed to mean?" I was instantly stung,

namely because I was under the reverse impression that everything is always about Laney.

"Well, let's see, now." Her tone was suddenly acerbic. "First it was about *you* going to NYU, when we'd all planned to go to UVM. Then it was about *you* never having time for anyone. For years. And about *you* coming home for holidays and getting the hell out of Dodge as fast as you possibly could. Every fucking time. Now it's about *you* getting a fancy fucking job at some cosmetics company in New York and *you* leaving again. It was supposed to be about *us*, Kitty, but instead it's YOU, YOU, YOU!"

"Laney, relax." Her cheeks were flushed a rich crimson, and my heart was beating faster than a speeding bullet, minus the superpowers, which might have come in handy for a quick disappearing act. "It's not like I'm never coming back. I'll visit as often as I can, and we can resume the master plan as soon as things are settled for you and the baby." *The baby. Wow.*

"You know what, Kitty? Just forget it."

"I don't want to just forget it, Laney. I want to make this okay."

"Oh yeah? What does Grant think of your little agenda?" Her mouth was spread in a tight, thin line. "You just planning to discard him too? I thought you were going to be together forever."

"I'm not discarding anyone." My eyes pooled with tears. I thought she might be a little annoyed that I was leaving so abruptly, but I never expected this reaction.

"You know Grant's never moving to New York, right?"

"That's not true! We just haven't ironed out the details yet."

"Keep telling yourself that, Kitty. My dad's going to give him a promotion. He'll never leave Manchester."

"I don't understand why you're so angry."

"Because I'm fed up. Fed up with your antics. And fed up with you."

"But we're best friends."

"No—we *were* best friends. Or wait—sisters, right? Isn't that what we always said? Would you abandon your pregnant sister?"

"But I'm not abandoning you!"

"Just go, Kitty."

"No. I'm not leaving until we work this out."

"Obviously, you've made your decision. You're going to New York when? Today?"

"Yeah." I hunched my head, unable to look her in the eyes.

"You're a bitch."

"Laney!" Tears were pummeling down my cheeks now. No one had ever directed that word at me. "You don't mean that." I tried to catch my breath amid erratic sobs.

"Yes, I do. You're a bitch, Kitty. Just like your mother was."

I staggered backward, as if physically wounded by Laney's verbal assault, and then ran from her bedroom, down the stairs, past Carol Drake, and out their front door. I walked aimlessly around our neighborhood, vacillating between untainted rage and a pressing desire to race back to Laney and tell her I'd stay. By the time I got home, my dad was waiting for me, worried.

"Carol Drake called. She said you were hysterical when you left their house." He looked at my mottled face and pulled me into a warm embrace. "Do you want to tell me what happened?" I shook my head vigorously against his chest. I couldn't even repeat Laney's words aloud, much less to my dad. "Grant called too. He sounded really upset. He said he's coming home early."

"Let's go now." I pulled away. "I want to go now."

"Where?"

"To New York."

"What's the rush, sweetheart? Don't you want see Grant before we leave?"

"I need to get out of here. I'll go finishing packing."

"Kitty . . ."

I shook my head again. "I'm ready."

Present Day

Katherine

Katherine tapped her heavy gold Montblanc pen—the one she'd received as a five-year anniversary gift from the company—on her desk and stared distractedly at her computer screen, the dense paragraphs of a legal document muddling into blobs of gibberish. It had been a grueling week of meetings, events, conference calls, and generally playing catch-up. It was hard to believe she'd been out of the office only for a few days. Somehow, her short trip to Vermont had felt more like a time warp, transporting her back to a different era. An era when things weren't nearly as intense.

Not that her week with Laney had been altogether relaxing, but—at the very least—it had detached her from the daily grind and reminded her that there was a whole world of people out there who did not wake up at six a.m. and check their voice mails before brushing their teeth. Or shun egg yokes. Or wear designer platforms to walk their dog. Or attend more than one gala in an evening. And those same people probably greeted each other with one kiss, *on* the cheek, rather than blowing three in the air, as if they were French. It was easy to lose sight of normality when your life was like Katherine's.

Work aside, there was the all-consuming bomb Laney had dropped right before Katherine returned to New York, rendering it nearly impossible for her to concentrate on anything else. Nearly. After all, Katherine had the willpower to overcome even the most obstinate, all-consuming bombs, and there had been a handful over the years, though none of the personal variety. There'd been the time that, at the eleventh hour, one of Blend's partners in China had decided to pull out of a deal, which would have created a domino effect so widespread that millions of dollars would have been lost. Katherine had, without hesitation, walked out of her office with nothing more than her purse, gone directly to JFK, paid top dollar for a first-class ticket to the Far East, and had—in typical fashion—saved the day. Three years later, when the head of public relations had sent out a press release with Jane's name spelled incorrectly—Saks, as in the department store, rather than Sachs—and three different major magazines had supposedly gone to print, Katherine had flown in quick succession from Illinois to Minnesota and then on to Kentucky, where their printing presses resided, to make sure, with her own two eyes, that the error was rectified.

Those were the sorts of all-consuming bombs that Katherine was accustomed to handling, and she always did so with her trademark flair and good sense. This news about Grant was different. Immediately after Laney had told her, she'd lost it, causing Laney to panic a little. For one, Laney had never been—and apparently still wasn't—terribly good about knowing what to do when people got hysterical. There was also the fact that Laney realized it might not have been her place to say anything. Katherine had pulled herself together in short order. Mainly because she was embarrassed by her outburst, but beyond that, she didn't want Laney to feel like she had to console her. They weren't there yet. And Katherine didn't like making other people feel uncomfortable, because that only served to make her uncomfortable.

She'd spent the car ride back to New York cross-examining herself. Had there been signs that Grant intended to propose? Why had she been so oblivious? How could she have been so rash as to walk out on someone who was so obviously devoted to her, just because he couldn't relocate his life at a moment's notice? Who did she think she was to expect that? And so on and so on. Her emotions had pingponged from regret to resentment to rage, and then back to regret. But did she regret it—leaving? What if she'd ended up as dissatisfied with her life in Vermont as her mother had once been?

Katherine had been so drained by the time she'd finally reached her apartment that all she'd been able to do was crawl into bed, assume the fetal position, and go to sleep. The following morning, she'd been a little disoriented, expecting to smell the familiar aroma of pancakes and maple syrup wafting into her room from the hotel hallway. Before long, though, she'd snapped right back into her usual routine. She'd run on the treadmill while scanning e-mails on her iPhone. She'd done her hair and makeup while editing a consumer report. And she'd slipped into one of her best suits and her highest pair of heels while reminding herself of Jane's mantra: *I always wear my most flattering outfit on my shittiest day.* Then she'd jumped into a taxicab and headed to the office, where she'd been certain that distracting herself from thoughts of Grant would be a piece of cake.

Not so much. Every time a man had walked past her, even if it was only Nick from the mailroom, she thought it was Grant. Every time Brooke had stepped in to tell her there was a call for her, Katherine had irrationally found herself hoping it was Grant on the line. And at night, when she'd finally come home to her empty apartment, after a full day at the office followed by a cocktail party or two, it'd been unbearable to try to keep her mind off of him. She'd lie awake for hours, trying to recall exactly the way he'd looked, even smelled, that night at Carol's house. She'd replayed every nuance of their conversation, searching for meaning where there was none. Ultimately, she'd found herself in a purgatory of sorts, on the precipice of sleep, caught between the past and the present, unable to let herself dream, for fear she'd awake to a less-desirable reality. Had Grant planned how he was going to propose? What would that have been like? She'd never had a story like most women, a story to wear as a badge of honor no matter how loveless their marriages were now. Those were the thoughts that bounced around Katherine's head and, regardless of how hard she'd tried to quiet them, she couldn't.

She'd wanted to pick up the phone so many times and call him, if only to hear his voice. But what would she say? What could she say? *I miss you. I want to be with you. I think I still love you.* She didn't even know herself. Either way, this was a conversation they needed to have in person, and possibly the only thing that had kept her going was knowing that she'd see him again over the weekend.

Of course, there was also the matter of Laney. She'd softened somewhat throughout the course of the week, no doubt. But she was still angry. And while Katherine couldn't quite understand why her anger hadn't waned at least a little in over a decade, she did know one thing. She wanted to fix it. Not just because it needed fixing, which, under normal circumstances, would have been reason enough for Katherine, but because she wanted her friend back. More precisely, she wanted her sister back, even if she had to take all the blame.

"Eh-hem."

Katherine looked up from her laptop to find Jane Sachs standing in front of her, resplendent in a royal blue St. John suit paired with four-inch, nude patent leather Manolo Blahniks, her expertly painted face an advertisement for the company she helmed, if only as a figurehead at this point.

"Hello, darling." Jane smiled. "It's nice to have you back." Jane hadn't been in all week; she rarely made an appearance at the office even that often. She preferred to work from home, her lavish duplex in the Upper West Side's exclusive Dakota, a building mainly recognized post–December 8, 1980, as the location of John Lennon's murder, a tragedy that had only increased the value of the real estate.

"Jane, how are you?" Katherine jumped up from behind her desk and walked toward her boss, expecting three air kisses, but instead she got a hug. Jane didn't really do hugs, at least not until now.

"I ought to ask you that." She sat down in one of Katherine's purple leather club chairs and motioned for Katherine to return to her own desk chair. "I was so sorry to miss Luella's funeral."

"Well, you didn't miss much. She wanted to be cremated. She told her lawyer absolutely no funeral. She didn't even want a reception."

"That makes sense."

"I thought so too."

"And you're okay?"

"I am. It's sad. I mean, she really was the closest thing I had to a mother, but I know she lived a great life."

"Do me a favor?"

"Anything."

"Don't say that about me when I'm gone."

"Okay." Katherine laughed.

"Well, listen. I have to run. Lunch at Bergdorf with Aerin Lauder, but I wanted to personally thank you for handling that issue with Marcus Wallaby with such skill, especially while you were in Vermont. He's a tough bastard, and I hear you made him very happy. This, my dear, is why I hired you all those years ago."

"Oh, right. Absolutely." Katherine nodded. She'd forgotten about the Marcus Wallaby situation completely. Marcus Wallaby was a major investor in Blend, and Brooke had reminded her multiple times that he needed attention, but somehow, it had still managed to slip her mind. And Katherine never allowed anything to slip her mind, unless it was a meal.

"All right, then. I'm off." Jane tossed a kiss in Katherine's general vicinity. "We'll talk next week."

As soon as Jane was out of sight and earshot, Katherine buzzed Brooke. "Can you please come in for a minute?" Brooke materialized almost instantly. "Do you know what happened with Marcus Wallaby?"

"Tom Birnbaum said he'd handle it." Brooke looked nervous.

"I see." Katherine exhaled. "Can you tell him to come up?"

"Sure thing."

"Oh, and Brooke, I know I've been distracted this week, but I wanted to thank you."

"For what?"

"You handled things very well in my absence, and it didn't go unnoticed. Well done."

"Thanks!" Brooke beamed and her chest puffed just a little. "I'll go get Tom."

Ten minutes later, Tom appeared in her doorway, wearing a sheepish expression. "Katherine, I'm really sorry. Brooke couldn't reach you, and she asked me what to do. And it was Marcus Wall—"

"Tom, relax. I'm not upset." She smiled and pointed to a chair. "Quite the contrary. I owe you a heap of gratitude. You saved my ass."

"Oh, thank you. Man, I never thought I'd hear you say that." He giggled almost manically. "That guy's a lunatic."

"No kidding." Katherine leaned forward, resting her elbows on her desk. "So, tell me: how is Judy doing?"

"Great!"

"Really? Isn't she still on bed rest?"

"Katherine, I swear to you, a couple of weeks at home and she's a changed woman."

"What do you mean?" Katherine had known Judy for ten years, even before she married Tom, and *changed woman* was not a phrase she ever expected to hear in reference to her.

"So, I guess her mom bought her all of these baby books and magazines to keep her occupied. And she's been going online. Honestly, I don't think she even had the chance to realize she was pregnant until now. Anyway, all of a sudden she's completely obsessed with ordering clothing and toys, and designing the nursery. She thinks she's going to *build* the crib, Katherine."

"Are they hard to put together?" Katherine had never assembled anything, much less a crib. "Judy is pretty capable."

"As if! She actually wants to *build it*. Like, from *scratch*. She said all the cribs on the market are death traps, and she'll be damned if our little bundle of joy has to sleep in one of those generic pieces of shit. Sorry, just parroting her."

"Okay. Isn't it a little late for that?"

"Apparently, the baby sleeps in a bassinet for a while, and of course Judy thinks she'll be in Bob Vila shape roughly a week after giving birth."

"Have you tried to discourage the idea?"

"At this point, I'm not discouraging anything. Judy also said she's going to take her three-month maternity leave and an extra three months of unpaid leave. Then she'll see how she feels."

"See how she feels about what?" It was all a little shocking to Katherine. She couldn't even begin to imagine Tom's bewilderment.

"About going back to work!" Tom flailed his arms in the air. "It's crazy, I know!"

Katherine wasn't sure what to say. But somehow learning of Judy's about-face was making her yearn for a place where designing nurseries and taking maternity leave were not considered taboo.

"Go home, Tom." Katherine closed her laptop, slung her Birkin bag onto her arm, and stood to leave.

"What?"

"You heard me. Go spend time with your wife. It's Friday."

"It's also noon."

"And?"

"And nothing."

"Get out of here before I change my mind." Katherine smiled. "It's time for both of us to go home."

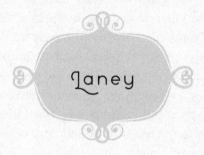

Laney

"So?" Laney trailed Katherine through Luella's house, from room to room, watching her absorb the full extent of the work that had been done.

"This is amazing." Katherine's head pivoted from left to right and right to left like a spectator at a tennis match. "I can't believe you got so much accomplished."

"Well, I can't take all the credit. The cleaning crew you hired was really thorough, and Rick's guys did the painting and fixing." Laney couldn't hide her satisfaction. Katherine was visibly impressed by her efforts, even if she hadn't done most of the physical labor. "I did finish packing up the stuff from Luella's closet that we want to sell, and I set aside a bunch of the dresses you'd expressed interest in. I was thinking maybe we'd each pick one piece of jewelry as a keepsake."

"That's a nice idea." Katherine smiled placidly. "I hope

you'll take the pearl choker. I can't imagine it looking better on anyone else."

"Thanks," Laney said, and smiled back. She'd had the week without Katherine to think about things. She'd even talked to Grant and Rick about it, which—despite her initial resistance—had helped her see things in a new light. Not that she was suddenly over it, but the wrath that had once resided in the pit of her stomach, ready to erupt at the sheer mention of Katherine's name, was gone. And, she supposed, on the heels of a lot of encouragement from Rick, the right thing to do was to talk to Katherine. She knew they could never go back to the way things had once been, but as Rick had gingerly explained to her, when you're that close to someone for such a long period of time, so much so that the person becomes more like a family member than a friend, there are bound to be disappointments, disagreements, and sometimes major fallouts. It wasn't that Laney didn't under-stand that. Of course she did. But it was harder to digest when it was you. Wasn't it always easy to look at things im-partially when it was someone else's life, someone else's hurt feelings, someone else's bitterness? How many times had she seen a show on television where two best friends, sisters even, had wanted to kill each other over something or other, and thought it was so silly that they'd get that worked up over whatever it was? She'd always rationalized that with herself and Kitty it was different. And, until now, she'd been certain that no one understood where she was coming from. That everyone—Rick, Grant, her mom, and Gemma—were all out to get her, taking Kitty's side over hers, just because.

It wasn't black and white, though. She had enough sense to realize that. There were still moments when the mere thought of Kitty leaving all those years ago tied her up in a million tight knots. "Talk to her," Rick would say. "The only way to move on, friends or not, is to talk to her." She could practically hear his words reverberating in her head.

"So, what's left?" Katherine followed Laney up the stairs to Luella's bedroom.

"You're lookin' at it." Laney pointed to a small dresser in the back of Luella's closet. "I was going to try to go through it last night, but then Gemma wanted to go see the late viewing of *He Hearts Me*, and after that my brain was dead."

"I heard it was terrible."

"You heard right. All those celebrities, and still a waste of fifteen bucks."

"For both of you?"

"Yeah, why?"

"Amazing. It's double in New York."

"And that surprises *you*?"

"I guess not. I always forget how cheap the cost of living is up here."

"It's all relative. The salaries are lower too, believe me."

"Oh, I'm sure. I didn't mean . . ."

"Don't worry about it. You didn't offend me." Laney walked toward the dresser. "Shall we?"

"Go for it." Katherine stood behind Laney while she opened each empty drawer.

"I think our work might be done here." Laney pulled at the last drawer. "This one is stuck. Let's just leave it. Rick can carry it down for us tonight. By the way, you should have seen the estate-sale lady's eyes light up when she saw all the loot."

"I'll bet." Katherine maneuvered around Laney. "Let me try that drawer. I haven't spent the last decade working out for nothing." She yanked on the handles and then yanked harder, until the drawer released a little, the momentum catapulting Katherine onto her rear end.

"Damn, you are strong." Laney knelt down next to her and peered through the crack. "It looks like there's a piece of paper taped to the back and a little plastic bag floating around." Laney tried to open the drawer farther, but ultimately settled on sticking her arm through the opening. "I can't get in there. You try. Your arms are skinnier."

Katherine wedged her arm, elbow deep, into the drawer. "Got them!" She handed the plastic bag to Laney and unfolded the piece of paper. "It's just a series of numbers. Looks like a combination to something."

"Oh. My. God."

"What?"

"It appears our sweet Luella liked the doob."

"What's the doob?"

"Weed, marijuana—whatever you want to call it." Laney held up a single, neatly rolled joint.

"That is hysterical. Although it doesn't seem like Luella."

"It's always the ones you least expect."

"Or maybe she was using it medicinally." Katherine frowned.

"Maybe." Laney searched through her purse. "Voilà!" She revealed a lighter, which looked to be about twenty years old. "I knew I'd find a use for this eventually."

"You're not going to smoke that. Are you?"

"Not by myself." Laney grinned mischievously.

"Well, I don't do drugs." Katherine shook her head disapprovingly. "Plus you don't even know what that is."

"It's a joint. What else would it be?"

"I don't know. Some weird herb."

Laney sniffed it. "Nope, weed. And it smells good." She lit it without hesitation, took a long, smooth toke, and passed it to Katherine. "Come on, don't be such a Goody Two-shoes."

"Fine." Katherine pinched the end carefully. "I'll have you know this is peer pressure at its finest."

"I'm okay with that," Laney deadpanned. "You could use a little loosening up."

"*Me*?" Katherine inhaled and then blew out a puff of smoke, coughing fitfully.

"You don't think you're uptight?"

"Maybe a little."

"A little. Right. Keep telling yourself that."

"Shut up!" Katherine passed the joint back to Laney, and they took alternating drags until it was gone.

"So, listen. I need to talk to you." Laney's eyes were glassy, and she had an insatiable urge to inhale a Big Mac and supersize fries, but her munchies would have to wait. Luella's stash was just the haze-induced courage she needed to break the ice with Katherine.

"Now?" Katherine could barely focus.

"Why? Do you have somewhere to be?" Laney giggled even though it wasn't funny.

"I don't think so." Katherine twisted up her face.

"Good. Because I'm only going to say this once." Laney took a deep breath. "I was wrong."

"About what?"

"About trying to get in the way of you moving to New York after college. For saying what I did about you and your mom. And then, you know, ignoring your calls. I'm sorry."

"No, I was wrong. I should have been there for you." Katherine looked like she was trying to make sense of her thoughts. "You were always the strong one. I know that's not an excuse. I just assumed you'd be okay. Actually, I knew you would. I wasn't so sure about myself."

"Oh, please. You were a genius. You would have been fine even if we'd never met."

"You're wrong, Laney. I don't think you realize this, but you saved my life. I could have come to Manchester and been a loser like I was in Bennington. But you saw something in me—God knows what—and you burst into my world like a bat out of hell at the very time when I needed you most. I wouldn't have survived without you." Katherine's eyes welled with tears.

"I depended on you too."

"It never seemed that way."

"Probably because I didn't want you to see it. I've been known to be stubborn."

"You?" Katherine feigned shock.

"Very funny." Laney rolled her eyes. "I should have told you that. And I should have let you go to New York without wrecking everything. I was jealous."

"Of me?" Katherine pointed at herself. "You were perfect."

"I was pregnant and stuck here. You were off to New York to steal *my* dream. Or at least that's how I saw it back then. And then I couldn't even talk to you about what I was going through. I was so angry, and it's taken me this long to realize why."

"But you have everything I don't in Rick and Gemma."

"I know. I didn't see that, though. I couldn't. I was too focused on being furious that you'd left."

"You know what's funny?"

"What?"

"I always thought you'd be the one to leave. From the minute we met, I was saddled with the fear that one day you'd realize you made a mistake. That you'd realize I wasn't best-friend material and that you could do better. But you never faltered. You were so fiercely loyal, time and time again. Still, I couldn't escape my own insecurity that you'd disappoint me eventually. The irony is that I disappointed you in the end. I disappointed everyone."

"Kitty, you have a huge career. I'd hardly say that's disappointing."

"Are you more impressed with my bank account or your daughter?"

"Come on . . ."

"No, really. I mean, does anyone that actually matters care that I have an important title and a hefty savings account? Does any of that amount to anything if I only have myself? I'm thirty-four years old. I live alone. And all I do is work."

"Believe me, I wish I had the successful career you do."

"You have a great job."

"Yeah, but I have Tina. And I fucking despise that woman."

"She really is annoying." Katherine laughed, fracturing the sober mood. "I was desperate to put her in her place on your behalf, but I figured it would piss you off."

"It would have."

"Have you ever thought about doing something on your own? Oasis seems like the only gig in town, and—from what I can gather—you run the show anyway."

"I'd love to, but in case you haven't noticed, we're not that rich."

"There must be a way. You'll have the money from the house soon, and interest rates on loans are fantastic right now."

"I've thought about it, especially when Tina goes on one of her crazy rampages. But we couldn't cut it financially, even with the inheritance. Gemma needs to go to college."

"I understand."

"Plus, it's a shitload of work to open a spa from the ground up. Tina bought Oasis when it was already a well-oiled machine." Laney shrugged. Her high was already wearing off. "I wonder if we could carry the dresser down ourselves. It doesn't seem that heavy." Laney stood up and pushed it away from the wall. "Look what we have here."

"What?" Katherine jumped up.

"A safe." Laney motioned to the piece of paper in Katherine's hands. "Let me see that."

"Maybe it's full of marijuana. What if Luella was a drug lord?" Katherine's eyes widened.

"You watch too much TV." Laney turned the dial in one direction, then back in the other, and again three more times until they heard a soft click and the door released to reveal two small black velvet boxes—one with Laney's name and the other with Kitty's, and a letter-sized white envelope, with "My Girls" on the front.

"Open the letter first." Katherine peered over Laney's shoulder.

"Thanks, Angela Lansbury." She tore at the envelope and pulled out a one-page note written in Luella's elaborate cursive.

My Dear Girls,

If you're reading this together, without attempting to strangle each other, then my work is done. I'm sure you're wondering why I went to such great lengths to reunite you. Now I can tell you.

Once upon a time, I had a friend who died too young. She'd asked me to come see her in her final days; she wanted to tell me about her illness—an inoperable brain tumor—in person. But I kept delaying the trip over and over, saying I was too busy with one thing or another. Who can even remember now? Whatever it was, it couldn't have been as important as being there for her. Even though I didn't know why she wanted to see me, not supporting her when she needed me most is one of the greatest regrets of my life. That and not going out with Gregory Peck when he asked.

Beyond that, I'm afraid it was my fault, at least in part, that the two of you fell out, as it was me who pushed Kitty to go to NYU and then again to go to New York and take the job with Jane. As Kitty knows, I always saw a great deal of myself in her, and perhaps, since I'd never had the opportunity to pursue such a dream, I didn't want her to pass it up. I should have explained that better at the time. I should have done a lot of things differently, but that's what regret and forgiveness are for. I hope you girls are able to forgive, because in all my years—and there were many of them—I've never known two people so well suited to look out for and support each other.

All right, then. Enough sappy talk for the moment. If you've found this letter, then you've also found two boxes. The one with Laney's name holds my wedding band. Wear it if you'd like or give it to Gemma one day. It represents the most wonderful time in my life. The one with Kitty's name is my engagement ring, which I hope one day— though it may not be traditional—you'll be able to use for yourself. Hint. Hint.

Oh, and one last thing. Sorry about the mess. I fired my housekeeper because I couldn't bear to let anyone watch me fade.

My final wish is that you'll each find true happiness in your lives separately and together. Every woman needs a best friend or a sister. And you were both to each other. I hope you will be again.

Much love,
always and forever,
Luella

Katherine

"**M**ornin', Kitty Kat." Katherine's father sat hunched over the kitchen table, the *New York Times* fanned out in front of him. "How'd you sleep?"

"Really well, thanks." It wasn't strictly the truth. She'd nodded off easily and happily, having received a text message from Grant just before midnight, asking if they could meet at their spot for lunch the next day. But she'd awoken at three a.m. and had been unable to fall back asleep, tossing, turning, and agonizing about what she was going to say to Grant and what he was going to say to her. Did he have an agenda? She sure as hell didn't, except to finally deliver a lengthier apology for walking out on him all those years ago.

Their chemistry had been palpable at Carol's house on Thanksgiving Day. At least it had been to her. Since then she'd questioned herself over and over until she was no longer sure of anything, not even her own intuition. Was it absurd to think she could fall back in love with someone after ten minutes of conversation twelve years too late? Or had she never fallen out of love in the first place? Conversely—and possibly more realistically—were her heightened emotions conditional? Once she went back to New York permanently, would Grant become a distant memory all over again, leaving her acute longing in Vermont, where it belonged? These were the uncertainties that had kept her alert in the middle of the night, forcing both her eyes and heart to remain open. But open to what? Grant wasn't available. And Katherine wasn't a home wrecker. If the option even existed.

There was also the not-so-small matter of finally opening up to her dad. It was time to release the burden once and for all, and she'd finally found the strength within her to do it. Perhaps it was a result of mending things with Grant and Laney, or Luella's regret over her own lost friendship, but suddenly Katherine couldn't hold it in any longer. She had to come clean, consequences notwithstanding.

"There's coffee in the pot, if you'd like." Her dad motioned toward the counter.

"Caffeinated?"

"Is there any other kind?"

"A man after my own heart." Katherine walked toward the cabinet to retrieve a mug, kissing her father on the top of his head on her way.

"It's so good to have you here, Kitty Kat. No use in staying at a fancy hotel. Chez Hill is five stars all the way."

"You've mentioned as much." Katherine laughed. "At least, oh, a million times."

"Has it been that many? I guess I'm becoming senile in my old age." He folded one section of the paper and swapped it for another.

"Listen, Dad, I need to talk to you about something important." Katherine poured herself a cup of coffee and joined her father at the table. She was wearing an old pair of pajamas from high school—festooned with pink and purple hearts—that she'd found in the bottom drawer of her bedroom dresser at four a.m. For whatever reason, Hazel liked to keep the house at 64 degrees, and Katherine had been freezing her ass off in a La Perla chemise.

"That sounds ominous." He put the newspaper down and stacked his hands on the table in front of him. "What's on your mind, Kitty Kat?"

"I don't even know how to say this, Dad." Katherine took a deep breath, preparing herself for the worst. He could be angry with her, she knew, and he had every right to be.

"Is everything okay with you? You're not sick, are you?"

"No, no. Nothing like that. It's . . ." Katherine shook her head, tilting it downward. How could she even look him in the eyes? "It's about Mom."

"Okay, what about her?"

"The day she got hit by the car . . ." Her voiced cracked and her eyes flooded with tears.

"Yeah?"

"It was my fault." Katherine lifted her head to gauge his reaction—a look of horror, no doubt—but his face was still soft and kind, albeit blanketed with concern.

"What do you mean?"

"We'd had a fight in the supermarket. She'd said I couldn't have a cookie because I was chubby, so I called her Mommy Dearest." Katherine was crying now. "She hit me. In the face. In front of everyone. And then dragged me outside by the arm. So . . . I told her I hated her."

"Kitty, calm down." He reached across the table and took her hands in his.

"She stalked off in front of me. She was so mad, Dad. And that's when it happened. It was all so fast. One minute I hated her so much. I did, Dad. I hated her. Then she was gone." Katherine sobbed, trying to catch her breath. "I'm the reason Mom died. I never told you because I was so ashamed. If you don't want to speak to me ever again, I'll understand."

Katherine's father took a long, deep breath; stood up; and walked around the table behind her, wrapping his arms around her shoulders. "I love you, Kitty. What happened to your mother was not your fault. Do you hear me? You were a child. It was not your fault. I'm just sorry you've had to shoulder the weight of this burden for so long."

"I'm so sorry, Dad." Katherine inhaled and exhaled slowly, over and over, allowing the warmth of his embrace to soothe her.

"You have nothing to be sorry about. I only wish you'd come to me."

"I couldn't. I'm sorry."

"It's okay, Kitty Kat. It's okay." He held her for another minute and then took his seat across from her again.

"You have no idea how happy I am that you don't hate me." Katherine smiled faintly, wiping her blotchy red eyes with her hands.

"I could never hate you. And, as it happens, I also have a confession to make. I've been waiting for the right moment, but I've been a bit of a chicken about it."

"Seems like a good time now." Katherine laughed unsteadily. "You're not really a woman, are you?"

"Nope. Nothing that salacious." He cleared his throat. "So, I never told you this, but I actually knew Luella before we moved to Manchester."

"Okay." It wasn't even remotely what Katherine had

imagined he'd say, not that she'd had anything in particular in mind. "Knew her how?"

"Kitty, Luella was best friends with your mother's Aunt Mary."

"What?" She'd only heard about her great-aunt Mary a few times in passing, and not since her mom had died.

"That's right. Mary lived in Iowa, in the town where your mom grew up, but she and Luella had been roommates at Mount Holyoke when they were girls and had remained best friends. When your mom moved to New York to pursue acting, Mary had asked Luella to keep an eye on her, you know, just kind of be available in case anything happened, since Luella spent so much time there."

"Right." Katherine nodded, intrigued by the wealth of unanticipated information.

"So, then your mom met me and moved to Bennington, which was even closer to Luella. As you can imagine, Mary was thrilled, because she worried about your mom. For good reason."

"What does that mean?"

"Well, Kitty Kat, your mom was a complicated woman. I'm sure you've figured that much out. These days, they'd probably have a diagnosis for it. Depression? I don't know. She was always an enigma to me—still is. Some days she was happy and light—a pure pleasure to be around. But she also struggled. Nothing drastic. I think she saw leaving New York as a failure and never really wrapped her head around the fact that being a wife and mom could be as rewarding as having a successful acting career. So, you know, with that, her being so far from home and the fact that she was always a little unpredictable, I suppose Mary felt relieved to have a trusted friend nearby."

"I see." If anyone could understand the abandoned-career

part, it was Katherine. Wouldn't she too have viewed leaving New York to become a wife and mother in Vermont a colossal failure?

"Your mother loved you, Kitty. Make no mistake about that. She didn't express it as much as she should have, and when she did it didn't always come out the right way, but she worried about you. For you. She told me often that she knew you'd make something of yourself one day. Maybe that's why she was hard on you. She wanted you to be everything she felt she wasn't."

"Maybe." Katherine sat quietly for a minute. "So did Mom and Luella ever meet in person?"

"No, we never saw Luella or anything like that. But when your mom died, Luella reached out to me and said the house next door was available. She knew about you and felt strongly that a fresh start was in order. Actually, she was pretty instrumental in our move to Manchester. I guess she figured you might need a woman to talk to from time to time. Neither of us had an expectation that you'd develop the bond you did. Believe me, the fact that she became like a second mother to you went way beyond her initial motivation of honoring a debt to an old friend."

"Okay. But I don't understand why you didn't just tell me."

"Honestly, we both thought it might make things more complex—explaining that there was this connection to your mom. In order to give you a fresh start, we felt there needed to be a totally clean slate. And the last thing I wanted was to turn you away from Luella."

"Interesting theory."

"Maybe I was wrong. Who knows? I was a man who'd just lost his wife and become a single dad. I had no idea what I was doing. All I cared about was making sure you were going to be okay."

"You did, Dad. And I am. I may not have had a mother in

the traditional sense, but I had more people who loved me than most kids do—between you and Luella and the Drakes." Katherine reached across the table and took his hands this time. "You made the right decision."

"I did the best I could."

"So, what happened to Aunt Mary? Is she still alive?"

"Sadly, no. She ended up passing away a few years later. Brain tumor. Luella was real broken up about it."

"Oh, my God. This all makes sense now."

"What makes sense?"

"Luella mentioned Mary in the letter she left me and Laney. She just didn't say who she was exactly."

"That's our Luella. Always a little mysterious."

"You said it."

"Actually your mom and Mary are buried next to each other, with your maternal grandparents."

"In Iowa." Katherine knew that much.

"Right. Mary felt strongly about it, and I wasn't really in a place to argue at the time. I even thought it might be easier for you as a kid, not having to feel like you needed to visit her grave all the time."

"Sure." Katherine exhaled. "Though it would be nice to be able to go there now."

"I see that."

"I mean, you absolutely did the right thing, Dad. It's not that. I guess it just would have been liberating to tell her . . ." Katherine trailed off.

"Tell her what?"

"That I understand." Katherine thought for a moment. "That I finally get why she left New York."

"Why's that?"

"For love. The dream is kind of empty without that. Don't you think?"

"Yes. Yes, I do." Her father stood up and walked toward her.

"Thank you, Dad." Katherine stood too and he folded her into his arms again.

"For what?"

"For everything."

"My pleasure, Kitty Kat." He squeezed her tightly. "Now, you just need to promise me you'll come visit more often."

"I promise."

Four hours later, Katherine was perched on a cement wall at Adams Park, the spot where she and Grant had made out for the sixth time. She'd counted up until the twentieth, assuming that at some point Grant would get tired of dating her and that she'd want to remember exactly how many times he'd kissed her. After breakfast with her dad, predictably the best egg-white omelet she'd ever had, courtesy of Hazel, Katherine had showered in her old bathroom, which was roughly one-third the size of her bathroom in New York and half the size of the one at the Equinox. She'd taken extra care straightening her hair and applying her makeup in a magnifying mirror she'd borrowed from Hazel, just enough to highlight her best features but not enough to appear as though she'd tried too hard. Next she'd dressed in a pair of dark skinny jeans that made her butt look extra firm and a shamrock green cashmere sweater to complement her emerald-colored eyes, not that Grant would notice or even see it under her hefty shearling coat. Still, this would be the first time in more than a decade that she and Grant would be sitting face-to-face in broad daylight for an undetermined amount of time. And even if they couldn't be together, even if she couldn't reach out and touch him as she so desperately wanted to, was it so awful to want to look her best?

"Hey, you." Grant appeared, seemingly out of nowhere,

punctuating Katherine's daydreams—same place, same players, another lifetime. She looked up, slightly startled, though not as anxious as she'd expected to be. Somehow he still had a calming effect on her.

"Hey, you." She beamed and stood to kiss him, but he pulled her into a bear hug instead.

"I think we're past the formalities. Don't you?" He smiled, revealing the dimples that had once made every girl at Manchester High School swoon—a fact that had secretly delighted Katherine, especially after they'd become an item. He sat down on the wall, and Katherine joined him. "So?"

"I think I made some headway with Laney yesterday." It was hard not to stare at him, to recall the way his nose angled slightly to the left or the way his lips were always marginally parted even when his mouth was closed; or to check to see if the three freckles next to his right ear were still there and, if so, whether or not one of them remained moon shaped.

"She told me." He ran his fingers through his auburn hair, and Katherine had to prevent herself from doing the same. "I'm glad. She's carried around a lot of angst for a long time. Some of it justified; most of it not. But you know Laney. She doesn't exactly get over things quickly."

Wasn't that the truth? Katherine could remember like it was yesterday the time their friend Lisa had asked Spencer Atkins to the eighth-grade "Under the Sea" dance after Laney had declared she was waiting for him to ask her. Laney had been livid. She'd sworn up and down that not only would she never speak to Lisa again, but she'd make sure no one else did either. Ultimately, Lisa had told Spencer to go with Laney, and Laney had forgiven her, until their falling-out at Karen Mann's sweet sixteen, which probably would not have been nearly as massive of a falling-out if not for the Spencer fiasco two years earlier. That was Laney for you—wildly loyal until you crossed her.

"I've noticed." Katherine cupped her hands over her nose and mouth and blew warm air into them.

"If you're cold, we can go someplace inside." He moved a small paper bag he'd brought with him in between them.

"I'm okay." More like frozen to the core, but she didn't want to seem high maintenance. What if Michelle loved sitting on cement walls in thirty-degree weather? Plus she knew why he'd asked to meet there. In addition to it being the site of their sixth kiss, it was also the place where he'd given her his class ring, a significant gesture for a graduating senior, especially one dating someone younger.

"Good, because I brought us lunch." He lifted two wrap sandwiches, a large container of fruit salad, and two waters out of the bag. "I'm guessing you don't stay in such good shape by eating McDonald's, so I brought a healthful selection." Katherine laughed.

"What?" Grant was suddenly self-conscious.

"Nothing. It's stupid."

"Tell me!"

"It's just that most people don't know the difference between *healthy* and *healthful*. I'm pretty sure it's one of the most common verbal and written mistakes in the English language."

"And here I thought you were going to tell me how handsome I am."

"Nah."

"Gee, thanks!"

"I think you know that already." Was he flirting with her? Was it inappropriate to flirt back? She needed to change the subject fast. "I owe you a better apology than the one from Thanksgiving." Katherine shook her head. "Wait, that

sounded ridiculous. I know any apology won't even scratch
the surface."

"Water under the bridge, Kitty."

"No one is that forgiving, Grant. Laney told me." She
couldn't even say the words.

"I know."

"How is it that you don't hate me? Seriously."

"First of all, I could never hate you." He stared into the
distance. "And, anyway, Luella came to me."

"She did?" This was news to Katherine.

"Yup. Shortly after you left, she asked to speak with me.
She explained the whole thing—how she'd pushed you to
leave. And she said that if I loved you, I'd let you spread your
wings, because if I held you back, there was a good chance
you'd end up resenting me for it. She also said that if we
were truly meant to be, then you'd come home or you'd ask
me to come to New York. But you never did." He turned toward her again. "Don't get me wrong, Kitty. I was pissed
and hurt for a long time. I half expected you to appear on
my doorstep for three years after you left, although deep
down I knew you wouldn't. Sometimes I'd think I saw you
in town and I'd even follow the person for blocks, just to
make sure it wasn't you. Or the phone would ring on the
anniversary of our first kiss, and I'd think, *Maybe that's her.* I
suppose at some point I realized I was holding on to a ghost,
and I found a way to move on."

"To Michelle."

"Not immediately. There were other women in between."

"I don't need to know."

"Good, because I'm not going to tell you." He laughed
softly. "Honestly, Kitty, I think I was mostly disappointed
that you didn't have the respect to tell me in person."

"It wasn't like that, I promise. After the fight with Laney,

I was just so raw and, not that this is any excuse, but it felt like you didn't want to move to New York, like you expected me to either stay or wait on you to decide. I didn't have the luxury of time."

"I know, but you still should have told me you were leaving. Running away wasn't the answer."

"You're right. What I did was unforgivable."

"Not unforgivable; just selfish."

"I'm sorry. I should have called you. I thought you would reach out. You were always the bigger person when it came to that kind of stuff, and then when you didn't, I felt rejected. Kind of ridiculous, since I was the one to leave. And then when Laney refused to talk to me, I guess I figured you would too."

"Laney and I weren't one in the same, although sometimes it felt like we were to you."

"I know. But it wasn't like that, honest."

"Here's the problem, Kitty." He took a deep breath and then exhaled. "Okay, I'm just going to lay it all out on the table, because at this point I can't come up with a better solution." He paused for a moment, furrowed his brow, and then continued. "I still have feelings for you. Strong feelings. I've been driving myself crazy over it these past couple of weeks. I'm in a relationship, for God's sake. And I don't know what to do, because I don't even know if you love me too. Or even if you were interested, how we could ever be together. It's nuts! You live in New York. I live in Vermont. You go to galas at the Plaza. I go to barbecues at my neighbor's house. You eat caviar. I eat meatloaf. It's stupid, right? Please tell me it's stupid."

"I can't." Katherine avoided eye contact, determined to quiet the voice in her head imploring her to kiss him. She couldn't let it happen this way. She refused to be the other

woman, despite the fact that every urge inside her was battling her better judgment.

"So what, then?"

"I don't know." She put her hand on his. "You're with
Michelle, and she seems great."

"That's the thing. She is. She's kind and devoted, and she
adores me. We've been together for a year and a half."

"Then what's wrong?"

"What's wrong?" He sighed. "What's wrong is she's not
you."

Katherine closed her eyes and let the wind beat against
her face. She'd imagined this moment more times than she
could count on both hands, and now that it had finally arrived, she couldn't do anything about it. "Grant, I can't tell
you to leave Michelle. I don't want it to be like that. You need
to make sense of your relationship with her on your own,
without me as part of the equation."

"Easier said than done." He slipped his fingers through
hers. "Just tell me one thing, Kitty. I need to know. Are you
still in love with me?"

Katherine tilted her head upward and their eyes met.
"Yes. I am." She smiled tenderly and caressed his cheek with
the back of her hand. "And, for the record, I hate caviar."

Katherine

I t had been another taxing week at the office, with only one
bright spot: a message from Grant on her answering machine every night when she got back to her apartment—
the flashing red light an antidote to her fatigued body and
even wearier spirit. They'd agreed not to speak on the phone
while she was back in New York. Katherine felt strongly
that it would marginalize his relationship with Michelle,
which wouldn't be fair to anyone. Grant had agreed, albeit
reluctantly, and much to her delight had found a loophole in
leaving her the sweetest, funniest voice mails that put a
smile on her face for the rest of the evening, no matter how
much work she'd taken home with her.

The more Katherine thought about it—and it was basically all she'd thought about in her spare time since leaving
Vermont—it was hard to believe that for the past twelve
years Grant, Laney, Carol, even her dad and Hazel had been

living their lives as she'd gone about pursuing her career at Blend like it was the one valuable thing in the world. While she'd been sitting at her desk, poring over ad copy or running meetings or traveling across the globe to secure major business deals, Laney had gotten married and raised Gemma. Her father and Hazel's symbiotic companionship had evolved into true love. And Grant—well, Katherine wouldn't dare let herself contemplate how many women he'd dated before committing to Michelle or, even worse, what their courtship had entailed.

Of course it had crossed her mind through the years that Grant could have moved on with someone else, but since she didn't know for sure, she'd allowed all of the characters from her past, including Grant, to remain just that— characters frozen in time. But now things were different, and all of a sudden she felt an urgency in her gut and in her heart. She didn't want to miss one more day, one more minute with him. The idea of Grant being with anyone but her made her feel sick, quite literally. Why did it all have to be so complicated?

She'd taken off early from work again on Friday, unable to concentrate on anything other than the thoughts whirring inside her head. What if Grant had decided, in the past seventeen hours, that he'd made a mistake in leaving her those messages and that Michelle was actually his soul mate? Michelle was the loyal one, after all. And she could cook. Really, really well. That had to count for something. What if Laney had realized that forgiving Katherine and letting her in again, if only a little, was more than she could handle along with being a wife to Rick, a mom to Gemma, and a slave to Tina? Was Katherine fooling herself into thinking she could stride back into all of their lives that easily, as if more than a decade of milestones hadn't elapsed?

She'd arrived at her dad's house after midnight on Friday. Hazel had already been asleep, but her father had waited up. He'd even sat with her and sipped a cup of tea. If he knew what was going on in her mind, he didn't say as much. He just asked about her week and if she was ready for Luella's estate sale the next day. She'd said she wasn't sure. Could anyone ever be truly ready to peddle the entirety of a loved one's possessions to the highest bidder? He'd told her to remember that they were just that—possessions—and they did not make Luella any less a part of the woman Katherine had become. Then he'd kissed her good night and told her to get some rest.

They'd settled on having the estate sale in the gymnasium at Manchester High School. Katherine had speculated, and Laney had agreed, that Luella would not have wanted flocks of strangers infiltrating her home like a stampede of greedy scavengers, even if she was no longer around to witness it. And Katherine wasn't sure she could stomach it either. When Laney had suggested the high school and put in a call to the principal, offering a small percentage of the proceeds, the decision had been made. The sale had gone on all day, from nine a.m. until five p.m., and every last thing had been purchased. Katherine had tried to remind herself of what her dad had said—that these things were only possessions—but there had been moments when the enormity of the situation had overwhelmed her. She'd asked Grant not to come to the estate sale, explaining that she preferred to see him alone when they could really talk, when she could give him her full attention, and when she looked her best, though she didn't tell him that last part. Mainly she wasn't sure how she was going to feel about everything, and the last thing she wanted was for Grant to see her fall apart. Katherine had never prescribed to the theory that men loved a damsel in distress. And she wasn't about to start now.

"I guess that's it." Katherine surveyed the cavernous space with its vacant tables and bare drop cloths.

"I can't believe there's nothing left." Laney's shoulders were hunched, and if the somber expression on her face was any indication, she felt the same way as Katherine did—empty.

"I know." Katherine reached for her purse, fishing through it to retrieve the keys to her dad's Subaru. "I think I miss her more now. That probably sounds stupid."

"No, it doesn't." Laney sighed and then looked up as the gymnasium door squeaked open. "Here comes Principal Wasserman. She said she'd check in when the sale was over."

"It looks like you ladies did well." Rebecca Wasserman smiled warmly at Laney. She was a petite woman with strawberry blond hair and sharp features that belied the earnest expression on her face. "Hope the space worked well."

"It was perfect, thank you." Katherine extended her hand. "I'm Kitty Hill. Laney's friend. I used to go here, once upon a time."

"Nice to meet you, Kitty." She nodded. "Well, if you're all set, I have a soccer game to get to. It never ends!" She rolled her eyes playfully.

"Thanks, again, Rebecca." Laney waved as the principal made her way toward the exit. And then she pivoted back to face Katherine. "You ready?"

"Just about." Katherine retrieved a small, creased envelop from her purse and handed it to Laney. "So, this is about twelve years belated, but I found it when I was in New York. I figured better late than never."

"What is it?" Laney took the envelope, addressed to the house she grew up in, stamped and ready to mail.

"A letter I wrote to you after our fight. As you can see, I never sent it. I don't even know why I'm giving it to you now. I guess I just want you to have it, to know that I was thinking of you, and that I was, in fact, truly sorry. You don't have to read it if you don't want to."

Laney tilted her head to one side and gave Katherine one of her vintage *You can't be serious* looks. "Right, like that's going to happen." She opened the envelope and took out the letter, which was swathed in Katherine's flawless handwriting.

> Dear Laney,
>
> I don't really know where to begin. I'm pretty sure you hate me right now, and I'm still not entirely sure why you're so mad with me. I see now how leaving suddenly wasn't the right decision. I was just so upset after our fight. I love you, and I do want to be there for you during your pregnancy and to watch your baby grow up. I still want you all to come to New York. If you want to. Of course, I'll understand either way.
>
> Things here aren't as exciting as they would be with you. My job is a lot of hard work, and I haven't made many friends— certainly no one like you. I hope you can find a way to forgive me.
>
> For what it's worth, I'm sorry for every- thing. It doesn't have to be this way. I miss my best friend. I miss my sister.
>
> Love always,
> Kitty

"Wow. I can't believe you kept it all this time. How come you never sent it?" Laney turned her attention back to Katherine.

"I don't know. I guess I didn't think you'd receive it well."

"Probably true. Well, thank you for giving it to me now. I'll, um, cherish it forever?" Laney smirked.

"Oh, shut up!" Katherine swatted at Laney's arm.

"But seriously, thank you. At least I know you weren't a complete coldhearted bitch." Laney grinned. "By the way, Grant called while you were haggling with that fat lady over Luella's purple gown."

"How ridiculous was that?" Katherine laughed for the first time all day.

"I know! I felt like coming over and ripping it out of her chubby hands."

"So, what did he say? Grant." She delighted in the simple pleasure of saying his name.

"That you should meet him at Luella's house as soon as we were done."

"Got it." Katherine tried to hide the cocktail of exhilaration and anticipation that was simmering within her, but her effort was in vain.

"You still love him. Don't you?" Laney looked at Katherine with that glint in her eyes. The same one she'd had when they'd first met.

"I've always loved him."

"Don't be coy, Kitty. You know what I mean."

"Yes, I love him."

"Just don't hurt him again."

"I won't. I promise."

"Good. Because next time, I won't forgive you."

Katherine stood in the middle of Luella's hollow foyer, unsure whether to mourn the past or celebrate the future. There were so many beautiful memories tied to this house. And now it was time to let go. But how? Running away she could do. She had that down pat. Letting go was another thing altogether.

"Hey, you." Katherine swiveled around to find Grant smiling at her. She'd been so consumed by her own reminiscences, she hadn't even heard him come in the front door.

"Hey, you." She moved toward him, and he folded her into his arms.

"It's really, really good to see you." He kissed the top of her head.

"You too."

"Come on, let's talk." He took her hand and led her to Luella's staircase, where they sat on the fifth step, as close to each other as physically possible, his arm draped across her leg. "I broke it off."

"With Michelle?" Katherine's heart started throbbing like a fresh wound.

"Who else?" He laughed.

"Was she upset?" She adopted her most convincing somber tone, even though her whole body was tingling and she could barely catch her breath.

"She was, but she also wasn't surprised. She said she'd suspected for a while that things weren't what they should be and that when she saw the way I looked at you at Thanksgiving, she knew for sure. She's moving to New York to go to culinary school."

"Kind of ironic."

"Oh, you didn't get the memo? All of the women in my life leave me for New York."

"Very funny." Katherine nudged Grant with the side of her body.

"Come here." He touched her cheek and turned her face toward his, leaning in to place the softest kiss on her lips and lingering there just long enough. "You have no idea how long I've been waiting to do that again."

"About twelve years?"

"Something like that." He kissed her again. "I love you, Kitty."

"I love you too."

"I don't know how we're going to make this work, but hell if I'm going to let you go again."

She kissed him back, stroking the nape of his neck with her hands and, finally, running her fingers through his hair. She didn't want to stop, but something—a sudden flash of inspiration—made her pull away abruptly. "Can you let me go for an hour? I have something to take care of."

"Wait. What?" Grant stood up too, bemused and visibly anxious.

"Call Laney. I need both of you to meet me back here in an hour."

"Kitty . . ."

"Trust me, okay?"

"Okay."

An hour later, as promised, Katherine walked through Luella's front door to find Grant and Laney waiting on her.

"We weren't sure you'd show," Laney teased, though there was an underlying strain of truth in her testimony.

"Listen, before you tell us why you called this impromptu meeting, I just got off the phone with the Realtor." Grant paused, as if preparing to deliver bad news. "There's already been an offer made on the house. A good offer."

"That's great!" Katherine beamed.

"It is?" Laney didn't seem to agree.

"Don't you think?" Katherine looked back and forth between the two of them, taking in their solemn expressions.

"I guess. I mean, I know that's what we wanted. The money and all, but it still feels sad." Laney appeared stung by Katherine's unabashed nonchalance. Grant too. "I love this house."

"I don't think it's sad." Katherine shrugged. "I'm sure the next owner will love it as much as we did."

"Okay." Grant shook his head at Laney, who clearly had more to say on the matter. "So, what's up? Why did you ask us to meet you here?"

"Right. About that." Katherine smiled meaningfully. "No one else is going to buy this house."

"What's that supposed to mean?" Laney arched an eyebrow.

"No one but me."

"So the offer . . ." Grant trailed off, his mouth hanging open.

"That would be me." Katherine nodded.

"You're going to move here?" Grant was perceptibly stunned.

"What about your life in New York?" Laney prodded, equally shocked.

"Don't you worry. I have a master plan."

K atherine looped her arm through her father's and inhaled deeply, filling her lungs with the sweet scent
of spring and focusing her attention down the aisle,
where the priest was standing at attention—arms folded in
front of him—underneath an elaborate canopy sheathed in
pale pink roses with sprays of blue hyacinths and white lily
of the valley cascading around him. Initially, Hazel had
wanted to do everything herself, given that the wedding
was in her own backyard, but Katherine had insisted on im-
porting Julie Case, Manhattan's most coveted wedding
planner—someone who could attend to every last detail
while unencumbered by the personal investment.

The result was spectacular, even better than Katherine
had imagined it would be. Julie and her bridal brigade had
transformed the modest half acre into a virtual Garden of
Eden, with enough flowers, it seemed, to blanket a football

field, and enough flickering candles to light up the neighborhood once the sun had turned in for the night.

"You ready, Kitty Kat?" Katherine's father looked at her, a wide smile animating his face.

"I should ask you the same thing." She beamed back at him, leaning over to kiss his clean-shaven cheek. She could tell he was nervous.

It was hard to believe it had already been six months since Katherine had purchased Luella's house. She hadn't been able to move in immediately, as there were renovations to be made. After all, Katherine liked things the way she liked them, and even if she had shed some of her edge since returning to Vermont, being particular was one aspect of her personality that was unlikely to wane. More than that, she wanted to make Luella's house her own, presuming it would be more than a little creepy to leave it just as it was. She hadn't planned to live there full-time at first. While things with Grant were obviously heading in the right direction, there'd been no telling what would happen in the long run. And there was also the issue of her job at Blend.

She'd gone back to New York for the few weeks until Christmas, ready to set her master plan in motion, and everything had played out just as she'd orchestrated. Katherine's first order of business had been to do a little research into Tina, Laney's boss. Something about her was shady, and Katherine was determined to find out the specifics. As it turned out, Katherine was spot-on. Tina and her husband were irreversibly behind on paying their bills and, therefore, driving Oasis on the fast track to bankruptcy. Laney later admitted that there had been signs of financial disarray, but she'd always disregarded them, assuming that Tina had plenty of money to sort it all out, and that said issues were merely a consequence of Tina's laziness, rather than her dwindling bank account.

It wasn't Katherine's intention to destroy Tina's life, although humiliating her had been gratifying; she'd let Laney deliver the news of her eviction. What Katherine really wanted was to co-own Oasis along with her best friend. After that was taken care of, Katherine had invited Jane Sachs to lunch, something they'd done only a handful of times over the years. She'd broken the news that she was leaving Blend, albeit not entirely, if that was acceptable to Jane. She'd proposed that she could work as a consultant, based mainly in her Manchester "office," otherwise known as Luella's house, and that Oasis—which she planned to quadruple in size, catering to all of the wealthy tourists who swooped in for ski and golf seasons—would carry and sell Blend products. Jane had said she was sad to see Katherine leave, but that she'd expected the day would eventually come—in fact, she was surprised it hadn't come sooner. She'd said that Katherine had played an instrumental role in growing and running the company, concluding with one final declaration: "Luella would be very proud of you."

Katherine had decided to sell her apartment in New York and buy a smaller two-bedroom in an equally posh Upper East Side building, between Park and Madison Avenues. While she wouldn't be commuting regularly, there would be days, perhaps even a week here and there, when she'd need it. Three months after her relocation to Vermont, Grant had moved in with her, and they'd taken the money from the sale of his house to update the swimming pool, fill in some landscaping, and redo the patio, which included an extravagant outdoor living area and kitchen. Apparently, one thing Grant had taken away from his relationship with Michelle—barring some hideous furniture—was a penchant for cooking, which worked out quite conveniently, given that Katherine couldn't scramble an egg.

"Ready as I'll ever be!" Katherine's dad squeezed her hand, and they commenced their short walk down the aisle, all 120 eyes of their sixty guests monitoring each and every choreographed step.

"I'd say so. How long has it been?"

"Just about seventeen years."

"That's scary. Now I feel really old."

The ceremony had been breathtakingly poignant. Hazel had written her own vows, of course, and they'd read like a Maya Angelou poem. Her father had fumbled a bit through his, which had read more along the lines of "Roses Are Red, Violets Are Blue," but they'd been charming nonetheless. Their unconditional devotion had been profound, and while Hazel had gazed into her groom's eyes, Katherine and Grant had exchanged affectionate glances. The reception had outdone Hazel's expectations—at least that's what she'd told Katherine repeatedly, thanking her again and again, more profusely each time, for not only facilitating and paying for everything, but for giving her father the nudge he'd needed to finally propose. When all was said and done, everyone in attendance was drunk on the finest champagne and the infectious love in the air.

"Have I told you how gorgeous you look tonight?" Grant snuck up behind Katherine, wrapping his arms around her waist and nestling his nose into the side of her neck.

"It never hurts to say it again." She turned around, kissing him firmly on the lips.

"And you're a knockout in that gown." His hands wandered down her back to her rear end, where he groped unabashedly.

"It was Luella's." Katherine reflexively blinked away the tears welling in her eyes—it had been an emotional evening all around. "You don't think it's too much?" Laney had convinced her to wear the sprawling white gown after admiring it on her during their impromptu dress-up session. She'd insisted that it didn't look bridal at all and—on the heels of consulting with Hazel, who'd said that not only would she definitely *not* be wearing white, but that if Katherine didn't wear the dress she'd be disappointed—Katherine had relented. They all knew it would mean having a small piece of Luella with them on the big day, even though no one had said as much.

"Not at all." Grant brushed a wisp of hair off her face and tucked it behind her ear. "And the earrings look perfect with it." Katherine had made a special trip to the vault while in New York to unearth the emerald studs Luella had gifted her on her seventeenth birthday, and Grant was right: they did look spectacular with the dress.

"What about this?" Katherine tugged on the delicate silver chain around her neck to reveal the familiar cursive "K" dangling beneath the top of her dress.

"Oh, my God!" Grant laughed. "I can't believe you still have it." He shook his head, staring at the pendant in his open palm. "I remember being completely terrified that you were going to hate it. Even the saleswoman at Mancini's knew I was a wreck."

"I love it." Katherine looked down at Grant's hand, and he tilted her chin up toward him again.

"And I love you. More than anything."

"Anything? Hmm. I like the sound of that."

"That's right. Even more than my new outdoor kitchen."

"Wow, I'm really flattered now."

"Yup. Thought you'd appreciate that. I mean, I think we

can agree that the pizza oven could give any woman a run for her money."

"Without a doubt." Katherine giggled. "Though may I point out that I've yet to sample one of your fabulous gourmet pizzas."

"I'm honing my skills." Grant pulled Katherine closer, until their faces were nearly touching.

"Is that so?"

"Oh yeah. I got mad skills in more places than one, baby." He placed three soft kisses just under her left earlobe. "Now I just need to make an honest woman out of you." He motioned toward the altar with his head. "Kind of puts you in the mood, huh?"

"Oh, I don't know." Katherine smiled flirtatiously. "What if I'm not the marrying type?"

"You'd better be. I haven't waited this long for nothing." He kissed her on the lips decisively, pulling back briefly to further his point. "That necklace was an investment. Make no mistake about it."

"Can you two *please* get a room?" Laney interjected, approaching with two glasses of champagne. "Here, take these. Something else to do with your mouths."

"Excuse me. I was just talking to your best friend and business partner here about finally making you two sisters for real. You know, when the time is right."

"Don't be ridiculous." Laney rolled her eyes in the dramatic fashion that only she could. "Kitty and I are already sisters. We always have been."

Emily Liebert is an award-winning author, *New York Times* bestselling editor, and TV personality. Her first book, *Facebook Fairytales*, is available across the globe. A graduate of Smith College, Liebert's second novel is set to publish in September 2014. She lives in New York with her husband and their two sons.